P9-AOF-917

# *MURDER*
# Loves Company

by John Mersereau

Introduction by Tom & Enid Schantz

The Rue Morgue Press
Boulder / Lyons

# Introduction
# John Mersereau and the World's Fair

THE YEAR 1939 saw two rival world's fairs in the United States, one on each coast, and each provided the setting for a contemporary mystery novel. Just as both fairs were economic failures, so were the novels inspired by them, especially the one set on the East Coast. *Murder at the New York World's Fair* was written under the pseudonym Freeman Dana by Phoebe Atwood Taylor, the creator of Asey Mayo, otherwise known as the Codfish Sherlock, and was commissioned by none other than Random House founder Bennett Cerf. Taylor struggled with novel, missed a deadline or two, and finally turned in a product that she obviously didn't have much of her heart in. She was paid $250, a fair advance for the time considering that only 900 copies were printed on its publication in 1938, as the final preparations for the opening of the fair were getting underway. The book would not be reprinted until 1987, by which point all of Taylor's other mysteries, including the eight featuring Leonidas Witherall and published under the pseudonym Alice Tilton, had been reissued by Foul Play Press. Today a fine first edition in dust jacket of *Murder at the New York World's Fair* fetches five times the money Taylor was paid to write it.

While Taylor had already achieved fame as a mystery writer, John Mersereau, the author of *Murder Loves Company*, set at the San Francisco World's Fair, officially known as the Golden Gate Exposition, was a relatively unknown pulp magazine writer who had previously published two adventure novels, both of which had been made into silent movies. *Murder Loves Company,* published in 1940, was the first of only two full-length mystery novels he would publish before service in World War II interrupted his writing career. Whether Mersereau had read the Freeman Dana novel is unknown, but it's unlikely, given its small print run and failure to attract a wide audience. The idea for *Murder Loves Company* was developed over the kitchen table when Robert Hyde, an old friend from Mersereau's student days at Berkeley, showed up to pitch possible plots. Mersereau figured the fair, which was already under way, had definite commercial value as a background for a mystery. Later writers have also recognized the appeal of using a world's fair as a setting for crime fiction, usually, however, choosing the 1893 Chicago Columbian Exposition, no doubt because of the exploits there of serial killer H.H. Holmes. Robert Bloch first used this setting in his 1974 *American Gothic,* followed nearly thirty years later by Nancy Wikarski's *The Fall of White City* and Alec Michod's *The White City.* A nonfiction study of Holmes and the Columbian Exposition, *The Devil in the White City* by Erik Larson, won the Edgar for best fact/crime book for 2003.

The Golden Gate Exposition was held on the man-made Treasure Island, one of three major public works projects undertaken in the San Francisco Bay Area during the Great Depression, the other two being the Bay Bridge and the Golden Gate Bridge. The fair itself, of course, was only to be a temporary occupant of the 400-acre island, which was built as the site of a future airport. The long-term tenant was to be Pan American airlines which intended to operate its clipper service from there.

Construction of the island by the Army Corps of Engineers began in March 1936, before either the Bay Bridge or Golden Gate Bridge was finished. Some 287,000 tons of boulders were dumped off the Yerba Buena shoals, creating a lagoon a mile long and two-thirds of a mile wide. Dredges working 24 hours a day pumped up sand, mud, and fossils from the sea bottom to fill in the lagoon. A causeway was built connecting it to Yerba Buena Island, so that cars traveling to the exposition could get to the island via a future Bay Bridge exit. It was given the name Treasure Island because the silt washed into the bay by the Sacramento River contained enough gold that a hard-working miner could pan a dollar's worth in a day.

Once there was ground to break, ground-breaking ceremonies took place, with the flags of various nations borne to the ceremony by members of the San Francisco Chinatown Boy Scout troop. Photos of the event prominently show the American flag sandwiched in between the flags of two nations, Japan and Nazi Germany, that we would soon be at war against. Organizers of the New York World's Fair valiantly tried to derail the San Francisco effort, even appealing to President Franklin D. Roosevelt to intervene. Roosevelt refused, probably because he saw both fairs as an indication of the American spirit and proof that his New Deal was bringing the Depression to an end.

Fair organizers were so successful in cautioning the public that opening day, February 18, 1939, might bring long traffic delays that people stayed away in droves, with only about two-thirds of the 200,000 fairgoers expected showing up. Attendance never caught up to expectations and vendors beseeched fair organizers to lower admission charges or to rebate rents. However, Chicago fan dancer Sally Rand's Nude Ranch, where a bevy of beauties dressed only in cowboy boots and G-strings pitched horseshoes, rode burros or played badminton behind plate glass windows for the edification of fair-goers, managed to attract 65,000 visitors willing to pay a quarter apiece during the first week alone, perhaps because ticket-sellers were notorious for their willingness to accept fake IDs. As an attraction, it certainly outdrew one holdover exhibit from San Francisco's first world's fair, held in 1915. Stella, a painting of a reclining nude with a machine-powered heaving bosom, had been a hit two and half decades earlier, but in 1939 she couldn't compete with nude badminton.

Those attractions were off the Gayway, a carnival-like arcade where barkers pitched games and freak shows to passersby. Much of the action in *Murder Loves Company* takes place at or near the Gayway. If some of its concessions make the fair seem a bit tacky, they pale in comparison with the architectural style, or styles, chosen by the organizers. *Time* magazine called its Pacific Basin motif, with

its odd mixture of Mayan, Cambodian, Indian and Burmese struc-
tures made of plywood and stucco that was tinted in hues of aqua,
gold and beige, an "exotic chowchow of the ageless East and the
American West." The most prominent structure, a 400-foot tall campanile called the Tower of the Sun, was derided by one and all, but
Ralph Stackpole's Pacifica, a blocky, enigmatic 80-foot female figure, drew rave reviews, perhaps because, as fair historian Richard
Reinhardt wrote, it bore an "eerie likeness to an overgrown automobile ornament." Stackpole was so enamored of his creation that he
suggested—in vain—that a permanent version of her be built on Alac-
traz Island as a Pacific equivalent of the Statue of Liberty.

Very little of the actual fair remains today. The airport was never
built and the island was turned over to the military not long after the
fair closed its gates for the last time in the fall of 1940
    Thousands of GIs passed through the gates on Treasure Island
on their way to combat in the Pacific.

If the buildings were a bit gaudy, the flora were spectacular. Thou-
sands of flowers and trees were planted on the island, including doz-
ens of huge ancient olive trees that were the descendents of trees
planted by the Spanish friars who tended the missions during
California's colonial period. To insure that the trees survived trans-
planting, each one was dug up with an enormous root ball weighing
several tons. Those are the model for the trees that Professor James
Yeats Biddle, the young University of California professor of horticulture, so vigorously attempts to protect in *Murder Loves Company*.

Although *Murder Loves Company* was one of the earliest mysteries with a horticultural background (Sergeant Cuff enjoyed his roses
in *The Moonstone*, Hercule Poirot had a passion for vegetable mar-
rows, and just about everyone knows that Nero Wolfe spent several
hours each day with his orchids), Mersereau was not an expert gardener, according to his son John Mersereau, Jr., who added, with a
barely suppressed chuckle in his voice, "unless you count the time he
spent cutting down trees as a logger."

Mersereau was born in 1898 in the northern Michigan peninsula
town of Manistique, but his father's ill health forced the family to move
to California around 1907. Following graduation from Oakland High

School, where he was editor of the school newspaper, the young Mersereau hiked the Oregon coast, worked as a mule-skinner, served as a fireman on Oakland's last horse-drawn ladder rig, and then homesteaded near Mariposa in the Sierra foothills. He also began selling short stories to the pulp magazines. Three times he entered the University of California at Berkeley, remaining enrolled for two weeks, two months, and finally two years.

In 1927, he married Winona Beth Roberts, with whom he had "the two stalwart" sons, Charles and John, Jr., referred to in the short biography he included in the Lippincott edition of *Murder Loves Company*. Things began looking up for the Mersereaus. Two of John's adventure novels, *Whispering Canyon* and *The Checkered Flag*, were bought for the movies and in 1925 he had inherited a large sum from his parents, although most of this was lost in the crash of 1929. In spite of this setback, Mersereau moved his family from Oakland to a new house he had built in the Berkeley hills in 1931. Although his son John said his father was happy about the move, he obviously had some reservations about the area, referring to "the antagonism of those cold, soulless hills" in Chapter Eight of *Murder Loves Company*. He called Berkeley the ideal setting for a college, since the hills drove people inside. "Rigid and virgin, they kept aloof, conceding nothing. Student and teacher alike felt the withdrawal and buried themselves deeper into books."

The Mersereaus spent their winters in Berkeley and their summers at "The Roost," a house he had built in the Santa Cruz mountains near Los Gatos. It was here where he met another Las Gatos writer, Owen Atkinson, in 1933. The two collaborated on a number of pulp magazine thrillers under the pseudonym Richard Race Wallace. Atkinson turned one of these stories into a screenplay which was filmed as *The Pool Where Horror Dwelt*, starring Wallace Beery and Mickey Rooney. In 1938, the Mersereaus bought a rundown resort, which they rechristened "Garbled Gables," not far from The Roost. It was here that Mersereau wrote *Murder Loves Company* as well as *The Corpse Comes Ashore,* published in 1941 and set in the Caribbean, featuring as its sleuth-hero the exotically if somewhat improbably named Captain Xenophon York.

After the Japanese bombing of Pearl Harbor in December 1941, Mersereau enlisted in the Navy at the age of 43 and was commissioned a lieutenant, serving as a speechwriter for the Twelfth Naval District. After the war, he was transferred to Washington, D.C., where he teamed up with Alan Bosworth (author of *Run Silent, Run Deep*) in editing a navy recruitment magazine. After he was discharged from the service, he sold Garbled Gables and moved to Santa Barbara, where he built a house with his own hands, as he had done in Los Gatos, although he had no training as a mechanic or a carpenter. It was there that he and his wife became close friends with Margaret Millar, already a very successful mystery writer, and her husband Kenneth, who was later to achieve literary stardom and best-seller status as Ross Macdonald. Mersereau continued to write, but his stories failed to find a market—the pulps were dying—and he was finally forced to take a job he hated as a dispatcher for the California Highway Patrol.

In the early 1960s, the Mersereaus visited Mexico, fell in love with the country, and eventually built a house on the shores of Lake Chapala, outside the village of Ajijic near Guadalajara, where they lived until 1972. They then moved to Forsythe, Missouri, where they lived until John died in 1989 and Winona in 1993.

Mersereau lived to 91 in spite of continuously smoking a pipe, the only habit he seems to share with James Biddle, the hero of *Murder Loves Company*, and consuming vast quantities of chocolate syrup, taken neat. He was a close friend in the 1930s to Haakon Chevalier, the University of California French professor who is said to have attended Communist Party meetings and later urged Robert Oppenheimer to give the secret of the atomic bomb to the Soviets, since they were our allies. (Chevalier said he was framed). Mersereau didn't share Chevalier's beliefs, taking what his son John referred to as a cynical approach to politics.

Both Mersereaus were far more interested in badminton than politics (one wonders if they had watched those badminton matches at Sally Rand's Nude Ranch on Treasure Island), helping to organize clubs in Los Gatos and Santa Barbara.

The Mersereaus' life had as many ups as it had downs, and certainly John's writing career didn't head in the direction he might have liked. But his son said that neither his father nor his mother were ever bothered by having to endure somewhat straitened circumstances at times, as long as they were able to live life on their own terms.

No one would argue that *Murder Loves Company* is one of the great forgotten mysteries of the 1940s, although the book has its obvious charms, not the least of which is the appealing and innocent courtship of its two principal players. But it is its remarkable portrait of what life was like in Northern California before World War II, when one could jump into a car and get out into the country in no time, that begs a rereading after all these years. The landscape of that period is irretrievably lost to the bulldozers, as are the wonders of Treasure Island and its fabulous exposition, but they'll live on forever in the pages of *Murder Loves Company*.

**Tom & Enid Schantz**
**Lyons, Colorado**
**June 2004**

We're indebted to John Mersereau, Jr., for his willingness to share his memories of his father, as well as to Richard Reinhardt whose *Treasure Island: San Francisco's Exposition Years* (1973) is an engaging and poignant recollection of what it was like to visit the Golden Gate Exposition as a teenager.

## CHAPTER 1

IT WAS ONE OF THOSE BALMY spring evenings when Professor James Yeats Biddle could rejoice in the possession of a sport convertible coupe instead of some model a little more conservative and practical.

*Xantippe,* she was called. And she droned faithfully along, with the merest hint that her rings were *passé* and that possibly she could use a new set of teeth. Her top was booted down, giving her a fast and rakish look for all her years. But signs at frequent intervals announced the speed limit on the great Bay Bridge, and meticulously Professor Biddle kept the speedometer needle hovering at forty-five.

And just as carefully, he kept his eyes averted from the figure seated beside him. He could look forward with equanimity to his address before the Associated Women Executives. He could be paternal in his academic contacts with jitterbug coeds. But it was another matter to be so unexpectedly and intimately isolated with this disturbing young woman of the *San Francisco Sun-Telegraph.*

James maintained a neutral silence. He was under no obligation to play the host. His companion had, after all, thumbed a ride. At least, he told himself, she had connived at it.

When he was calling at the offices of her paper on quite another matter, the night city editor had tossed her into Xantippe.

"Professor Biddle, this is Kay Ritchie," was what had passed for an introduction. "She's covering your Associated Women's program in Berkeley tonight. How about giving her a lift across the Bay? And maybe tell her what your talk's going to be about? She's hell on these business Amazons, but her horticulture may need cultivating."

So here she was. And behaving abominably. Twice, she had gasped when Xantippe swerved an inch or two. A nervous passenger was extremely annoying. And there was no provocation. He had merely let his eyes glance fleetingly toward the lights of Treasure Island gleaming like a magic jewel through the thin mist in the harbor far below.

How could this Miss Ritchie understand his paper on "The Flora of the Golden Gate International Exposition"? She had been positively insulting on his first tentative reference to the saline tolerance of olive trees.

"Can't we save that, Professor Biddle?" she had said. "It's such a perfect night, and this is the first time I've been on the bridge in an open car. It's different. It sort of frightens me. But I like to be frightened sometimes, don't you?"

It was one of the hoariest of classroom tricks. Professor James Yeats Biddle classified it instantly. When you caught a student unprepared he would drag out a red herring by asking you a question.

It was a technique that had always irritated James. It irritated him now. He gave the young woman a look to indicate as much, but something went wrong with his disapproval.

Xantippe's dash light showed that this Kay Ritchie's eyes were shining up at him from beneath the brim of a crazy little peaked hat of Tibetan influence. Her lips were slightly parted. She had a pert, inquisitive nose, and her chin, lifting from the fur collar of her coat, was firm and yet softly round.

She had looked only competent back in the *Sun-Telegraph* editorial rooms. But now she seemed contradictingly small and feminine. Just at this moment she gasped again as a horn blared raucously. Resentfully James swung Xantippe closer to the bridge railing.

"If you get so easily frightened, Miss Ritchie," James observed acidly, "why did you ever choose to become a girl reporter?"

Miss Kay Ritchie seemed, without moving, to attain distance and dignity.

"I'm not a girl reporter," she answered crisply. "I'm a newspaperwoman."

James failed to see the distinction. He had not realized that the newsgathering fraternity has its Brahmins and its Untouchables. He only felt that he was back on safe ground again. He looked straight ahead. The hour was too early for the great evening crowds to be descending on Treasure Island. Traffic was comparatively light, but he gave his most careful attention to Xantippe.

The night air was sharp and invigorating. James liked the feel of the wind tugging at his hair. He liked the sharp stinging sensation on his scalp. He liked to think he could still take it with as keen enjoyment as the college kids in their weird jalopies.

Perhaps, without realizing it at the time, he had chosen Xantippe's youthful lines to call attention to the fact that he was the youngest professor on the Berkeley campus. Perhaps he should have worn evening clothes tonight instead of Harris tweeds. Maybe he was just making a holy show of his youth and his success.

Xantippe was secondhand. But she was his first and sole dependent. He might have splurged when he became consultant to the horticultural division of the Fair. But he had chosen Xantippe because of her sterling merits, and with the blessings of Consumers' Research. And, damn it, he preferred an open car!

Kay Ritchie said, "I still can't believe, Professor Biddle, that you've gotten those lovely flowers to really grow on Treasure Island. Some of them can't have a saline tolerance of much more than fifty at the most."

James gave her an oblique glance, and was reassured. She was working for the *Sun-Telegraph* now. He smiled, relaxing somewhat the stiffness of his jaw.

"Have you been cramming?" he asked. "Or are you really interested in my subject, by any chance?"

"I've been cramming," the girl admitted. "I'm supposed to whip my assignments, not let them whip me. I'll hand it to you. You've made the island into a magic place. But of course that doesn't cut any ice. I suppose you realize you're playing second fiddle to those female Simon Legrees, the A.W.E.! They're newspaper circulation, but they stop mine like a tourniquet."

Grinning rather in spite of himself, James drove Xantippe under the Exposition overpass and into the tunnel bored through Yerba Buena Island. As they approached the eastern portal, his hand drifted to the horn button on the steering wheel. The cavern echoed and reechoed with the blast. James glanced guiltily at the newspaperwoman at his side to see if she had detected his childishness.

"I was hoping," she said, "that you'd do that."

James concentrated on the road. He wasn't quite himself tonight. Miss Ritchie's approval was disturbing. She seemed to know it, too. It gave her an advantage over him, somehow.

For James's part, he knew by now that Miss Ritchie regularly split her infinitives down the middle as though, like oysters, that was the only way to get at them. But she was a writer. She could manhandle grammar as she chose. They all did. And intruding adverbs were no defense against her wise young eyes.

Xantippe emerged from the tunnel and shot out onto the long cantilevered span, the reigning marvel of the modern world. The moon shone down on the glinting silver of the bridge. Directly below were some of the deepest waters of the bay. Ahead, the wide roadway declined slowly toward the still distant toll station and the twinkling lights of the East Bay cities. To the left, Treasure Island appeared again, with its yacht-filled anchorage and the joyous illumination of the Gayway.

"We started," said James, "with five thousand parts of chlorine per million. It took two hundred wells and months of pumping to reduce the content eighty percent. Natural rainfall and sprinkling cut that down again. We licked the small remaining fraction with chemicals." He allowed enthusiasm to creep into his voice. "Aside from uncounted shrubs and flowering plants, we've brought in four thousand trees. We have fifty olive trees perhaps more than a century old, among the oldest in California, and we haven't lost a one!"

"Don't tell the women executives that," advised Miss Kay Ritchie. "Forget your statistics. Get breathless, you know, the way those writers about disease germs do! Have the pumps stop dead. Let the island start to sink. Your back is to the wall. But you stand there, fighting. You won't give up. You…"

James laughed. "I couldn't," he cried. "I'm too honest. I just helped do a big, orderly job."

This was not false modesty with James. He liked to quote figures with rows of zeros after them. They were exciting to him. But he didn't expect to thrill others. The removal of a fifth of a billion gallons of salt water, for example, or the bringing in of a hundred thousand tons of topsoil and seventy thousand shrubs. It was the magnitude that impressed him, not the hazards of the work.

"Those olive trees, for instance," he went on. "We found them on ranches in the Santa Clara Valley. Just to play safe, we say they're at least sixty years old. But they may have been planted in the early 1800's by mission neophytes. There's real romance for you, digging up California history by the roots!" He shrugged. "But our part was routine stuff. We just boxed the trees and barged them up from a landing at the south end of the bay. Why, I've had twice as many actual thrills in my own cottage, growing tomatoes in the living room!"

Kay Ritchie looked skeptical.

"More overproduction," she sighed. "I suppose before long the government will be paying you to plow your rugs under."

"I'm serious," insisted James. "It's hydroponic culture, without soil, you know. I have ripe tomatoes right now, in February, and the vines are as big as Christmas trees."

"I'll bite," the girl surrendered. "I might even get a short article out of it for one of the Sunday syndicates. If you wouldn't mind, I could get a couple of pictures with my Leica..." She stopped short. Her hands lifted in dismay. "I've forgotten it! We've got to take shots of those women, whether we run them or not. And it's payday!"

James couldn't follow her rapid-fire reasoning.

"Is there some rule," he asked, "against taking pictures on payday?"

"Not a rule," said Miss Ritchie. "Merely a newspaper practice. The cameramen get drunk on payday. It's a sort of tradition. One of them is supposed to show up tonight, but you can't be sure after four o'clock."

Miss Ritchie's distress was genuine, and James rose to the occasion.

"It's just twelve of eight," he said, glancing at his wristwatch. "If we step on it, we might have time to go back."

"But they don't allow U-turns on the bridge." Miss Ritchie's voice lifted in a cry of protest as James flipped the wheel around. "You can't do that!"

"I did it," James demonstrated complacently. Xantippe was heading back toward San Francisco now, and the nearest approaching car was still all of two hundred yards away. "We endangered no one. An emergency existed. And there isn't a speed cop within miles."

The distant wail of a siren interrupted him, singing the gambler's dirge. Resignedly, Xantippe began to slow down. Kay Ritchie screamed.

And then James, too, saw the thing coming at them. It was the nearest of the cars approaching from San Francisco. It was traveling at tremendous speed, curving toward them in a wide arc. It was heading directly for Xantippe.

By a mighty wrench at the wheel, James managed to pull out of the path of the juggernaut.

The oncoming sedan passed inches to their left and with a rending impact, almost head on, struck the raised ramp. The car seemed to stop entirely for an instant against the massive railing of the bridge. The doors popped open. The roaring motor died convulsively. In slow motion, it seemed, the sedan rolled over and over, twice. And in the roadway lay two bodies.

"Are you all right, Miss Ritchie?" James asked, shakily. The girl nodded mutely. Her face was white, but her jaw was set. She fumbled for the catch to open the door. "Maybe I can help," said James. "You stay here. It may be pretty bad. Don't look."

Kay Ritchie said, "It's my job to look. That's what they pay me for."

As they alighted, a white traffic car ground to a stop beside Xantippe. Before the siren had stopped churning, two speed officers were springing out. One ran across the roadway, carrying flares. The other, young but thoroughly efficient, beckoned peremptorily to James.

"Here, you," he called. "Give me a hand."

The sprawling figures in the road were roughly clad in boots and overalls. They were Japanese laborers of middle age, gardeners, probably, James guessed. And they were dead. He was sure of that, even before the speed cop examined the second man. James was surprised that he could watch so callously. But the wells of human sympathy within him seemed to be dammed up by some curious circumstance. He was puzzled. He couldn't quite put his finger on it, but it was there. Something incongruous. Something he couldn't understand.

The speed cop suddenly cursed softly beneath his breath and jerked his head at James.

"Look here," he said. "Feel this. And now this." James felt, reluctantly. The frown cleared from his face. Of course, that was it. One of them was still warm. The other was cold and stiff.

"It's murder!" said the officer. "One of these guys was already plenty dead before the crash." Then, abruptly, "What's your name?"

James told him. "You can find me either through the Berkeley phone book or the U.C. directory," he added.

"We'll find you," promised the officer. "We don't forget drivers who make U-turns on this bridge!"

Disconsolately, James wandered over to the wrecked machine, where Miss Ritchie had located the registration card.

"The car belonged to Harvey Bell," she said. "San Francisco address."

"If you value your public, you'd better see that other cop," James suggested. "He'll tell you there were two Japanese in it and that one of them had been murdered."

Miss Ritchie's mouth opened for an exclamation, but none was audible. She hurried off. It amazed James to see how quickly thin lines of traffic could thicken into a jam. Flares were burning smokily. An officer was getting the lines of cars on the move again. A police motorcycle, with wide-open siren, was streaking down the bridge.

Efficient fellows, those highway cops.

James poked his head through the warped doorway of the wrecked sedan. The interior was bright with the glare from cars creeping past. James reached through the twisted steering wheel to guard against fire by turning the ignition off.

He also flicked the switch of the smashed headlights. As he withdrew his hand, the button on his cuff caught on something. By its elasticity it was evidently a taut rubber band. The band snapped loose, stinging his wrist, and the hand throttle, with the retarding spring released, clicked forward on the steering post.

In a moving car, the device would have raced the motor at top speed. And this sedan had been really moving.

James's inspection was interrupted as a motorcycle drew up while he was still fiddling with the throttle. A sharp voice ordered him in unequivocal terms to be on his way.

"I'm driving a press car," James said, with dignity, but he prudently retreated to the rail. It was only fair, he thought, that Miss Ritchie should get her story if she wanted it. Perhaps she even worked on space rates. He didn't want to be a handicap when chance had given her a break.

With studied unconcern, he turned and looked down on the dark bay. In the movies, reporters bawled out the law and got away with it. But James was satisfied to be ignored.

Casually, he watched a long sleek motor yacht glide out from beneath a bridge arch close by. Seventy feet below and a little to the right, he could see it cutting through the thin, low-lying mist. A blue pennant with a white diamond center fluttered from the truck of a short mast. And a radio somewhere on the vessel was broadcasting a modern symphony.

With sudden agitation, James remembered to look at his watch. He had only ten minutes to get to Wheeler Hall. He hurriedly rejoined Miss Ritchie.

"Could you come, now, Miss Ritchie?" he suggested as urgently as he thought polite.

The girl nodded.

"Yes," she said, "we can't keep the paper waiting any longer. We'll have to rush."

James slid into the seat beside her.

"After I get turned around there's something I want to tell you about a rubber band—"

"Turned around!" interrupted Kay Ritchie incredulously, too harassed to pick up the proffered clue. "You think I'm going to lose this scoop?"

James wasn't listening. He was cramping Xantippe's wheels, intent on the turned back of a traffic cop.

"They'll give me a ticket, I suppose," he sighed. "But it's really safe enough, and I can't be late—"

Miss Ritchie reached over and pressed down on Xantippe's horn, hard, and with her free hand she beckoned to a familiar and literal-minded speed cop.

"I'm with the *Sun-Telegraph,* remember?" she told him imperiously. "I'm covering Professor James Yeats Biddle's lecture in Berkeley, and we're late. We have to turn around."

"Lady," the officer told her, with a tremor in his voice, "you're already turned around! You're going to San Francisco, see? Now scram!"

Miss Kay Ritchie was smiling sweetly up at the astonished professor. "The *Sun-Telegraph,* James," she said.

## CHAPTER 2

JAMES FELT TOO SHAKEN FOR bed. You can't have it brought so forcibly to mind how crime runs rampant in your fair city and not brood over it a little.

Why should people kill? Glandular, James supposed. Not enough Vitamin C. Too much in the shadow of roofs and walls. And probably not pleasant roofs and walls, either, but the gray, soot-stained cubicles to which so many of one's brothers voluntarily condemned themselves.

James surveyed his own gentle circumstances. A living room pleasantly warmed by an open fire of smooth-barked and fragrant eucalyptus logs. Well-shaded reading lights that brought out the deep, satiny glow of redwood walls. High shelves sweetly burdened with good books. None of this cheap detective stuff. A dining alcove, glassed and gaily chintzed. And beyond that swinging door a modern kitchen with every facility Mrs. Pringle's limited imagination could conjure up.

Beyond another door his comfortable, three-quarters bed with the covers turned triangularly open and pajamas laid out. Remote and spotlessly tiled, James's bathroom offered its homely comforts. This picture captured James. He would shave, thereby saving ten minutes, precious minutes in the morning. And if on the morrow five o'clock shadow overtook him with its stealthy menace, he was at least a lonely bachelor with no near relations to mourn for him.

James removed his coat, vest, and shirt. He ran the water till it came scalding hot and then filled his soap-bottomed mug. The lather felt fine.

He applied it well, and then, with short hoe-like strokes of a new blade, scraped it methodically off.

He observed his face as it came out clean and naked from this daily ritual. His nose was peeling disgracefully as usual. This resulted from riding in an open car and from having a nose with a too well indicated bony structure. His chin had a masculine and independent look, but he considered his mouth too large, the lips too full, which was supposed to indicate a sensual disposition. His matter-of-fact gray eyes, however, had always managed to see things in a conservative light, for which circumstance he was grateful. Black and still plentiful hair was beginning a threatening retreat from his forehead. Nothing imminent, however. And his heavy eyebrows always astonished him with a devilish, faunlike look which Hymie said gave women the impression that he was making advances to them.

For better and for worse it was his face. And at least he had never considered improving it by plastic surgery.

At this point he doused it generously with straight alcohol and finished off with a towel. He liked the tingle of the ardent spirit. He preferred it vastly to any emasculating, superimposed perfume.

Now what? James still didn't feel like bed. He put on his overalls. His tomatoes didn't really need attention, but fortunately, they could always take it. He could be fussing about with his spraygun in man's unceasing war against blight and insects and it always brought a profound peace to his spirit.

He surveyed his tomatoes with pride. They pushed upward into light and being out of long plate-glass tanks. You could see their roots, frail and tenuous, groping blindly for the invisible stream-born sustenance. You could see the green, glossy fruit swell and shade into crimson or gold according to their birthright as the sustenance was found. Almost you could see the secret of life. There was just one slight process that remained secret, one link of missing knowledge. Always it was like that. Science had pushed its boundaries to the very shadow of the goal. Nature always held for downs on the one-yard line.

Several colonies of aphis were discovered and routed. James had nearly attained the peace of mind with which he liked to approach his lonely bed, when against usual practice the doorbell rang. A student worrying about a test on the morrow? There was no test. One of the associated women executives after his autograph? No, God send! That would be merely a subterfuge.

James was on his way to the door. It would be Paul Hyman, inevitably. Hymie didn't have any sense of when a day had been long enough. There was always time for one more effort in Hymie's day. What did Hymie want? He always wanted something.

What James could never have imagined was the fact which now faced him: the ingratiating visage of Miss Kay Ritchie.

"Swell," she said. "You aren't in bed. You even seem to have been at manual labor. I hope I don't interrupt."

James had stepped back with surprise, and it became unnecessary for him to invite the young lady in because she was in already.

"Well," James began. "To what…"

But Miss Ritchie took the initiative. She wasn't exactly shy, but it was hard to think of her as forward, either. The thought would be critical, and it was hard to be critical about Miss Ritchie. She was a very personable young woman.

"I feel guilty," she said. "Frankly, Professor, it's my conscience. Here I've gone and solidified myself with the *Sun-Telegraph* and probably at the expense of your friendship. Oh yes, it was a scoop all right. They couldn't deny it. When one of their girls is practically present at a murder they can be very decent. But I'd hate it if you didn't forgive me, for making you late to your speech and all."

"The women executives were furious," James recalled with relish. He was mollified. His feelings toward Miss Ritchie softened easily, he found.

"I can't afford to lose a friend," she was saying. There was a little wistful ring to the words that quite touched James. "I haven't many, for some reason or other. I get around. But there's so much difference between an interview and a buddy. Of course this is an interview."

"I'm flattered," said James.

"You needn't be," Miss Ritchie pricked his balloon with what he recognized as a refreshingly sharp tongue, "it's not you the city editor's afraid of. It's the Associated Women's Executives. They throw their weight around. But you're just some kind of professor or scientist. You don't cut any ice. We don't interview you unless you come in on a steamer and just took the curl papers out of your hair and have something to say about the American girl."

James had gradually retreated into the protective shelter of his tomato vines. From their jungle fastness he surveyed Miss Ritchie thoughtfully.

"Doctor Livingstone, I presume," she mused quaintly.

She had an air about her, she did. The professor warmed to her in spite of himself. On general principles he was suspicious of women, especially women in business. And of all women in business he was most suspicious of women in the business of reporting. But this one seemed different. She was a human being, one like himself, or at least as he fancied himself, a person of intelligence. More than that, she was a receptacle for all manner of odd, half-satisfied cravings. In other words she was somebody you thought you could safely confess to.

"These are my tomatoes," he said. It wasn't much of a confession, but it was a starter. And actually there was one whole large class of individuals he hoped would never learn that he had tomatoes, such folk as throw beer bottles on the highways, scratch windows with diamond rings, shoot the digits out of signposts, and leave ferny places strewn with crumpled paper cups and napkins. No good comes from those minus quantities in human form. And a stranger is always suspect, until you feel a warmth, until by some frailty he reveals himself, becomes vulnerable, and you take him by devious paths into your heart.

"I thought probably those would be your tomatoes," said Miss Ritchie. "Now, please, may I have your speech? You see, I went to Wheeler Hall first, and you had stopped talking already. I thought professors always talked for quite a while. I didn't dream there was any hurry."

The professor found himself digging in the desk for the notes of his lecture. There was something about this girl. She got what she wanted.

"I bet it's fun raising tomatoes," she said. "Especially in such an original way."

"It's not original with me," James corrected quickly. He was always careful not to take any credit he had not earned. Self-advertising scientists were anathema to him.

"I wish I were a man," said Miss Ritchie regretfully. "I know what I'd be. I'd be a detective. Don't you wish you'd taken up that instead of just teaching? Don't you, in your secret heart?"

"I can't say I do," James denied shortly. He was unable to visualize himself as any sort of a detective.

Miss Ritchie had a faraway look in her eyes. "I think it would be so lovely to dust lamp-black about and find the fingerprints and the murderer and all," she said, dreaming aloud. "Of course that tonight wasn't a lovely murder at all. There wasn't any mystery. The man was just dead, that's all. And accidentally the man who was driving the car was killed in the crash while trying to dispose of the body. And the car was a stolen car that belonged to a man named Harvey Bell. And he went into the police station at the Fair and reported his car stolen even before it was wrecked. And everything was pretty legal and boring. I mean, considering that after all, it was a murder. Because of course it must have been. One body hot and one body cold. But there wasn't any mystery. It was all clear. If I were a detective I'd want to solve baffling murders. Only baffling ones. Don't you think that would be fascinating?"

"Well, hardly," said James. He was distinctly chilled. He had nearly forgotten the unpleasant episode on the bridge and now Miss Ritchie brought it back in all its sordid glory.

And what especially annoyed him about Miss Ritchie's monologue was the creepy and sinister fascination of the subject, which he had always cautiously avoided. One shouldn't succumb to the baser inheritances, was James's firm belief. And yet Miss Ritchie frankly admitted her shame and thereby forced him either to agree with her or to lie. James loathed hypocrisy, and yet he had lied, so now he felt a just resentment. "I think you will find the notes clear enough for your purposes," he said.

It was a dismissal, crude and direct.

He saw disappointment flash across Miss Kay Ritchie's face and hide quickly in a dimple to the left of her small, red lips.

"I must go," she said, and smiled a rather forced smile. "I seem to always have to go some place. There's always a hurry. I have to get your paper into print so the A.W.E. can read it tomorrow morning with their three-minute eggs and phone the editor if I slipped up on anything."

Inexplicably James didn't want her to go. Having just dismissed her he wanted to reach out now and pinch the lapel of her sleek little brown fur coat, to keep her near, in sight and in hearing. She seemed so small and yet so much of a woman, not like the farmerettes in his classes, self-important and callow and overimpressed with their recently acquired majority. Miss Ritchie was so much more adult than any of them, and yet so frankly childish. "Here," said James. "You haven't met Cinders."

Cinders arched his café-au-lait back and paraded proudly for the lady. Miss Ritchie stooped and petted him. Cinders' Siamese whiskers vibrated with pleasure, and he made a sound like a train going over a trestle at a great distance.

"Very distinguished," said Miss Ritchie. "Do you get on well together?"

"Tolerably," said James. "I envy him his ability to avoid stumbling in the dark. And he is jealous of my tomatoes. Otherwise we get on well." An inspiration came to James. "Look," he said. "I have a bottle of very fine old port…"

Miss Ritchie examined him quite intently for a second, evidently to assure herself he wasn't just being polite. Then he saw a magic smile glow all over her face, and he wondered how he could ever have considered hurrying her off.

"I'll have to use the telephone," she said. "They'll let me do a tightrope act on the deadline if they know I'm coming. They're really almost human about that."

James understood her to be talking about her bosses of the *Sun-Telegraph*. He liked her attitude toward bosses. James also had bosses, and he felt that here again he and this young woman spoke a common tongue.

"Gracie," Miss Ritchie was saying over the telephone, "give me Ed." Then followed a promise to Ed about the A.W.E. lecture. It was in the bag, she said.

James didn't purposely listen. But if somebody talks in a clear and engaging voice in the next room it doesn't make any difference if it is your business or not. You hear what she says.

"I thought it was a pretty good one myself," she was telling Ed. "Practically to order." Then Ed said something and Miss Ritchie said "What?" and sounded puzzled. "Listen," she gasped. "Say that again!"

James felt mildly jealous of Ed. He wished Miss Ritchie knew him that intimately. It would be pleasant to be called "James" by somebody like Miss Ritchie. Or, and the professor almost blushed at the thought, to be called "Jim!" He busied himself getting the port and two glasses.

Lost in the clamor of his thoughts James didn't hear the conclusion of Miss Ritchie's talk with Ed. But if he had not been present at the transformation James would not have believed a mere telephone message could so stimulate anybody.

She faced him with her eyes wide and her jaw tensed, electric with excitement.

"Do you know what they found?" she demanded. In spite of himself James felt an odd tingle at the back of his neck.

"Traces of cyanide!" said Miss Ritchie. "Cyanide gas!" There was an insidious contagion to Miss Ritchie's malady. James felt himself coming down with it. As he poured a glass of port his hand trembled, and as he presented the glass he slopped it clumsily so drops ran down the slender stem and dripped off the base onto his green broadloom rug.

James tried to get a grip on himself. What had happened on the bridge tonight was just something unpleasant to be put out of mind as promptly as possible by any healthy and right-thinking person. Of course there was the problem of that rubber band, but it wasn't any affair of his. Two total strangers they were, and Japanese at that. It was probably some sort of tong thing, if Japanese had those. Certainly it had nothing to do with a professor of horticulture at one of the world's largest and finest universities.

James poured himself a port and downed it rather too fast.

"He was murdered with cyanide gas," repeated Miss Ritchie. "And we thought…"

"You thought," James corrected. He had not thought about it at all. At least, well, he hadn't thought about it any more than he had to, and that was too much. "If he was murdered it had to be done with something," James heard himself say. The words were out before he could stop them. He didn't want to talk about this thing. He didn't want to be disturbed. He just wanted—

"But I don't mean the victim," said Miss Ritchie, her voice awestruck. "He was just killed with a conk on the head, probably. But the other one. The murderer! The one we thought was driving the car. He was the one that was poisoned."

James poured himself another glass of wine. Temptation was strong within him. It wasn't liquor. It wasn't love. What he wanted, he realized, was to make this young lady's eyes look even wider and lovelier than ever.

"We thought he was killed in the crash!" said Miss Ritchie. "And all the time he was poisoned!"

"Naturally," said James.

"I don't get it," said Miss Ritchie. "What do you mean, *naturally?*"

"That explains the rubber band," said James.


CHAPTER 3


"FOR TUESDAY PREPARE THE chapter on the crop-thinning of prunes and apricots for size," commanded Professor Biddle. He removed his spectacles and snapped them into their case with a punctuating click. It was only two o'clock, and his last class for the day.

His students filed out, released and clamorous, a bunch of large-sized children. Most of them weren't interested in crop-thinning. They were there because they needed a unit from one to two o'clock on Tuesdays and Thursdays, or because they thought it would be a pipe course. Maybe ten out of a hundred would ever actually get out on the land and practice what he was trying to force into their minds with the sweat of his own brow and the example of his own enthusiasm.

Often he felt lonely, lost in a sea of bobbing heads. They were not of his epoch, these kids. They thought of him and his subject as merely the dull and unavoidable adjuncts of bonfires in the bowl, pajamarinos, junior proms, big games, houses, and calf-love.

For years he had tried to show students how we live in a teeming jungle, how utterly dependent we are on plants, and how we have created a partnership by making plants dependent on us.

A few students got the idea and became fired with the allure of chlorophyll, the magic color with which the smallest blade of grass traps the mighty sun.

A few girls went out of his classes into marriage and brightened their lives and the lives of their families with window-boxes of geraniums and borders of cinerarias. And a few men became farmers and lived in the peaceful sunlight with not much money but a lot of satisfaction. Those students were a teacher's reward.

James had the whole afternoon to play with. The campus was sparkling with springtime green. The campanile shone white and aspiring. Today its bells had the special windy sound of March bells, though it wasn't yet March.

James thought of Kay Ritchie. This seemed her kind of a day, clear, sunny, and vivid, the kind of a day to have a good time. He found his feet leading him gently downhill. Treasure Island! It called him.

Sometimes James found his thoughts so closely wedded to action as to be almost indistinguishable from it. It seemed, with hardly any interval of time, that Xantippe was left deserted in a parking lot and James found himself on the high throbbing deck of the ferry.

The bay was choppy and blue, reflecting a February sky rinsed clean by a winter of forty inches. Seagulls glided hopefully along abreast of the galley. The ferry plunged forward with a deep, surging strength, as though pulled by an irresistible lodestone toward the magic island.

And what an island! Its cream and golden towers reared above the salt waves. It was an Aladdin's palace, incredible beyond human dreams, an Atlantis reversed, a gleaming city that overnight rose out of the sea.

Even before the ferry nosed into the slip James observed that the palms were doing finely. He took more than a proprietary interest in the planting. His advice had been freely asked and given, and as it was a gift, he felt doubly responsible for his counsel.

He disembarked with a crowd of chattering students and made his way along the flower-bordered walks. Stately lines of *Phoenix Dactyl-*

*ifera* clashed their fronded swords in the Pacific trade winds.

It had been lot of trouble, moving those giants. Some of them were heavier than a house, heavy and awkward. And the highways, a maze of wires and overpasses and antiquated bridges, had limited them to ten-ton loads.

But the trees had marched. Look at them, then try to deny it! And they made a brave show. They were worth all that trouble.

Palms were all very well, but James progressed toward the yacht harbor and the Fine Arts Building. It was there he would find his first love, his pets, his olive trees.

He had mothered them like an old hen. More than a hundred years old, they were. Their inception was lost in the haze of a half-seen past. Shades of the Padres, of bronze-skinned Indians, of Russians down in their hidebound boats from Sitka hunting sea-otters in the bay!

These were the things James's olive trees made vivid before his eyes. These very trees had seen those days. Their gnarled old trunks had been graceful saplings then. No one knew who had planted them or who, during the summer droughts of their sapling days, had felt the cut of the thong into his shoulder as the *olla* tilted to give its quenching draught to the young roots.

There were fifty trees in all. There were many other olive trees on the island, but these hoary graybeards were James's passion. They came from the Werner ranch, which was part of an old Spanish grant.

With each tree, carefully boxed, came eight tons of the soil it had grown in. Somnolent in their rugged age, the trees could hardly have felt the change. Not a root was touched, not a gnarled branch severed. And yet here they stood, gleaming gray-green in the sea-swept air. And here a short year ago the striped bass stemmed the tide between Yerba Buena and Alcatraz.

James wandered happily down his double aisle of trees. The chattering, milling folk about him gave him a sense of well-being. America was at peace. Let the rest of the world dish up its daily war. Here was civilization, peace, and the olive branch. The branch and the bole and the root were here, and the peaceful soil.

James was arrested suddenly by the unexpected. A small handtruck and spraying equipment stood at the side of the walk. Sawhorses deflected pedestrians with the time-honored message, supposititious no doubt, that men were at work.

One of the olive trees, one of his trees, was covered with a fumigating tent. Why would they be fumigating an olive tree? Peace, that faery will-o'-the-wisp, began to evade James.

Why had he not been consulted? Why? Why?

The only workman in evidence was a chunky individual with cauliflower ears. James promptly addressed him.

"What goes on here?" he demanded. James couldn't have been more outraged if he had found somebody meddling with his safety razor. These trees weren't actually his, of course, but by the love and attention he had put into them he felt that he had made them his.

"Who authorized this work?" James demanded again. "I don't recall—"

"Scram, buddy," advised the workman. He was a most unpleasant looking man. His ears were distorted to the point that they hardly appeared human. They looked like sprouting nodules of coral or mushrooms misshapen by having to squeeze through a crack in the pavement.

"I want you to know I—"

"Dis gas is bad for guys wid neckties," said the lout. "Scram outa dis, buddy."

Clearly, James observed, he was no physical match for such a person. He must have reinforcements. And there were some questions to ask, plenty of questions. He was about to leave the shrouded tree when he was stopped by a gentleman with a camera, a sallow complexion, and Panama hat that concealed all but a fringe of fiery red hair.

"Can you tell me what is being done to that tree?" the man asked. His words were too carefully enunciated to allow of his being taken for an American. James thought him probably one of those redheaded Italians from the Piedmont district of Mussolini's area.

"I can't say," James answered truthfully, "but I intend to find out."

The redheaded gentleman rejoined a lady, quite a strikingly beautiful lady, who had stood aloof a couple of paces during the inquiry.

"He does not know but he is going to inquire," the man related accurately, and the two walked off together, stopping once at a distance of some fifty yards to look back.

A line from *Macbeth* popped into James's head, full fledged. "Fear not," it said, "till Birnam wood do come to Dunsinane!" James recaptured the context from some cobby interstice of his brain. The messenger's report: "I looked toward Birnam, and anon, methought, the wood began to move!"

James's recourse to Shakespeare was interrupted by a remark at his elbow.

"Must have some kind of scale," was the comment. James accepted the diagnosis as being addressed to him and turned to encounter a venerable but rugged-looking old gentleman in a suit of shiny black mohair.

"Must have the scale," repeated the patriarch. "I can't figure any other reason to tent over a tree like that. Seems kind of silly to start doctoring a tree that's lived through what they have."

"Exactly," said James. It was more than silly. He departed rapidly in the direction of the administration building. He was annoyed and his mood was spoiled.

But at the very door of the administration building James paused. The wheels of authority being once set in motion spin on to tiresome lengths. Also, he rationalized, why allow one's self to be fussed? Why not relax and enjoy the afternoon? And why not enjoy it with somebody? With somebody like Miss Ritchie, for instance? Why not Miss Ritchie herself?

The professor palpitated absurdly on his end of the telephone. He was making a date. What of it? It was done, constantly. Everybody he knew lived from one date to another by a calendar of intimate celebrations. Not saints' days, perhaps, but at least offerings to devotion of some sort.

James called the office of the San Francisco *Sun-Telegraph.*

She was there. She would come. She would love it.

He hung up the receiver with a glow of excitement stirring in his veins. Kay Ritchie. It was a nice name, small and neat, like herself. If you said the name over she appeared instantly before your eyes, her brown hair very fine and smooth and dodging unexpectedly behind pretty little ears that heard everything.

He waited at the West Ferry building, and almost before he began to look for her she was there.

"You really did forgive me, didn't you!" she laughed. Her hand was very silky and cool and satisfactory to the feel, not wiry with energy, or flaccid with self-effacing, but firm and confiding and neat, like her. James let go of it reluctantly.

"Forgive you?" he said.

"For making you drive me to my paper last night and making you late for your paper. I mean, when I came around to see you I thought you were maybe just being nice because you couldn't help being nice, being a nice person. But you wouldn't have called me up today if you hadn't wanted to see me, would you? That sort of convinces me."

"I didn't want to see you at all," said Professor Biddle. "I wanted to show you my olive trees, because I'm so proud of them, and because it's spring, or something."

Miss Ritchie nodded. "I wondered if you might call up," she admitted. "I mean it was so chummy and nice seeing you peering out of your tomatoes last night. I thought we kind of hit it off."

"I thought so," said James. "And it seemed to me we ought to go on the roller coaster. I've never been on one."

"Haven't you?" Her nose wrinkled with disbelief. "Well, I suppose I ought to say I haven't either. But the fact of the matter is—you see, I wasn't born yesterday, James. Do you mind if I don't ring in the Philadelphia title? And you can save a lot of syllables by calling me Kay. You're sort of sedate, aren't you? I thought at first you were an impossible stuffed shirt. Then quite by chance something seemed to break the ice. I heard it crack. I suppose it was that accident."

Her little heels clicked a syncopated accompaniment to his long strides as they made for the Gayway. Her chatter was the most pleasing sound he had ever heard, he thought. It went on and on.

"When people go through something unusual like that, even though it happens in a few seconds, it seems to me it's just as though it adds years onto their friendship. As though time isn't really just a certain measure that can't change, but has different gears, and sometimes you're in high and sometimes you're in low."

James nodded. "My olive trees are very old," he said. "Old with all kinds of years. Such years as 1849, for instance, and 1917."

James and Kay threaded their way among a thickening crowd as they approached the Gayway. Everywhere was laughter and the hum of excited voices. They entered through the arch of the Pagoda. "There it is," cried Kay. "The roller coaster!"

James bought two tickets to "The Race Through the Clouds," and presently he and Kay were strapped side by side into a seat and moving deliberately uphill, no longer masters of their fate.

"I'm not sure I'm going to like this," said James, but Kay reassured him.

"I was scared the first time," she said. "You see, things that scare you don't get tiresome like other things. Murder, for instance. I know I'll always be just crazy about murder!"

"Really, Miss—uh, Kay!" James objected. Why did she have to pick this moment to mention death and destruction? The car had reached the summit now. It was about to plunge into the most fearful abyss.

"Any really decent girl would scream and start grabbing for landmarks," shouted Kay as the wind began to whistle. "But you see I love to be scared, James. I just can't carry on the way men always expect a girl to."

By now they were plunging at a ghastly speed, and even Kay's words failed her. It was James who was grabbing at landmarks, and he found Kay's firm little hand very comforting and steadfast. He held it until after incredible convolutions the car arrived back at the station again.

"Well," said Kay. "That really was something, wasn't it!"

James was speechless for the ensuing minutes. They wandered down the sparkling madhouse of the Gayway. Freaks and frolic, hawkers and bells and horns, and laughing crowds created an effervescent effect of Mardi Gras.

"Let's go on something else," Kay begged. She had her arm tucked confidently into his, and when she spoke she twisted her face around and looked up at him in the most pleasing way.

They went in the skyride to get a view of the island. It lifted them up and up.

"Look!" said Kay. "A beautiful yacht sailing down toward Treasure Cove. You can even see a little blue flag with a white diamond at its masthead. Does that mean the owner's aboard? I wish I knew about yachts."

James remembered that boat. He had seen it gliding under the bridge just after the wreck.

There was one thing about Kay. She didn't have to be answered. She didn't even expect it. She carried on all by herself, practically automatic. "I don't know about yachts either," James said. But suddenly he wished he had a yacht, because Kay would be pleased.

He thought of other ways he could please her. If he could just find her something sensational for her paper, that would probably please her most of all. It would probably entail thinking against his will about such distasteful matters as that affair on the bridge.

"James, James!" she was demanding. "Look at that lovely lagoon and the Japanese pagoda and bridge and everything! Isn't it exquisite! And look at the fountains and the statues. And the people! They look like ants!"

"Look at my olive trees," said James. "There they are. All of them. They were good-sized trees before the prairie schooners weighed anchor for the West. They—by the way, Kay, would you like a story for your blessed *Sun-Telegraph?*"

"Oh, James! Would I!" No doubt about it. Kay had a natural appetite for news.

"You'll have to be patient," said James. "It's quite a long story. It begins with different kinds of scale. You are aware, of course, that trees are afflicted with scale?"

Kay sighed. "I thought you were going to tell me something hot, James. There's no news angle in scale, I'm afraid."

"But I'm not talking about the common black or San Jose scale," said James. "I'm talking about red scale. Black scale, for instance, shows a preference for such ornamental hosts as pepper trees. It spreads to oranges and lemons and other fruit trees and does a certain amount of damage but is very easily controlled with an oil spray."

"Oh, James," begged Kay. "Must I listen? I'm not so very good about such things, really."

"You'll have to listen if you want the story," said James. "Of course if you prefer I can call in a reporter from the *Evening Star.* Come to think of it, I know one quite well. A likeable fellow…"

"Well, go ahead about the scale," said Kay. "I'm listening."

"I was telling you about the black scale," said James. "I believe it has been known to afflict olive trees, though it has decidedly no preference for them. And being on intimate terms with my olive trees, I can say definitely that while they *might* have black scale they *haven't* got it."

"I see," said Kay. Her voice was gloomy, remote. James realized that they had had a better time being frightened together in "The Race Through the Clouds" than they were having now. In the unselfconsciousness bred of terror he had grabbed her hand and to have is to hold. But on the subject of scale he was most at home and most himself. Professor James Yeats Biddle never grabbed anybody's hand. It wasn't done.

"The red scale," said James, "is a much more cantankerous character. He must be routed by means of fumigation. He does not, however, attack olive trees."

"What, never?" said Kay listlessly.

"No, never," said James. He was enjoying himself. He was enjoying himself because presently Miss Kay Ritchie would be demanding this recitation all over again and hanging on his words. Hanging on them. "Red scale is often found on lemon trees and oranges," said James. "Never on olives. Is that clear?"

"Quite," said Kay. "Proceed."

The car reached bottom at this point and the attendant came around. "We'll go again," said James. "It's so peaceful and quiet up there."

"It's all of that," Kay agreed. The car took off.

"Well," pursued James, "I thought you might be interested to know that my olive trees are being treated for red scale. In other words, somebody, for reasons of his own, is fumigating my olive trees for a disease they could not possibly have. And the treatment for that disease, the treatment for red scale, my dear, is cyanide gas."

Kay's eyes grew round and dark.

"Cyanide!" she breathed. "But that's…"

"Exactly," said James. "I thought you might be interested."


## CHAPTER 4

JAMES HAD LOOKED FORWARD to a reaction from Kay, but he wouldn't voluntarily have closeted himself for a skyride with a wildcat.

"Then, then—but I've got to get out of here!" she screamed. "Do you realize what that means, James? Why—" Kay Ritchie's agitation made her inarticulate. "Why, then fumigating your old olive trees was just somebody's subterfuge for murder! And those men on the bridge—I've got to get that story out, James! I'm going to jump!"

The giant ball had just started to climb, but James suspected the ground was farther away than it looked to Kay in her excitement. He restrained her by force.

"Oh! You're mean!" she cried, wriggling and impotent. "How can I sit here patiently for ten minutes while somebody else digs up the story and gets my scoop?"

"Nobody's going to get your scoop," James promised. "And what's more if you wrote it in your present state of mind you'd get it all wrong."

Reluctantly she abandoned the struggle. Anybody could see now that the sphere was too high to jump from, and James withdrew his restraining arms with a sigh of regret. Only a gentleman would have used reason. Force was so much more alluring. Well, at least he had combined the two.

James was breathing rapidly. You couldn't hold something like that in your arms without knowing it. And he felt definitely more breathless than the exertion warranted.

"What do you mean I'd have it all wrong?" Kay demanded now, the pair of little wooden buttons on the shoulders of her coat marshalling themselves to pinch hit for chips. "I guess it doesn't take a college professor to put two and two together. After all, cyanide in a man's lungs. The man found dead half a mile in a beeline from a tree that's being unnecessarily fumigated with cyanide. It's as plain as the nose on your face. It was all planned. It was premeditated murder intended to look like an automobile accident."

"If you wanted to put out a match, my dear Kay, would you send for the fire department?"

Kay pouted. "I don't see the parallel."

"Why assemble half a ton of canvas and pumps and spraying material just to murder a man?" James inquired practically. "If cyanide is your dose, why not drop a grain in his coffee? So much neater."

Kay was incensed. "Well, all right. You know so much. What's your explanation?"

James pulled out his pipe. "Mind?" he asked. "It's quite airy up here."

Kay took a deep breath. "You imprison me against my will by your superior masculine strength, and then you ask me politely if you may smoke. Go ahead. I suppose I ought to bow."

"That's what I have against murder," James explained patiently. "People can't help getting wrought up about it. Look at you. You're all wrought up. First thing you know there's another murder."

"I suppose that's why the man who was driving the car had cyanide in his lungs!" Kay deduced more gently. "I mean, he must have killed the other fellow with a conk on the head. And then somebody else killed him with cyanide gas, which didn't take effect immediately and he had a chance to drive that far before he cracked up. That must be it."

James puffed broodingly on his pipe. "Most distasteful affair," he commented. "I wouldn't have a thing to do with it. No, I wouldn't. Except that it seems to have something to do with my olive trees."

Kay was waiting, searching his face. She looked so pretty he didn't say anything for a minute but just blew rings at the golden figure on the "Tower of the Sun," and out of the corner of his eye took in a much more seductive figure.

"I'll ask Angus what he thinks," Kay resolved. "Inspector Angus McDuff. He's head man on the Homicide Squad. He's my pal. He won't let me take any bum steers."

Resourceful she was, too. All she had to do was mention the name of another man, and James suddenly felt much more inclined to oblige her with anything she wanted.

"We'll go over to the olive trees," he said. "I'll show you the setup. But I can't believe anybody would assemble that much machinery for a mere murder."

"But if I could just trace the man who brought the fumigating stuff and find him, why it would solve the murder!" Kay's eyes sparkled with detective sheen.

"You don't have to trace him," said James. "At least if the person who brought the equipment is the one who's operating it now, why—"

"You mean there's somebody?" Kay stared with disbelief.

"A very unpleasant somebody," James specified. "A gent, if you know what I mean. A gent with cauliflower ears."

"Let me down!" wailed Kay. "I've got to interview him! He'll get away, James. Don't you realize? Murderers don't just stick around till you get ready to attend to them!"

"He's been sticking around for a while, evidently," James pointed out. "Furthermore, it might not be safe to interview a murderer. The fellow was a most unsavory type."

"Oh, dear," wailed Kay. "Won't this vehicle ever go down? I don't care how unsavory he is. Of course he's unsavory, or he wouldn't be the murderer. What a scoop!"

"But, my dear girl," James argued out discouragingly, "to get back to your own words, 'murderers don't just stick around.' Doesn't that almost convince you that the person down there now is not the murderer? And that in allowing him to get his story in print you might be deceiving your public?"

"You're impossible," said Kay briefly. "Why didn't you call the police?"

"Because they're always reprimanding me," said James. "And besides, I wanted to let you know first, so you could get your scoop."

Kay was somewhat mollified, but she said, "I don't think Angus McDuff will like it. And I certainly hope the man is still there."

The car was nearing the ground.

"At last!" rejoiced Kay. Once her little feet touched terra firma James had difficulty keeping up with her. She didn't hold his arm any more. She tripped on half a pace ahead of him. She was a businesswoman, now, business bent, and he could like it or lump it. Well, he liked it.

Kay dodged into a phone booth and called her pal, Angus. "You must call him Inspector McDuff," she warned James. "He's very dignified. He won't let anybody but me call him Angus and he's very pleased with my sleuthing and he's coming right away."

James felt a pleasant little twinge of jealousy. What was pleasant about it was that he had a right to be jealous. He didn't know where that right came from, but surely it was there.

Perhaps it was the subtle way that Kay threw her pal, Angus, at him, tacitly spurring jealousy, perhaps it was that which gave James a proprietary place. Anyway it was a place in the sun, and he basked in it.

James was surprised to find Mr. Sperry and several other members of the Fair administration gathered before the cyanide tent. The man with the cauliflower ears was out of evidence.

James introduced Kay. "Miss Ritchie has heard the mystery of the cyanide tent," James confessed. "My indiscretion."

But Mr. Sperry seemed relieved. "Then we can talk about it freely," he said. "I don't understand it. Nobody seems to have given orders. When it was reported that the trees were being mistreated I thought of course it was an erroneous report and that you had arranged whatever attention they were getting. Now it appears you don't know anything about it either! I've sent for the head gardener. He'll be here presently."

"I talked with the gentleman who seemed to be in charge," said James. "He was a forceful individual. Biceps, and all that. Not to mention his cauliflower ears."

"The man with the cauliflower cars!" Kay wailed. "He's gotten away from me, James. And it's all your fault!"

"You say somebody reported the trees were being misused?" James reminded.

"Two strangers," said Mr. Sperry. "They declined to leave their names. She was rather a strikingly beautiful woman."

"I know," James remembered. "And he had red hair."

Mr. Sperry nodded eagerly. "Those were the people."

Kay was consumed with admiration. Her eyes as they feasted on James were positively slavish. "How did you ever know that?" she whispered.

James grinned. It was fun having somebody look at you like that. He walked over to the green tarpaulin and around it till he came to an overlap in the material. It was drawn tightly closed. He unfastened a cotton rope and lifted the flap. The tent smelled of nothing but the wholesome greenery of the tree. But as he stooped to step into the tent there was a little wail of anguish from Kay.

"Oh, James!" she cried. "Don't go in there."

Even Mr. Sperry remonstrated with a "Say, Professor…"

But James entered doughtily. There was the pleasant, early California aroma of olives and the fabric smell of sun-baked canvas. But more than these, there was the smell of freshly turned loam. And at his feet James saw in the green dimness a rectangular hole a couple of feet wide and perhaps six feet long, half refilled with moist earth, a hole the size and shape of a door. Or a coffin.

James backed out into the open and Kay gave a little gasp of relief. "Oh, James," she scolded. "I wish you wouldn't do things like that! Have some consideration for other people. Why, in a few minutes you might suddenly—"

He couldn't believe it, because it was still a little difficult for him to see clearly in the bright outdoors after the green shadow inside the tent, but if he had been able to believe his senses he would have thought he saw tears in the eyes of Kay Ritchie! No. That couldn't be.

Kay's pal Angus came up now with reinforcements, and James was introduced.

Angus McDuff was a stalwart Scots copper of severe mien and canny black eyes. The R's in his diction had been bullied but not tamed. He acknowledged James with a perfunctory politeness. It was clear he had no great respect for the cap and gown.

"Professor Biddle has been so good as to take practically complete charge of these trees for us," Mr. Sperry explained, by way of a buildup for him. James appreciated it.

"And he saw at once that cyanide wouldn't do olive trees any good," said Kay.

"Nor if the professor got this outfit in here will it do him any good either," Angus McDuff observed unexpectedly.

"But I didn't," said James. "Anybody knows that olive trees don't have red scale. And that cyanide—"

"Maybe so and maybe not," said the inspector. He motioned to his cohorts. "Yank that tarpaulin off there, and if it don't smell good clear out of it. We'll get to the bottom of this. A man has been found murdered and another dying of cyanide gas a mile from these trees, Professor!" said McDuff.

"Not dying, Inspector," James corrected. "Dead."

"Found dead, with another stiff beside him," said Angus, "but observed driving the car, Professor. Dead men drive no cars, Professor."

"Possibly," said James. "At least I can see how a tolerably intelligent man might hold that opinion, Inspector McDuff."

By this time McDuff's men had removed the tarpaulin and uncovered the hole in the ground.

"A grave!" shrieked Kay. "James! Angus! A grave!"

Mr. Sperry nervously shushed her up. He evidently felt that if it *was* a grave it shouldn't be called to the attention of the holiday public.

"But people would be thrilled!" said Kay. "People love murders. Oh, Angus, dig it up, please! Please dig up the body!"

An overwrought gentleman with a forehead furrowed deep with care now joined the group. James knew him well. Mr. Krantz was a sturdy, hard-working American of German parentage. He was conscientious, even to a fault, and was the Exposition's head gardener.

"Mr. Krantz," said Mr. Sperry, "would you be so good as to explain to Inspector McDuff how this fumigating equipment came to be here?"

Mr. Krantz wagged his head helplessly. "I don't know, sir," he said. "Day before yesterday it showed up. I didn't think nothing of it. It's something of the professor's, I say to myself. Me, I'm just the head gardener. I don't boss nobody. Everybody bosses me. I see this canvas, like. But I don't know if it's my business or somebody else's business. I decide I'll mind my own business and that's that."

"Now if you could provide a couple of men with shovels, Mr. Krantz," directed Inspector McDuff, "I think that will be all we'll want of you for the moment."

"Oh boy!" Kay rejoiced. Her taste for crime was positively gustatory. "The body!"

"It seems a silly notion to dig out all that dirt," James objected.

"I'll decide as to that," said Inspector McDuff stiffly.

"The body!" insisted Kay.

"Uh, if you please, Miss Ritchie," Mr. Sperry put in uncomfortably. Several passersby had turned startled heads and were on the point of stopping.

"You won't have a scoop if you shout your body from the house-tops." This admonition from James put Kay somewhat under control for a short time.

Two gardeners with shovels were spirited out of the bushes by Mr. Krantz and set at dealing the dirt to left and to right.

"This is nonsense," said James. "A waste of time."

The contents of the hole had just been freshly replaced, so it was quickly emptied. There was nothing at last but the hard, original limits of the hole.

"No body!" Kay was highly incensed. "Imagine! After getting our hopes up."

"Of course there wouldn't be a body," said James. He was becoming more and more annoyed with everybody: with the inspector for being so pompous, with Kay for being so noisy, with Mr. Sperry for being so discreet. And lastly, with himself for getting mixed up in this. Why did he?

It wasn't any concern of his. Suppose there were fifty bodies in that hole in the ground. What difference did it make to him? And why try vainly to tell these misguided people that there would be no body? Why not just let them dig and find out, which in any case was what they had done?

The inspector's disposition became even more acid after James's prognostication about the hole had been proven correct.

"Miss Ritchie," he demanded, "I don't want to be too tough on one of your friends and all that, and Mr. Sperry, I know you always believe the best of everybody, but what I want to know is, how did the professor know there wasn't going to be a body in that hole?"

"The idea was ridiculous," said James tactlessly. "You can't expect to find bodies distributed about here and there just because they're your hobby."

The inspector's eyes narrowed. "Well, my hobby isn't olive trees, Professor," he countered. "And I'm glad of it, right now. I wouldn't want to be in your boots, frankly!"

"This is all a waste of time," said James. "Kay, let's clear out of this. I never was interested in murder and I'm fast getting a positive phobia about it."

"And if this is a waste of time, how would you spend it better?" demanded Inspector McDuff sarcastically.

"I'd watch all the gates and catch the man with the cauliflower ears," said James. "Though I suppose it's too late."

"The gates *are* being watched," said the inspector. "And I also suppose that likely it's too late. Do you know why it's too late? Because you didn't call us immediately, Professor. Because, Professor, you saw fit to obstruct justice!"

Kay was twisting her handkerchief in small nervous fingers. "Now, Angus," she said, pleading James's cause. "Don't be too hard on James. He just wanted to call me first because he isn't interested in such things as murder and doesn't know anything about them, and he was afraid he'd make some mistake."

The inspector showed his teeth in a steely grin. "He made a mistake when he didn't call headquarters," said the inspector. "And doesn't it strike you as odd, Miss Ritchie, that a gentleman above such sordid matters as common murder should be so sure there wasn't a body in that hole?"

A sudden light came into Kay's eyes. "But Angus! Of course! It's clear as day. How could there be a body in the hole when they were in the car that crashed on the bridge? Don't you see? They changed their plans!"

"Bodies don't change their plans," Angus answered grimly.

"Silly," laughed Kay. "I don't mean the bodies changed their plans. I mean the murderers. They had a hole all dug, and then for some reason they decided not to use it, and one of them came back to fill it up. Then James came along, and the man was frightened and went off. And that's all there is to it. It's the solution, Angus! Don't you see? James was right all along. He's awfully clever, Angus, really. He's much brighter than professors generally are and a lot brighter than he lets on."

"That's just what I think, Miss Kay," said Angus McDuff. "That's my opinion in a nutshell. I think the professor knows a lot more than he lets on, and I'm going to find out what it is."

"I'm fed up with this business," said James irritably. "It's something I didn't want to mess around in in the first place and now I've had enough and to spare. Come on, Kay. I'm through."

"No, Professor, you aren't through," said Angus McDuff evenly. "You'll be at the morgue tomorrow at ten o'clock. We're having an inquest at that time. I'll want you to be there and tell what you know about a couple of murdered Japanese. I'll want you to tell what you know about cyanide, too. And why you would get it in here for olive trees. And maybe just for the hell of it you'll tell how you knew there wasn't any body in that hole. And why you didn't want us to dig there. And why you obstructed justice!"

"But I can't be there at ten o'clock," said James. "I have a class."

"Ten A.M., Professor," said Angus McDuff. And he wasn't fooling.


CHAPTER 5


JAMES TIPTOED UP THE AISLE and slipped into a vacant seat beside Kay Ritchie. He was fifteen minutes late, and he felt a pleasant glow of self-esteem as he met the glowering, tired eyes of Inspector McDuff. He didn't like officious people. It was part of every citizen's duty to put such public servants in their place. And if the inspector chose to make an issue of it, that would be all right, too. James didn't propose to cringe. Besides, if it became really necessary, he could always blame his tardiness on Xantippe. Her waywardness was unpredictable. It was an act of God.

"You're late," whispered Kay Ritchie.

"So I am," James whispered back.

He looked around the inquest chamber critically. The stout gray-haired man sitting at an isolated table with McDuff beside him was probably the coroner. James tabbed him with that title, anyway. The twelve men ranged behind them on stiff bright oak chairs would be the jury. They looked dejected and half-sleeping. Even the young fellow giving short, crisp answers to the questions drawled at him looked much less impressive in civilian clothes than in his traffic officer's uniform of yesterday.

James yawned. He'd seen everything that happened when the sedan was wrecked. He wasn't interested in this routine stuff. For that matter, he didn't have much use for inquests. He had never attended one before, but he had the definite feeling that they were a waste of time. They were red tape, that was all. The authorities knew the men had been murdered, so why didn't they give all their efforts to tracking down the criminal?

James shrugged irritably. He had read a few detective stories because they were a favorite relaxation of Woodrow Wilson, whom he admired. It was hard work for him, however, for he always raced the homicide squad to a solution. As a rule he pinned it on the butler a step ahead of New York's Centre Street. And it was no trick at all to pick out the black-sheep brother from Australia and get the jump on Scotland Yard.

But nowadays, as James understood, the writers were learning to do a better job of it. The blunt instrument, he believed, was now definitely frowned upon. And the bittersweet smell of almonds was *passé,* although the deadly curare poison of the Amazon jungles still popped up occasionally, according to the reviews.

The one unvarying fixture must always be the dumb detective. And there was a role that Inspector Angus McDuff could fill without changing a shoelace!

James cast a glance of unveiled hostility at McDuff. The inspector, quite arbitrarily, had coerced him to attend this lugubrious occasion. Small wonder that thinking people were getting frightened about fascism!

An elbow digging into James's ribs put to flight his stirring social consciousness. He looked down at Kay and saw that she had purposely roused him from his moody cerebrations.

"Look!" the girl whispered excitedly. "We're entertaining royalty, almost. That's *the* Mrs. Porter Cartwright entering from the wings. Who said there was no future for chorus girls?"

James looked obediently, ignoring Kay's feline thrust. A woman was, indeed, entering from the corridor. And what a woman! James yielded to few men in his firm indifference to mere feminine beauty. He went in for personality and character. But Mrs. Porter Cartwright had something that was not akin to these, and James was fascinated.

She was rather tall for a woman, slender and poised. She was young and blonde and very beautiful. She walked down the aisle with lithe grace, a faint patrician smile curving her full, lightly painted lips. Her dress of clinging, dark blue crepe was in exquisite taste. Her smiling eyes, silently thanking the attendant who scurried forward to show her to a seat, were impersonal but gracious. She was God's perfect female. She was chewing gum.

"James," whispered Kay, "your mouth is open. And I think someone is paging you."

He looked up, startled, and was conscious of a stir of chairs. The speed cop had finished his testimony. "Professor Biddle," a voice repeated. Kay gave him a gentle shove.

"Remember," she said, grinning, "they haven't got a thing on you!"

He took the vacated chair beside the table. After exchanging hostile glances with McDuff, James went through the opening ritual. He admitted his identity and that he had been proceeding on the Bay Bridge toward Berkeley shortly before eight o'clock on Wednesday night.

"And," asked the gray-haired man, glancing at a note pad, "you made a U-turn at some distance west of the toll plaza?"

"There were extenuating circumstances," said James coldly.

The coroner smiled a patient deprecation. He didn't seem to be the browbeating type, at all. There were a couple of elk teeth suspended over his comfortable embonpoint.

"We have no interest here in your motoring eccentricities, Professor Biddle," he explained, "except to establish that you were traveling west at the time the accident occurred."

"Yes," said James, "I was heading back toward San Francisco. I stopped, however, just before the sedan crashed. But it was just luck that it didn't hit my automobile."

"Please proceed," directed his interlocutor. "Describe what you saw. In detail."

James described what he had seen. He described the sedan crashing against the ramp, after its terrifying sweep along the bridge, and the two still bodies.

"They were both dead," he finished, "when the officer and I arrived."

"Is that just an opinion," snapped the coroner, "or do you claim professional knowledge in that field?"

"No." James shook his head. "But—"

"Did you hear the testimony of the medical examiner just now?"

"I guess I arrived a trifle late for that."

"Well, if you'd been here," the coroner went on, severely, "you would have heard Dr. Cronise state positively that one of the men was alive until he was thrown out of the sedan. He had absorbed enough cyanide to cause his death eventually, perhaps. But he had contusions that were certainly caused by the crash. And you can't bruise the body of a dead man, Professor Biddle."

"Then at best he was unconscious," James insisted stubbornly. "There must have been a third man in that car before it picked up speed—"

Inspector McDuff leaned forward suddenly.

"Did you see a third man?" he demanded.

"I was occupied at the moment," said James. "But a third man had to be there to adjust the rubber band that was holding down the hand throttle of the wrecked machine."

"What rubber band?" demanded the inspector.

"It snapped loose when I brushed it with my cuff."

"Why were you tampering with evidence, Professor Biddle?"

"I wasn't tampering," James cried, exasperated. "The traffic officers had more than they could do. I thought they might not have turned the ignition off. I was afraid a short circuit somewhere might start a fire."

"I suppose you know," went on McDuff, inexorably, "that cars aren't allowed to stop on the bridge except in emergency. You know that pedestrians aren't allowed at all. Or do you make it a practice not to read signs?"

"I read them yes," James retorted doggedly. "I also know when an emergency exists. And furthermore I know a third man—"

"Did you see him? Did anybody see him? No, of course not!" Inspector McDuff answered his own bellowed question. His tired eyes were getting hot. He thumped the table with his fist. "I've checked up thoroughly. There wasn't a pedestrian came off the bridge at any time Wednesday night."

"He could have dived," James pointed out. "There's deep water right below."

"Seventy feet below, at that point," interposed McDuff, "and water nearly freezing cold. If a man dived, he'd have had to have a boat waiting to pick him up."

"A boat did pass beneath the bridge at exactly the time of the crash," announced James coldly. "I'm surprised, Inspector, that you missed such an important fact in your undoubtedly thorough checking up."

"You'd be surprised, Professor," McDuff answered grimly, "at just how many points we have checked up! Including the mystery boat you mention. It was the *Iolanthe,* Mr. Porter Cartwright's yacht. Are you accusing Mr. Cartwright of being mixed up in the murder of two Japanese?"

James was momentarily squelched, almost.

"Well, then," he said, "just try and find some other reasonable explanation for that rubber band."

"Here now," the coroner interposed crisply, "we want all the truth, but this debate has lasted long enough. The purpose of an inquest is not to play with theories. We're to establish facts."

"I've told you everything I know," said James.

"Except," amended the inspector, "how you could be so sure there was no body in that Treasure Island grave."

"Sorry," James retorted, in orderly retreat. "I was just playing with a theory. As you've so ably pointed out, I haven't a shred of evidence. We even seem to have lost the rubber band!"

"Thank you, Professor Biddle, for your cooperation," the coroner said, dismissing him hastily. And James, feeling a trifle wild-eyed and breathing heavily through his nose, stalked back to his chair beside Kay Ritchie.

Kay patted his arm as he sat down. James didn't know whether it indicated approval or merely sympathy, but he was comforted. He bent down to whisper to her, but his attention was attracted by the summoning of the final witness.

"Doreen Cartwright!"

Mrs. Porter Cartwright was always at her superb best in managing her entrances, James suspected. But she surprised him by proving to be a first-rate witness, too. If she leaned a little heavily on the broad A"so much the vogue in Hollywood, her statement still emerged in satisfactorily sharp focus. She had brains, she had. But why would she, a lady, chew gum in public? Were her nerves at the breaking point? What was there about this inquest to frighten Doreen Cartwright?

"I boarded the *Iolanthe* about seven-thirty on Wednesday evening," she said. "Mr. Cartwright had some sort of conference to attend and did not come with me."

"If you please," interrupted the coroner, "were you accompanied by any guests?"

"I was alone. It was just a whim. The night was lovely, and I thought it would be pleasant to circle Treasure Island. The lighting effects are magnificent. And one gets quite a new perspective from the water, don't you think? Moving slowly, as one can aboard a yacht."

"Yes, yes, I quite understand, Mrs. Cartwright," the coroner agreed. Glamour and gold were broadsiding him. He was sinking fast, James noticed. He was beginning to use a broad A, too!

"We left the island anchorage at once," resumed Doreen Cartwright, "and cruised under the east end of the Bay Bridge. At that time the crew was forward, all six of them, except for our Japanese cabin steward, who had just brought me my coat, my mink coat, on the after deck.

"As I recall it, the *Iolanthe* had cleared the bridge when we both heard a crash. We looked up, but there was nothing we could see, of course."

"And you saw no one plunge down into the water?"

"Positively not!"

"Thank you, Mrs. Cartwright," smiled the coroner. "Thank you very much. That will be all."

James sat there alone while the jury went into their huddle, as Kay had left him to telephone. Every time he looked up, it seemed, Inspector Angus McDuff was staring at him. It was very irritating.

But the verdict of the coroner's jury came quickly, after an interval so short that it hardly seemed dignified. It was the traditional formula. Time had been wasted and nothing proved. One of the Japanese had died, the verdict read, as a result of the bridge wreck, but he, as well as his murdered companion, had been a victim of "a person or persons unknown."

"Come on," said James. "Let's get out of here."

It was a change to be out in the light and air again with the high morning sun burning down on their heads. Out of the presence of death and darkness into the benevolent, life-giving sunshine.

"Oh, dear," said Kay. "I wish I didn't have to go straight back to the paper. But of course I must."

"Nonsense!'" said James. "You weren't covering the inquest for the *Sun-Telegraph.* You were summoned by the law. And even if you weren't called on to testify, you couldn't possibly be a cold-blooded newspaperwoman again today. You've been through an ordeal, and I have plans for you. You're going for a ride."

Kay smiled up at him. "It's fun to be bossed," she said. "I think I'll take a chance. Your story might get by."

James opened the portals of Xantippe and Kay uttered a little screech as she sat on the sun-baked leather.

"Spring is here," said James. "Hot days and cold nights. The sap begins to flow. And instead of having to go on my spring reconnaissance all alone I have you to go with me!"

"You're lucky to be out of jail, my man," Kay allowed. "I was so put out with Angus. He's like a bloodhound, that man. After you of all people! And it's my fault. I let him get off to a wrong start with you, somehow. You were like two bulls, goring each other. Really, it was quite frightening, James. Because, you see, I like you both. And I didn't want you to hurt each other."

"A very bullheaded sleuth, McDuff. You're quite right, my dear."

"Hush," said Kay. "Where are you taking me? Or is it none of my business?"

"It's none of your business," said James. "This is an unadulterated pleasure trip."

Xantippe skimmed along at her favorite lope, seeking out the broad slab of Bayshore Highway. They left a lot of antiquated railroad coaches sidetracked on their left, and on the right the half-settled hills of South San Francisco. The air terminal basked in the sun, awaiting patiently the inevitable day of the flying flivver. A few lone souls with wings dipped and banked over the field.

The brackish tide pressed in, skirting the traffic lanes.

"What are those rows of little sticks out in the bay, James?" asked Kay. She didn't say "Do you know what they are, James?" She asked him as though he, being the font of all knowledge, would undoubtedly know and satisfy her idle curiosity out of the sheer generosity of his nature.

"Oyster stakes," said James. He was glad he did know.

He wanted to come up to her expectations of him. "Oysters grow on trees," he said. "Especially cherrystones."

"Cherrystones are clams," said Kay. "Now I don't believe any of it."

They crossed arteries leading up into fashionable places such as Burlingame and San Mateo. He found the turnoff he was looking for, and they left the fast traffic behind them. After a mile or so over rough oiled chuckholes, he turned in at two blistered Victorian gateposts, stopping Xantippe short before a likewise blistered Victorian house.

The high blinded windows indicated the old-fashioned height of the rooms within. The gables zigzagged whimsically into an occasional mansard influence. Dormers protruded fringed eyelashes of gingerbread. And the whole anachronism pushed back the jungle with just a very gentle hand indeed. Another ten years, perhaps, and no paint pot would save it.

But the jungle thrived. A massive rubber tree crowded palms, acacias, and a spiny lemon into tangled confusion. Wisteria caught easy grips in

the jigsaw and diligently pried shingles off the roof. Bermuda grass under-
foot ran long, bamboo-like runners beneath the clapboards and appeared
unexpectedly at the window ledges.

"Goodness," said Kay. "This must be the wrong number."

James climbed the sun-cupped wooden steps and twisted a manual
doorbell which let out a jangle. Kay followed, a little bit on tiptoe. "Not to
disturb the ghosts," said James.

Kay grinned and flicked her skirt. "You're the most mysterious man,"
she said. "You don't tell 'em anything."

"I treat 'em rough, too," said James.

The door opened, and a middle-aged woman with faded skin laid the
towel, with which she had apparently just been wiping her hands, on the
umbrella stand, before she said briefly, "Yes?"

"Is Mr. Werner in?" James inquired, and then went on, without waiting for an answer. "It doesn't matter. He doesn't know me, and I am
acquainted with him by name only. But I wanted to show Miss Ritchie the
old ranch. Perhaps you don't remember. I am James Biddle. I was down
once in connection with moving the olive trees."

The woman's face hardened. "Mr. Werner isn't here," she said. "And
I'm sure he regrets selling the trees." James had the fleeting impression
that if he didn't put his foot in the door she would slam that oaken bul-
wark in his face. But it was only an impression, for she went on to say,
"Is there anything else?"

"I'm sure Mr. Werner wouldn't object to my showing Miss Ritchie
the ranch," James repeated.

"Oh," said the housekeeper. "Well, I'm sure I don't know. I'll call my
husband."

Without inviting them into the house, the woman half closed the door
and disappeared down the shadowy hall. In a half minute her voice was
heard raised in a plangent "Ree-eed!" And again, "Ree-eed!"

A muffled shout sounded in answer, and presently a stocky fellow
outfitted in various shades of original and accreted drab appeared around
the corner of the house. His trousers were filthy riding breeches which
didn't extend down far enough to meet his low shoes, leaving an interval
unaccounted for either by these or by heavy woolen socks, which were
gathered into wrinkles about his ankles by the sharp decline of his wedge-
shaped calves.

"Yes, sir?" he said. "Ma'am?"

James repeated his wish to show Kay the ranch.

Reed was more hospitable than his wife had been and led the way down an ancient, shell-bordered drive toward the rear. By comparison with the house the stables were in excellent repair. Several fine-looking mares faced them over the paddock fence, pricking alert ears.

"That girl to the left, there, she dammed the *Furlong,*" said Reed. "You've heard of *Furlong.* Everybody has."

James hadn't, but Kay came through. She said, "What a horse!" And James just looked impressed and let it go at that.

"Over there is the old adobe," said Reed. "We use it for tools and tack. Folks sold the old tiles off it last year. Got six bits a tile. Beat that? Guy said the Mexican women made them over their knee. I'd sooner have tarpaper myself. Dump used to leak. It don't now."

"I wanted to show Miss Ritchie where the olive trees at the fair came from," James explained to Reed. "She's seen them up at Treasure Island, but I thought it might interest her to see what's left of the old grove."

"And that ain't much," said Reed cheerfully. He took them past the stables in the direction of the bay. The old grove-site near at hand looked like a piece of shell-scarred Spain, sacked and desolate.

There remained a few culls of the old trees, enough to indicate where the rows had been. And there were deep craters to mark the sites of the trees that were gone.

"Old man carries on about missing his trees," said Reed, "but the ranch is better off without them old things. We'll get in here with a Fresno scraper one of these days and level this all off and make a fine alfalfa field of it. There wasn't no money in olives anyhow. Don't pay to make oil and the market for eating olives is flooded."

Reed's discourse was interrupted by the long musical note of an automobile horn. A handsome, cream-colored roadster rounded the corner of the barn and bounced gently down the lane toward them.

"There's the boss, now," said Reed.

James was prepared to see old man Werner, but when the car came to a halt a young man stepped out.

"Professor Biddle?" he said. "Miss Ritchie? Mr. Werner is my uncle. Mrs. Reed said you wanted to look around, and I wondered if I could show you anything you hadn't seen already. I've lived on the ranch since I was knee high." He turned away momentarily. "How is Girlie, Reed?"

"She's just fine, sir," said Reed. "She knows you're back. I hear her whinnying at you right now."

Werner's nephew was a prepossessing young fellow, eager-faced and intelligent-looking. James felt the familiar nervous twinge of jealousy, which had come to be almost a psychosis with him in the last two days.

And Kay wasn't the demure type with the downcast eyes. Her head was tilted back, and she was drinking the boy in. You couldn't blame her. He had on a pair of fawn-colored pants and a dark brown coat. His shirt and tie were two shades of blue, and he had that straw-colored Scandinavian hair and the smooth tan that goes with it.

James winced. Well, a girl had to do the best she could by herself. That was only reasonable. You couldn't blame a girl for choosing the best. And you certainly couldn't blame her for looking them all over.

"Mr. Reed has shown us everything, I think," said James. "I came down here in an advisory capacity before the olive trees were moved up to Treasure Island, but unfortunately I missed your uncle, both then and now."

"Uncle's up at the fair for a week," said the boy. "He has his little cruiser anchored up there in the cove and he's going to see the exhibits in style. It's just unlucky that you missed him. He hardly ever leaves the ranch unless it's to take some short trip with the boat."

"I think your ranch is lovely," said Kay. "And the horses are beautiful."

The young man's face lit up. "Reed and I manage to put out a nice pony now and then," he said. "It's speed we're after, you know. We breed them for the tracks. Those old girls in the stables, they just eat their heads off. You wouldn't believe what they get away with. That's one reason we talked Uncle into selling his trees. This flat land here would be the best spot on the ranch for another alfalfa lot."

"I told the folks that," said Reed. "Young fella, when you get me a work team I'll soon drag that out smooth for you."

"Well, it won't be long now," the young man said. "Maybe next week I'll have a team for you, Reed."

"We'd better be heading back toward town, Kay," said James. He took her elbow firmly between his thumb and fingers and felt relieved when she came along. He didn't know what he had expected, but how *can* you know what to expect with a girl?

Then he paused. "Thanks again for showing us the hospitality of the ranch," he said to the young man. "I didn't catch your name."

"Bell," said Werner's nephew. "Harvey Bell." He called after them as they reached the stables. "Come again," he invited.

James herded Kay into Xantippe. He ground on the starter and presently they were bouncing off toward Bayshore Highway.

"That name rings a bell," said James. "Did you get it?"

"No," said Kay absentmindedly. "What?"

"The car that was stolen and wrecked the other night—you haven't forgotten it? Well, it was registered to a certain Harvey Bell," said James. "Surely it's no coincidence that our friend is driving a brand-new car today."

"I thought he was a lovely man," said Kay.


## CHAPTER 6

IT WAS SATURDAY MORNING. Crop Rotation at 11 o'clock. Nothing before then. Blessed be nothing. James allowed himself an extra half hour flat on his back to enjoy the luxury of being replete with a new day's energy and of not being expected to spend it immediately in any way whatsoever.

He thought of Kay, mostly, and what a charming little baggage she had turned out to be. And he reflected how Cartwright's millions had only netted him a ravishing plaything, and how on the contrary Kay had sense under her saucy brown locks.

James heard Mrs. Pringle light the crackling fire in the dining room to indicate that breakfast was ready and she wanted him to eat it and get it over with, but with lordly unconcern he stayed right where he was, and even lit his pipe.

An avalanche of hot ashes down his neck, was, however, a fire he could no longer ignore, and he sprang out of bed with a sudden gust of energy.

There was already mail beside his coffee cup, which was one advantage of rising late. But a quick survey of outside indications dissipated his interest. There was a letter executed on the familiar stationery of the Hotel Raleigh. Horrors! It was spring again, and Aunt Millie was Honolulu-bound. James cursed briefly the whole theory of family ties and the invention of stopovers. Another weekend would be sacrificed to putting up a united front.

With a stab of his fork James ripped Aunt Millie's proxy from stem to stern.

Then without reading it he put it down again. Why spoil a beautiful morning? He picked up the *Sun-Telegraph* and undid its crisp folds. In a page of blaring captions his eye went unerringly to a byline name that had come to mean a surprising lot to him, a name that always evoked dancing eyes and red lips parted in challenge: Kay Ritchie.

It was a feature article recounting in a vivacious helter-skelter of punctuation and split infinitives how a certain Princess Tania Varnakov had been robbed last night. She was robbed, it seemed, of a fabulous article called the Ikon of St. John Chrysostom.

James wasn't interested in princesses of the contemporary variety. He doubted if a single one of them would react positively to the time-honored test of the twenty mattresses and the pea. He wasn't interested in crime of any sort, not even murder. No, not even murder, and certainly not robbery.

And it was his invariable wont to drop reading matter like a hot coal at the first incidence of a split infinitive. How could any writer who split infinitives have anything to say? Furthermore, he had never heard of St. John Chrysostom, and an ikon was a dull, primitive thing done in dirty blue and white enamel with a frame of tarnished brass.

But because the byline was Kay Ritchie, and because her particular brand of split infinitives had a peculiar charm for him, James became positively concerned over poor Princess Tania's loss of her St. John. The martyr had reposed clandestinely in her suitcase, the princess reported, until last night. And while she had been away from the room for a merest hour the dignified old fellow had disappeared. What made it touching was that she had already arranged to sell him downriver to the multimillionaire packrat of such antiques, Porter Cartwright. And since the princess had expected to live on the proceeds for the rest of her born days, St. John Chrysostom was evidently some shakes. Done in a mosaic of three primary colors, rubies, sapphires, and canary diamonds, he would have turned over in a bank for a cool hundred thousand, the princess said. But his antique value she placed at five times that, five times at the very least.

Then James gave a snort of glee, for the princess was staying at the Hotel Raleigh, and James's mind, skipping from crag to crag like a mountain goat, had instantly cornered the thief: Aunt Millie, naturally! The picture pleased him. It would be fun to take jellied consommé to Aunt Millie at Folsom Prison. He minded the time when he had been ill with mumps and unable to escape, and Aunt Millie had taken just such an advantage of him for six interminable weeks.

Encouraged by the picture of Aunt Millie in Folsom, James withdrew the contents of the egg-stained envelope and examined it.

Strangely enough, it was not from Aunt Millie at all. It was anonymous. And what it said was:

Advise your friend Kay Ritchie to lay off the Bay Bridge

murder. One murder may cause another, Professor. Murder loves company!

Bred to a fine scorn for anonymous poison-pens, James tried to dismiss this threat with a gesture of contempt and enjoy his second cup of coffee. But something was wrong. Probably Mrs. Pringle, against his positive orders, had purchased more than three ounces of coffee on Thursday. He had explained to her carefully that the essential oils of coffee lose their flavor and may even become rancid within three days of the roasting. And since Mrs. Pringle drank her morning coffee at her own home and James found an ounce each day to be amply sufficient for his own needs, it seemed unreasonable of Mrs. Pringle repeatedly to attempt to deceive him.

Forced into a corner, she had once explained herself. It made her look like a fool, she said, to go into the grocer's and buy three ounces of coffee.

"Mrs. Pringle," James called. And since she was always hovering just beyond the door, waiting to pounce on his dishes the moment he seemed reasonably through with them, she appeared promptly.

"I hate to mention the coffee, again, Mrs. Pringle," said James.

Mrs. Pringle was no dissembler. "But Professor!" she cried. "I've done just as you said I should. Three ounces it was, on, let's see, Thursday."

James dismissed her with an apologetic gesture of the hand and a slight mumbling sound. There was no mistaking truth. It wasn't the coffee, then. It was Kay. He was sick with worry. He couldn't eat. Why not admit it? What could be more childish than to deceive oneself?

James almost tipped over his chair as he dashed to the telephone. He called her room. There was no answer. He called the *Sun-Telegraph.* Kay Ritchie was due there any time, overdue, as a matter of fact. They didn't know why she hadn't stopped in. She was generally very prompt in the morning. Yes, they would have her call back immediately.

James hung up the receiver. He paced his green parlor rug, watching how the nap showed his footsteps more clearly when he was northbound than when he was southbound. Sleuthing. It was in his blood. He couldn't get away from it. He had been trying to keep out of this, but he couldn't keep out any longer. Nobody could make veiled anonymous threats against Kay and get away with it.

James relaxed the censor in his mind, and almost with relief he felt his thoughts stop whipping about senselessly like the rigging of a boat headed dead into the wind. He felt the strum of a full sail, now, and he gave her all she'd take.

That inquest had been a farce. He suspected it hadn't even satisfied Kay's bullheaded McDuff. But it had brought out some things. Some very interesting things. Good cuds to chew on.

Kay. He must find her immediately. Why didn't she call up? Where could she be?

James took out his handkerchief and wiped little beads of sweat off his forehead. He had to wait. If she had left her room just before he called she ought to be at the paper by now. She ought to have had his message and telephoned.

James tried to lose himself in his tomatoes. It was no use. He didn't give a damn about them. Let the ants bring in their cows by the carload. He didn't care. He wanted Kay Ritchie.

Then he knew what he had to do. It was a humiliating thing to do, but he did it. He called McDuff,

Those Hebridean R's skirled over the telephone in a surprisingly welcome way to James's ears. "Ahr, Prrrofessorrr, this is Inspectorrr McDuff."

When James had to humble himself he didn't make any bones about it. "Look, Inspector," he said. "I'm worried about Kay. She hasn't turned up at the paper this morning. And I've had an anonymous letter."

"Can you bring it over?" said McDuff.

"Right away," said James. "I want to talk to you. About that, and other things."

"Oh, and by the way," came McDuff's teasing drawl. "Don't be getting too grizzled about Miss Kay, Professor. She's got ten fine young officers watching out for her. She's here in the office now."

"Thank God for that!" James breathed. "Tell her to stay right there till I get there. I'm on my way."

James mounted Xantippe and sped toward the city. He had difficulty holding Xantippe down to her usual legal pace. She was no sooner sternly checked than she would begin a crafty and gradual acceleration again, intended to delude her master into false composure. Her duplicity was so far successful that twice, warned by a deep, earthy tremor and a sense of foreboding, James found the speedometer quivering in the upper fifties.

Kay in danger! Kay, receiving threatening messages. Kay, under the glazed, cold eyes of the underworld! Well, at least she was momentarily safe.

As he climbed the cold, impersonal steps of police headquarters,

James's heart had already begun to beat faster at the near prospect of seeing her. The officer at the desk indicated McDuff's office, and presently James was facing the impassive physiognomy of that kiltless Highlander.

"Miss Ritchie couldn't wait for ye," said the inspector.

"Damn!" James exploded. Disappointment and uneasiness again possessed him. "I told you over the phone to keep her right here until I—"

"Sure, and I did tell her," said McDuff. "But she'll meet you at noon under the olives. That's what she'd have me say."

"The devil!" said James. "Then there's nothing to do but wait till noon." He glanced at his wristwatch. It was a quarter past eleven.

Something in connection with his wristwatch was haunting him. Some sort of obligation bore down on his spirit with leaden insistence. Suddenly he had it. His class on Crop Rotation! He had cut a class!

The horror of the discovery chilled him. He believed there were instructors who habitually cut classes, but James had never cut a class. Never, either through error or design. And now he had done it.

What disintegrating effect was this young woman having on him? It was really frightening. For days he had neglected his tomatoes. He had admitted to himself a debasing interest in murder. Twice in the last hour he had exceeded the speed limit. And now he had cut a class. What next?

He withdrew the ominous letter from his pocket and passed it to McDuff. "Here," he said. "What do you make of it?"

The inspector read the note, folded it and tapped it thoughtfully edgeways on the knuckles of his large hairy hand.

"What do I make of it?" he said. "This, Professor. I make of it that nobody is going to stop Miss Kay from snooping around all she's a mind to. And that nobody has any intention of stopping her. And that she's in no danger. That's what I make."

James felt himself frowning. He didn't follow the inspector's logic and said so. "Then why should somebody write to me, threatening her?" he demanded.

"You like Miss Kay quite a lot, Professor," diverged the inspector blandly.

"Well, I won't deny it," said James. "But I can't see what that has to do with the problem."

"A great deal," said McDuff. And before James's eyes the inspector seemed suddenly to acquire the stature of an intelligence James had not suspected before. "Somebody who had in mind to dissuade you from probing in those murders at the bridge, somebody sufficiently clever, might have seen that it would do no good to threaten you direct. That note is no threat to Miss Kay, Professor. It's a threat to you."

"Me?" James surveyed the inspector incredulously. He wasn't joking, apparently. "But nobody has anything against me!"

"Yes, but you forget. What does it say in the note? Murder loves company. There's more truth in that than a lot of people would suspect, Professor. You've meddled in this a bit, at the island, and again over at the inquest. Apparently your ideas have come too close to some fact. Somebody's after you, Professor."

James felt his neck hairs bristle. The sensation was not unpleasant. It was vivid and stirring and tied him in sharply with a vast, human world he had been too unaware of. His reaction was more anger than fear.

"It's impossible," he said shortly. "But if it's true, they aren't going to scare me away. That's sure."

To James's surprise the inspector slapped him on the back.

"Atta boy, Professor!" said McDuff.

"You're convinced Kay is in no danger?" James wanted reassurance as to that.

"Positive," said McDuff.

And suddenly James found the inspector to be a genial and stalwart friend. His pal and Kay's. He felt quite moved by the discovery.

A whole host of questions came to James's mind. With McDuff as a congenial ally he felt no problem could be too obscure. Together they could get to the bottom of it with McDuff, inexorable as fate, sifting evidence through the fine mesh of his indefatigable self, and James furnishing the flights of imagination without which a realist like McDuff bogged down in the morass of his own findings.

"A girl's got no right messing about in a murder hunt," the inspector was saying. "But she'll not be kept out of it. She's off now on an angle she's sure is red-hot. A spy-ring idea she came by, God knows where. Trouble is that kid ought to be married. She ought to have something to keep her good and busy. A baby, that's what she needs. Why, she needs twins!" The inspector guffawed at his own wit.

James blushed. He remembered with difficulty the question he had been about to ask. "Did you track down the ownership of the cyanide tent and handtruck, and all that equipment?" he asked.

"I did," said McDuff. "There's big forces involved in this thing, Professor. I've a mind to let you in. I don't mind admitting you've shown me a thing or two. And what's more, I think you ought to know what you're up against, that is, what you may be up against."

"I'd appreciate knowing," said James. "I'm rather hot after this thing. I haven't said it before. But it's out now, and there it is. Tell me all you feel at liberty to tell me."

"I'll tell you everything," said McDuff. "First, the equipment came from Hollyoaks Farm, the tarpaulin and stuff you mentioned. My men traced it. It was a cinch. Second, you'll not guess who Hollyoaks belongs to. Not unless you know already."

- "I've no idea," James admitted. "I never heard of the place."

McDuff lowered his voice. "It's a big name," he said. "It's not one to throw about freely. The name is Cartwright, Professor."

"Ah," said James. "Husband to our blond friend, Doreen."

"See?" said McDuff. "A trifle too snug. A trifle too close-knit for comfort, this business. Two Japanese dead on the bridge, cyanide poison, Cartwright's cyanide equipment. And his wife cruising by at the time of the murder." McDuff's face looked tired. "I don't like it," he said. "I don't like to tangle with those big guys. But we got to do it."

"Not necessarily," said James. "Anyway, there's no hurry. Best not to rush into anything. The equipment may have been stolen."

"That's the point," said McDuff. "It wasn't reported stolen."

"What's their story?"

"One of the boys went straight to Cartwright. Those big shots don't take any water, Professor. Cartwright was bored with the idea that he should know or care if he had a handtruck and some canvas missing. It wasn't missed, and what of it, he said. And we could bring it back if we wanted to, he said. And the main thing was, don't bother him about trifles."

"Murdered Japanese aren't trifles," said James. He glanced at his watch. It was nearing noon. "Time to meet Kay," he said. "Thank you for your confidences, Inspector. I'll take care of then."

"And it's a straight trade, Professor," said McDuff with a stern grin. "I'll want to see that murderer on the spot before the week's out."

"It'll be arranged," said James. He shook the inspector's great hairy fist and went out the door.

Inspector McDuff turned to his desk phone. "Put a shadow on Professor Biddle," he said. "He'll be passing in half a minute."


## CHAPTER 7

THE FERRIES FROM SAN FRANCISCO were already disgorging crowds of morning visitors as James drove slowly along the Avenue of Palms. He parked Xantippe and toyed briefly with the idea of putting up the top. Clouds were banking in the west, and he had some time to kill before meeting Kay for lunch.

He stood there, one foot on the running-board, giving the matter sober thought. Actually, he had already decided to take a gambler's chance, but he always liked to rationalize such things. Then he'd be a victim of Fate, not carelessness, if the seat got wet.

The wind was from the north, a pretty good indication of fair weather. But the waters of the bay were dark as lead. Over toward the Golden Gate the prison island of Alcatraz frowned sullenly. Staring at it idly, James wondered what those hopeless criminals would be thinking, peering through their slitted windows at this enchanted place. He wondered if a desperate man could swim from there to here.

James stoked up his pipe and set out at a brisk clip toward the Northwest Passage. As he passed the taxi stand, a man in a gray overcoat stepped from a Yellow Cab. James noticed the coat. It was a ringer for one he had given away last winter, the one the moths had liked so well.

The sun was peering out of the clouds by the time he reached the Port of the Trade Winds. The water edging the Esplanade was smooth as glass. Small boats were scurrying about in the snug harbor, and a crowd had gathered near the hangars. Probably one of the Clippers was due from Manila and way points.

But James turned left at the fire boat wharf. He was early for Kay, but if he hadn't felt worried about her in spite of the sanguine McDuff, a short wait under the olives would have been only a pleasure. This byway between the Women's Club House and the Hall of Air Transportation, his favorite spot, was deserted now, except for a lone old man. And the cyanide tent was gone. There remained only a small patch in the paving to recall the "grave" that had so excited Kay and McDuff.

James was relieved to find no indications of damage to the adjacent olive tree. He looked it over thoroughly. His examination was finished before he became aware that he was not alone. Straightening up, he found that the old man loitering on the avenue was standing close by now, studying him suspiciously.

"I heard," the old man ventured, "that someone got bumped off here in a tent a couple of days ago. Served him right, I say, for ruining a fine old tree."

James agreed. It pleased him that someone besides himself should feel a personal concern about his olives.

"The tree is all right," he said. "It wasn't harmed."

"It won't help an old tree any, cutting the roots like that," the old man contradicted vigorously. "I wouldn't be surprised if the tree was to die."

"Is that so?" inquired James. He allowed his voice to be mildly challenging. It was the Socratic method he used so successfully with assertive freshmen students. You led them on by feigned humility and ignorance. You wheedled them out on the end of a limb. Then, when they led with their chin, you sawed it off. James deplored his mentally mixed metaphor, but he salvaged the main idea.

"Is that so?" he repeated. "Do you know quite a lot about olive trees?"

"I ought to," the old man said simply. "I saw these trees on my ranch almost every day for over sixty years."

"Oh!" James said, making the connection. "Then you must be Mr. Werner!"

"That's my John Henry," agreed the old man.

"I dropped in at your ranch yesterday with a friend," said James. "It's a real beauty spot, Mr. Werner. We had the pleasure of meeting your nephew, too."

"I wouldn't want Harvey to know I miss these olives," confessed Werner. "He got me a first-rate price for them and I never let on I wasn't tickled pink. But these trees were on that ranch before I was born. They were there, I guess, when my father bought the place in 1849." He paused. "Say, I didn't get your name."

"I'm Professor Biddle," said James. "These olives of yours were some of the first trees barged in here. I had a little something to do with handling them. They're special pets of mine."

Isaac Werner seemed delighted. The hand he held out to James was neither infirm nor soft.

"I'm sorry I contradicted you, and I'm pleased to meet you, Professor," he rattled on. "And just because that tree's going to die sure as hell is no reason we can't be friends. How about it? I'd like it a lot if you could come out to my cruiser for a little shot of bourbon to sort of square things up. Or don't professors drink?"

"I think I might sneak a short one anyway," said James, grinning, "if there's time enough. You see, I have a date."

"It won't take five minutes," promised Werner. "Besides," he added, with a shrewd sidelong glance, "women are always late."

Werner's boat, the *Corsair,* proved to be a tidy thirty-footer with a compact little cabin, two transom berths, and a miniature galley forward. It couldn't be very fast, James judged, but it was an ideal old pot for knocking around the bay.

"She's all messed up," Werner apologized, "but it's my own fault. Before I brought her up from Medbury Landing, Harvey warned me about the stuffing box. And she'd have sunk, I guess, if he hadn't showed up to see if I was O.K. Wednesday night. He never wanted me to run up the bay alone. And the bilge was flooding up around the flywheel before he got her fixed."

Werner set out two glasses and a quart bottle bearing a bonded excise stamp. He poured out two stiff jolts and handed one to James.

"Well, here's to crime," he said, chuckling.

"Mud in your eye," said James.

They tossed off the salute to friendship, and Werner smacked his lips.

"Perhaps I shouldn't say so," he admitted modestly, "having made it, but that's prime liquor for six months old. It gets that way from slopping around in a charred keg on the boat. If I hadn't told you, you'd never have known it, now would you, from real bonded stuff?"

"The bottle fooled me all right!" admitted James. He blew his nose, and surreptitiously wiped a couple of scalding tears from the corners of his eyes. "Shall we go outside?" he asked. "I—well, I'm a little troubled with claustrophobia."

"Sure." The old man nodded sympathetically. "You can't tell about people, can you? Here you're just a kid."

"Thirty-three," corrected James, "come Michaelmas!"

"Well, I'll bet, Professor, I could still do a day's work right alongside of you."

"I'll bet you could," agreed James, "right now."

The cool fresh air on the exposed deck restored him at once, however. From his vantage point, he looked curiously at the crowded ranks of motor and sailing craft drawn together by the magnet of the Exposition. And above them all, like a majestic liner surrounded by tug boats, loomed a long sleek ocean-going yacht.

"Now there's a real toy for you, Professor Biddle," commented Werner, with bitter sarcasm. "Just a little quarter-million dollar job! But what's a few dollars to a man who's squeezed poor devils off half the best ranches in California? Why shouldn't he give his wife a birthday present? And it made work for the shipyard crews in Kiel, Germany. But just wait," he prophesied darkly, "until we get the single tax working on land-hogs like Porter Cartwright!"

James hadn't bothered to notice the yacht's name. His attention had become fixed on the club pennant flying from a mast, a triangle of blue with a white diamond in the center. And Werner's chance remark explained the riddle that had been pricking James's subconscious mind. Again this was the yacht he'd seen sliding through the mist at the time of the Bay Bridge wreck on Wednesday night. It was the *Iolanthe,* the vessel that had brought Mrs. Porter Cartwright and her mink coat into the mystery of the two murdered Japanese. And Professor James Yeats Biddle was unchivalrous enough to believe most positively that lovely Doreen Cartwright had perjured herself on several counts.

As James watched idly, a motor tender came smartly around the *Iolanthe's* counter. A chic young woman went down the accommodation ladder. With what might have been a gay smile at someone on the deck above, she stepped into the launch and was whisked toward Treasure Island.

James watched for a moment, incredulous. Was Isaac Werner's ancient bottle playing tricks on him? No, definitely, the girl who had disembarked from the *Iolanthe* was an acquaintance. She had a date with him, in fact. She was Kay Ritchie.

It didn't seem seemly, James decided, to shout across the water. One couldn't simply yell at a girl. Besides, some damned fool in an airplane was droning around overhead, dreaming that he was Charles Augustus Lindbergh or at least another Corrigan.

With Werner's help James got ashore. But Kay was already lost in the crowd on the Esplanade. She was at the rendezvous under the olive trees, cool, immaculate, and waiting, when James came puffing up. And she was not alone. She was conversing with two people earnestly, a lady and a red-haired gentleman.

The couple's identity was unknown to James, but they were not total strangers to him. He had encountered them once before at this very spot. The man with the precise foreign inflection to his speech had inquired about the cyanide tent and the olive trees. And more than that, James remembered, it had been this Italian who had gone directly to the Administration Building to report the cyanide tent.

Kay did the introductions, and James was amused to observe how deftly she loud-pedaled his academic title, as if he were some bigwig rating at least a nineteen-gun salute.

"The Princess Tania Varnakov of Russia," Kay further announced, presenting him to the exotic woman with the perfect overbred features and the tawny feline eyes. "And her business manager, Mr. di Piazzi, of—"

Di Piazzi shrugged as he met her inquiring glance.

"Castes and nationalities," he responded in his stilted diction, "they are becoming a thing outmoded, is it not so? One is permitted to enter a bright new world of hope here in your America."

"But only if one has one hundred dollars to exhibit to the unpleasant practical authorities," amended Tania Varnakov. "Do not forget that, my Rubio."

She spoke softly. There was a pleasing husky modulation to her voice. But a stinging whiplash hidden somewhere in her words flushed di Piazzi's face with color. His heavy sensuous lips set in a smile that was really almost a snarl.

Princess Tania Varnakov laughed musically.

"We shall see very soon, I think," she said, "whether we were welcomed for our many undoubted virtues, or simply because we were vouched for by St. John Chrysostom!"

James abruptly recalled Kay's feature story in the *Sun-Telegraph*. In reading it, he had slid over the victim's name, one of those Russians. The fantastic value placed on the stolen relic had left him unimpressed. But he had taken rather a fancy to the sonorous syllables, the Ikon of St. John Chrysostom.

"You've had an unfortunate introduction to our country, certainly," said James, "if the morning paper reported facts."

"It was exaggerated a little, yes," smiled Tania Varnakov. "Antiques are worth whatever they will fetch, of course. To arrive at the actual valuation of St. John for his jewels, you would have to reduce Miss Ritchie's estimate by about one-half, perhaps."

"Two hundred and fifty thousand dollars," marveled James. The woman did not seem to be talking to impress him, so he was impressed. "Yet you can come out here and laugh."

"To forget for a moment, if I can. To relax," explained Tania Varnakov. "And Rubio works on his invention here, which will make him rich. Then he will no longer have to manage a temperamental woman who is careless with her jewels and really cannot sing!"

Di Piazzi appeared annoyed and even apprehensive. He retreated to the proximity of the camera tripoded beside a gnarled old olive tree.

"It is nothing," he said, disparagingly. "A device, merely, for the automatic adjustment of the lens and exposure according to the amount of light."

"An exposure meter," nodded James. "I have one myself that is very efficient and compact. But I'd like to have a look—"

"It is not to be seen," said di Piazzi, rather rudely. "It is not entirely my own, you understand. It is not patented. There are certain obligations to others."

"These evasions, you must humor them," interposed Princess Tania. "One must be patient with timidity. You see, my manager was made a prisoner in Mussolini's Ethiopian campaign. But he was not killed like other forced-down aviators. He was merely tortured by those savages." Her tawny eyes glistened with a humor that seemed almost as primitive as that of the natives of the Blue Nile highlands. "*C'est la guerre!*" she finished.

James said, "We really must go now, Kay." They had ventured, he sensed, into unknown, dangerous territory. In a backhanded way, and with a wholly obscure motive, Tania Varnakov had accused her manager of God-knew-what. And di Piazzi was close to the boiling point.

James sped the conclusion to the scene with a bow of finality. He was a strict isolationist. He wanted no part in the intimate differences between Russia and Italy.

"One moment! I have already asked Miss Ritchie," said the Russian woman, "if she could bring her young man to dance with us tomorrow evening at our hotel."

James looked at Kay. He thought that neither words nor telepathy were needed to convey his meaning. But he learned then that women, always so intuitive, can be entirely blind to suggestions not meeting with their approval.

"Couldn't we, James?" she asked. "I have nothing special tomorrow night, and the music at the Raleigh is wonderful."

James raised his eyebrows mentally at the naming of the hotel. It reminded him that the anonymous letter threatening Kay had been penned on Hotel Raleigh stationery. Tania Varnakov and di Piazzi were guests there, and they seemed to find some special attraction in this avenue where the cyanide tent had been in operation.

"Why, yes," said James, "yes, indeed. We'll look forward to it with pleasure."

The couples parted in an atmosphere redolent with high regard. James and di Piazzi even bared their teeth in what James thought was probably mutual dislike but which bore an outward resemblance to approval.

As he and Kay set out for their delayed luncheon, James puzzled over the morning's unexpected developments. Why, he asked himself, had they been invited to the Raleigh? Why had this Rubio, the "red one," protected so jealously the bulky gadget which he asserted was some sort of exposure meter? Was it only a camera? And why was Tania Varnakov so constantly goading di Piazzi?

"You don't have to be sulky, James," Kay's voice broke in upon his thoughts. "If you don't care to dance, why did you accept?"

"Why," he countered, "did you go aboard Cartwright's yacht this morning when you must know his reputation?"

"I went for information," she answered promptly.

"It must have been a successful quest," commented James, "the way you grinned up at someone from the foot of the accommodation ladder!"

"It was. I'm trying to trace those unidentified Japanese in the Bay Bridge wreck. Angus let me see the things taken from their pockets, James, and among them was a notation written in Japanese characters."

"What did it say? Or didn't McDuff have it translated?"

"It said 'One dozen iris bulbs.' "

"Very significant!" James commented dryly.

"But it was on the stationery of the Malibu Yacht Club."

"And Cartwright belongs to the Malibu," finished James. "Which I have discovered is what is meant by the pennant flying from the *Iolanthe's* mast."

Kay stopped. She was excited.

"But it is all significant. Can't you see? It all has to tie in with that equipment that came up from Porterville."

A man with a gray overcoat sauntered past.

"What equipment?"

"Didn't you read my story in the *Sun* this morning?" Kay asked, accusingly.

"I read it," said James. "All about St. John Chrysostom."

"I mean," explained Kay, patiently, "my feature story about Angus tracing the cyanide equipment to Cartwright's orange grove near Porterville."

"There wasn't anything about the murder," said James, "by you or anyone. I'm sure, because I was positively disappointed."

"But they couldn't have left it out," protested the girl. "It's impossible. It's news, big news. It would have had to be left out intentionally. Nobody could kill a story as hot as that!"

"Porter Cartwright did," said James.


CHAPTER 8


THERE WAS A QUALITY OF grassy bleakness about the hills of Berkeley, James ruminated, some subtle lack of accord between man and the outdoors, which made the place a natural setting for a college, a stopping place for restless transient youth.

There was a British taint to the landscape. That was it. It drove a man indoors. It made him seek out his hearth and his books from choice. He never had to be driven to them.

Not that the sun failed to shine. Not that roses frosted in the bud. The antagonism of those cold, soulless hills was more suppressed than that. Rigid and virgin, they kept aloof, conceding nothing. Student and teacher alike felt the withdrawal and buried themselves the deeper in books. The student, probably homeless for the first time, confused about so many things, sighed and accepted the alien land, weathered the receding tide of nostalgia, and spent four years hurriedly, departing with slight regret and forgetting at once.

The teacher, bound to the land by the circumstance of a job, did what the British do. He created a ceremony of his hearthstone and tea, built shelves to the ceiling, filled them with the imperishable warmth of dead hearts, closed out the fog-filtered day, and lit a lamp.

This cold Saturday afternoon was just one such perfect day to drive a man indoors. James had felt it coming on. Even at noon the sun had a watery, ineffectual feel to it. And by two o'clock you had to drive Xantippe with one hand and hold the brim of your hat down over your left ear with the other hand, because a harsh, determined blast pressed unceasingly down from the north and whistled in your ear in a way that made you think of croup kettles and goose-grease, mustard-plasters and aspirin.

James had lived here long enough to have become more than reconciled to such days. He looked forward to them with a deep, lusty satisfaction, especially if they fell on a Saturday.

"Catching up on your reading," was an expression that had always annoyed James. It had a sound of the intellectual *nouveau riche* about it, as though three Mondays had gone by without a washday, but now that one had servants one could get it all over with in short order. Or as though, for that matter, placing the most tolerant meaning on the words, one could ever, not to mention catch up, break even with the point at which literature stood when most of us were born.

All James ever hoped to do was to read rather hastily the world's finest treasures of verse and in the vastly accumulated written thoughts of man to run by chance upon his fair share of the choicest passages of prose. It was a sufficiently ambitious program.

Such days as this, then, were dedicated. And James went through the first motions from force of habit. He lit the fire Mrs. Pringle had laid, and as usual, it went out. Now he knew why, but for years it had mystified him. Mrs. Pringle thought of wood, not as something to burn, but as something to conserve. The moment he finished breakfast and left the house, Mrs. Pringle approached the fireplace with a kettle of cold water and extinguished the blaze, perhaps in fond memory of her first husband, who had been a fireman.

Returning hastily one morning for a handful of sophomore tests, James had caught Mrs. Pringle in the act. From then on he understood why those fires were so difficult to light again, because when Mrs. Pringle put out a fire it stayed out.

With fresh wood from the basket James finally qualified to be a second-class scout. He pulled the curtain a foot lower to shut out more of the cold daylight. Outside, in the street, a man with a gray overcoat was wandering by, looking up toward the house as though for a number.

James turned on the reading light by his favorite armchair. But as his eye roved familiarly from book to book he found that he was not thinking of them or their contents. He was thinking about Kay. And Inspector McDuff. And, of all people, Porter Cartwright. Life, raw and quivering, had intruded itself upon the professor's sacred habits. He couldn't shake it. The more desperately he tried to relax and attain his usual literary mood the more evasive that mood became.

He took a look at his tomatoes. They needed attention badly. The ants were at their old tricks and had established a half-dozen flourishing dairies on the tender and succulent extremities of the vines. James sprayed without ardor.

He tested the water in the tanks. The hydrometer reading showed his tomatoes to be in the last agonies of starvation, but the plants themselves apparently weren't aware of the fact. James rectified the situation from his stock of chemicals, but he was not excited. He was even undeniably bored, and lonely. He missed Kay. He remembered McDuff. He thought about Cartwright.

Paul Hyman would know about Cartwright. Paul always knew about everybody. To get ahead in this world you have to know about people, and Hymie was going to get ahead.

He called up Hymie. "How about a chat before the fire?" James asked. "And a glass or two of port?"

Hymie was delighted. He was all at loose ends. That was just what he had been waiting for.

Hymie's eager, genial face appeared presently in James's doorway, against the smoky outdoor daylight.

"Enter," said James. "I felt lonely. And I wanted to mention names. Come by the fire."

James had decided against port. Its effect was too soporific. He was puddling a pair of old-fashioneds on the sideboard.

"I meant to bring back your tuxedo," said Hymie. "There's one button missing off the sleeve. It wasn't on when I got it. I made sure."

"I'll have these drinks ready in a jiffy," said James.

"Not too strong, for me," said Hymie. Hymie never lost control of his tongue, although sometimes it might seem so, if you didn't know him.

"I said to myself, Hymie, take back Jim's tux. Maybe you'll want it again sometime. Then on top of that I forgot."

James slipped a cube of ice cautiously into each brimming drink, hooked a slice of orange rakishly over the edges, and conveyed one of the blended masterpieces to Hymie's outstretched hand.

"It's fine," said Hymie. "You missed being a big shot, Jim, a first-rate bartender. Too bad, Jim."

James saw his opportunity. If it hadn't arrived he would have made it, but he didn't want to be too obvious.

"Speaking of big shots," said James. "What do you know about this guy Cartwright, Hymie?"

A veil seemed to drop before Hymie's eyes. His voice became distant and vague.

"Why?" he said cautiously. "What about him, Jim?"

James considered a moment in silence before he answered. He didn't want to betray McDuff's confidences. But it was never something for nothing with Hymie. It was always a trade, a fair trade. If you wanted to find out something, you had to tell him something.

James saw the way to do it. He would have to be indefinite and give Hymie the idea, and yet not pin it down.

"I'm running foul of him," said James. "It's a business connected with those trees I helped move for Treasure Island. Cartwright gets in my hair. I want to get a line on him and find out what I'm up against. I understand he keeps an aura of sanctity about his name by donating to worthy causes. Is that true?"

Hymie turned his drink restlessly in his hand. He had hardly sipped it. "Listen, Jim," Hymie said suddenly. "I know you pretty well. And I know I could trust you. And we're sitting here all alone by ourselves with nobody listening in. But I'd never say a word against Mr. Cartwright in Berkeley."

James laughed good-humoredly.

"I'm not kidding, Jim," said Hymie. "He's a powerful man."

James examined the sharp, purposeful face of Paul Hyman. It had lost its easy impudence and had taken on instead an expression of deep caution. They finished their old-fashioneds in silence.

"I'll bring back your tux tomorrow, Jim," Hymie said.

It was a valedictory comment. James didn't try to stop him. But the moment Hymie was gone the scene became puzzling.

The whole Cartwright angle on the murders was more than puzzling. It was fantastic. The idea that anybody, much less Porter Cartwright, should employ half a ton of Cartwright equipment to get rid of two Japanese! What about Kay's story, then? Why was it quashed? It wasn't. It couldn't have been. If it didn't make the paper it was merely because it didn't have news value.

James made another attempt to settle himself with a book, but it didn't work. He telephoned the paper. Kay had left. He caught her at her apartment, her voice miraculously transforming the moment for him. He no longer felt irked and puzzled. Everything seemed suddenly solved.

"I was all wet about the Porter Cartwright menace," James told her. "People just fall in a fit at the mention of his name. It's a sort of hysteria. He couldn't have had anything to do with quashing your story. It just got lost in the shuffle. It was just a coincidence, that's all. Nothing to fret about."

"Oh," said Kay. "Well, add this up then. I was transferred this afternoon. Promoted to the society column. I suppose that's nothing to fret about, either."

"I think that's fine," said James. "You'll meet a lot of interesting people. It'll get you out of this sordid muckraking. And you'll be a lot safer."

"Out of it is right," came Kay's gloomy voice. "Just dandy, like a toboggan ride. Who said I wanted to be safe? A fine friend you turned out to be!"

"Listen, Kay," said James. He was serious now. "If you don't like your promotion then I don't like it either. You can count on that. And I think what you need is dinner. Dinner and dance, and then the best show in town."

"That's what Harvey Bell thought, too," said Kay. "And he thought of it first. Sorry, James."

James left the telephone in a rage. He was furious with himself for not getting Kay's Saturday evening promised by asking her sooner. Failing that, he was furious with himself for having asked her at all. Next he was furious with Kay for accepting Harvey Bell's invitation. Finally he was furious with Harvey Bell for having tendered it. His rage toward Harvey Bell was, on the whole, the least violent, because that handsome young fellow had shown sense, after all. He had recognized something superlative in Kay and he had gone after it, wasting no time.

It was rather terrifying to find yourself definitely, undeniably, in love. That was what James was discovering. Perhaps you first admit it to yourself in the moment when what you thought was yours eludes you, such a moment as this. When she says, "Sorry, James," and when the only consolation (which comes over you after a lot of agony) is that there was a note of goading malice in the words. Girls don't goad the men they're through with.

James felt reckless. Already today he had cut a class, downed a straight whiskey, and followed it up at his own leisure with an old-fashioned. Clearly he was on the skids.

It would be bad enough if he was now ready to go out and fit himself to a hair shirt and ashes. But penitence was not his dish. He scrawled a brief note to Mrs. Pringle, grabbed his hat and topcoat, and stepped out the door, banging it after him.

He just didn't give a damn. He had broken his perfect pedagogic record by cutting a class. He had broken his heart by foolishly entrusting it to a girl who would spend Saturday evening with another man. He had destroyed his personal integrity by admitting the gory fascination of a murder acrostic.

James knew what people did in a spot like this. They went out and got drunk.

Xantippe cleared the holy precincts of the campus at one bound, headed toward San Pablo Avenue, where men went in their extremity.

James reined in Xantippe to a restless and pawing lope. San Pablo, the primrose path, stretched before him all the way to Oakland.

His eye caught the neon sign of the Tropic Café. A hint of decadent rejoicing exuded from the place. James was in a dangerous mood, a Babylonian mood. He stalled Xantippe against the curb, abandoned her, and glared his way past the doorman and the coatcheck girl into the inner sanctum of the Tropic Café, the bar.

"Bourbon," said James, pronouncing it "berban" in the best tradition of desperate men.

It seemed that the Tropic Café was also a museum. Under glass bell-jars ranged at intervals along the bar were specimens of desiccated fauna and flora. There were recumbent shrimps, limp drawn and quartered cucumber pickles, rounded mounds of potato salad on rumpled sheets of lettuce, and flaccid portions of pumpkin pie.

James tossed off the bourbon and advanced the empty challengingly toward the barkeep. The ardent spirit flowed.

"Atta style," said somebody. It was another barfly, just another desperate man. But he was there first and he had a head start of James.

"Play bridge?" inquired the barfly.

James answered vaguely. He had always heard about humoring drunks.

"My wife, she doesn' understan' psychip-pids," said the barfly. "She jus' sez you dint half enough tricks. I'll show 'er. I'm fulla tricks. I'll show 'er."

James carried on a desultory conversation with the barfly. The conclusions arrived at were all indeterminate. But before his very eyes James saw the effects of drink, and yet he drank. Every time his glass was empty he filled it, and every time it was full he emptied it.

Finally it seemed to James that he had enough. He was no longer bothered by any of the things that had bothered him to begin with. There were a whole new set of worries now. He couldn't find his hat, for one thing, and he was sure the barkeep had underpaid himself for the drinks.

James found himself in the street. He looked about, forgetting exactly where he placed Xantippe.

There, before his eyes, not twenty feet away, was the man with the gray overcoat, the man he had seen at the Fair, the man who had paused before his house. They were the same.

A sudden rage possessed James. What right did this fellow have to follow him everywhere? Wasn't this a free country? They couldn't do this to him.

James approached the stranger with crafty indirectness, pretending he was going to pass him. When very near James whirled suddenly about.

"Follow me, will ya?" cried James. And his right arm swung in a devastating arc.

The man in the gray overcoat went down. But so did James, felled by the recoil of his own mighty swing.

They reclined for a moment like Indians around a campfire, their feet toward a central point. Then, rising slowly and towering over him, James saw the man in the gray overcoat. He was surveying James with an expression of ill-restrained wrath.

"Whatcha wanta sock me for?" demanded the mysterious stranger. "Inspector McDuff put me on you for a bodyguard."


## CHAPTER 9

LIKE A GALLANT OLD FIRE horse, James reared up from deepest slumber in answer to the bell. He threw back the covers and sprang out of bed. It was morning. The light stung his red-rimmed eyes. He felt terrible, but he was game.

Half-blindly, he stumbled over to the bureau to stop the distressing clamor of his "Happy Chimes" alarm clock. But there was something wrong. Both hands pointed approximately to the figure nine. The bell lever was already shoved over to the silencing position. The alarm couldn't ring, therefore, and it hadn't. This wasn't seven o'clock, anyway. It was Sunday, day of peace and rest.

"Damn that phone!" groaned James. "To hell with it!"

But he answered it, because people always answer telephones.

"Hello," he growled.

"And a good, good morning to you," came the answering voice of Inspector Angus McDuff, honeyed with sarcasm.

"What's good about it?" asked James. "And why can't detectives go to sleep once in a while and let honest taxpayers alone?"

"Why," countered the inspector, "did you slug that tail I put on you?"

"Why did I slug a tail? Oh, yes !" James caught on. "You mean the plainclothes man I knocked down last night."

"Why?" persisted McDuff.

"How was I to know you'd put a tail on me?" demanded James querulously. "It was nonsensical."

"You got a threatening letter, didn't you?"

"I can take care of myself," said James.

"Yeah? Well, better think twice, Professor, before you let yourself bump into that cop when he's off duty some dark night!"

"Not to change the subject," James interposed, "but I happened on a bit of information yesterday that may interest you. Perhaps you remember that a lady and a gentleman stood nearby, watching curiously, when I first saw the cyanide tent and the man with the cauliflower ears? I told you about that, didn't I? And that they later went to the Administration Building?"

"Yes, I've heard all that. Go on, Professor."

"I was introduced to that couple yesterday, at the same spot. They were an Italian named di Piazzi and the Princess Tania Varnakov."

"The hell you say!" McDuff was impressed. "The same dame who lost an ikon worth five hundred grand—perhaps?"

"Be more definite with your English, McDuff," requested James irritably. "Do you doubt that she lost the ikon or that it was worth five hundred grand?"

"Both—perhaps," said the inspector. He seemed suddenly in better spirits. "Thanks for the tip, anyway. I'll see what I can do with it. And by the way, have you seen the Sunday morning papers?"

"No," James told him, with emphasis. "And I don't intend to. If you'll leave me alone, I'm going back to sleep."

"By all means," chuckled McDuff. "But better take a gander at the paper first. I'm giving you a straight steer. It's worth a peek." And he hung up.

James wandered out into the kitchen and looked around disconsolately. His head was a little giddy. His tongue felt like a piece cut out of a camel's-hair overcoat. His stomach burned. A glass of ice water didn't help at all.

Dubiously, he opened a cabinet and took a bottle of authentic bourbon from the shelf. He'd heard somewhere, he remembered, that a morning-after chaser would put a hangover on the run. With a shudder, he unscrewed the cap and poured two fingers into a small glass, but he lacked the stern fibre of a real drinking man. The very aroma repulsed him. He went away from there.

But a cold shower did help, and after a brisk rubdown he was at least awake. The shower hadn't soothed his edgy nerves, and his stomach called for something that was cold and heavy.

He decided to be Spartan. He would walk the two miles or more down to Dad's Place for a chocolate shake.

As he left the cottage, James spied the Sunday paper lying on the flagstoned path. He picked up the weighty roll and slipped off the rubber band that neatly encircled it. Angus McDuff must have had some reason for such pointed advice.

One glance proclaimed the worst. Blurted it out. There it was, all in black and white: "PROF SOCKS COP…That's News!" He read on, fascinated.

A serious contender for the crown of heavyweight champ
Joe Louis has been found at last in that sanctuary of peace and

learning, the University of California at Berkeley, in the person of Professor Yeats Biddle of the College of Agriculture.

For reasons still undisclosed, the pugnacious professor tangled last night with one of San Francisco's finest in front of an Oakland hot spot on San Pablo Avenue, and the Berkeley Bomber uncorked a lethal wallop before he had even warmed up.

According to competent observers, Professor Biddle showed a neat feint with his left, then pivoted in approved style to turn loose a devastating right cross.

The victim, Peter Kelley, 28, asserts that it must have been a case of mistaken identity and, furthermore, that his foot slipped before he knew what it was all about. He even speaks wistfully of journeying across the bay to Berkeley in the near future, possibly in search of knowledge but more probably in search of the punching pedagogue. All of which appears to worry Professor James Yeats Biddle not at all.

"When I sock them," he says, "they stay socked!"

James read it to the bitter end. Then, with some slight show of passion, he flung the paper into his beloved iris bed and set out for town. Trouble came in bunches, he reflected, just when you thought you had the world by the tail on a downhill pull. First a pair of murders, then love, and now this pseudo-funny story with much-too-much left to be filled in by evil minds. The Dean would see it, inevitably, and even if the writeup had been genuinely humorous, the Dean wouldn't be able to find a laugh in a carload.

A passing motorist blared his horn as James swung into Euclid Avenue. He thought he detected furtive grins on the faces of a pair of coeds he passed on a campus trail, and there could be no mistake about the guffaw he heard going by Wheeler Hall.

"Here, here!" James warned himself as he passed through Sather Gate and left the campus behind, "you've got to brazen this thing through. You've got to pretend you think it's all a big laugh and that you don't give a damn. Above all, you must look as if you're in the pink and that you couldn't possibly have been lit up like a torch at the Tropic Café last night."

James squared his shoulders and pulled out his pipe. If it killed him, he was going to smoke. He paused deliberately in front of Jim Davis's sport shop to inspect a new display of badminton racket frames. Even on Sunday morning, Telegraph Avenue was a busy street. Anyone might see you here, and the athletic touch was definitely good.

James really felt much improved by the time he had perched himself on a stool in Dad's Place and ordered a milkshake.

"A choc malt," repeated the brisk youngster behind the counter. "And how's everything with you today, Professor Biddle?"

"Fine!" said James, sonorously. "First rate."

The soda jerk deftly splashed a blurp of thick chocolate syrup into the mixing mug while his too-wise, too-old eyes remained fixed quizzically on his customer. James hated him.

"Anything else, Professor Biddle?" he inquired.

"Why, yes," said James. "A couple of scrambled eggs, with a dash of Worcestershire sauce."

After this, Mrs. Pringle was an anticlimax. She wasn't due at the cottage until noon on Sunday, but she was there when James returned, and she was prepared to talk. But James beat her to the punch.

"The coffee," he said brusquely. "It will have to be purchased in two-ounce lots henceforth. Every other day. The toxic effects are becoming quite noticeable, I find—" The telephone jangled, and James escaped from Mrs. Pringle's merciless maternal scrutiny.

"Yes?" He took the call. "Oh, yes, Mr. Sperry…Of course I can come over if it's necessary…No, don't bother checking the soil again. It's quite obviously an isolated case. And there's no need for you to wait. I'll be there right away and take care of everything."

He hung up and turned to face Mrs. Pringle.

"Two of my olive trees at the exposition have been killed," he announced wrathfully. "Who would murder an olive tree, Mrs. Pringle?"

"My land!" marveled Mrs. Pringle. "How should I know, Professor?"

"Take the remainder of the day off," James hurried on. "Try to relax. You're looking peaked, Mrs. Pringle. Above all, don't take that old coffee home with you. It's toxic. Throw it out."

The bad news about the olives had made a man of him. At least he was on the mend. And he let Xantippe have her head as he hurried toward Treasure Island. The olive trees must have been damaged maliciously. But who could have purpose or pleasure in murdering a beautiful, growing thing? Was the tree old Isaac Werner had condemned one of the suffering pair?

James parked Xantippe in front of the Administration Building in the space reserved for officials' cars. From there, it was only a brief walk to his goal. He strode past the Magic Carpet without a glance at the cunning, lovely pattern of buds and blooms. Turning up Clipper Way he found the blighted trees.

Neither one had been covered with the cyanide tent, so far as he knew. They were a pair a few feet north of the walk leading to the side entrance of the Hall of Air Transportation. Both were badly wilted. The leaves had lost their soft, live gloss, and the young sprouts at the limb tips drooped. They seemed to be starving for lack of food and moisture, yet the sun was shining, the ground was damp, and there was no indication of any of the common blights.

James was checking over these points a second time when a husky middle-aged man came sauntering up. "Got a match, buddy?" he asked. James handed him a match.

"Smoke?" The intruder proffered a pack of cigarettes.

"Thanks, no," said James. "I use a pipe."

"Out here from the East?"

"No."

"A native son, eh?"

"No." James bent down and studied the tree trunk carefully. He could see that it wasn't girdled, but the maneuver was pointed enough to dismiss any ordinarily inquisitive pest. This intruder was not to be disposed of so simply. "Work for the exposition, do you?" he asked. James stood up deliberately and turned around.

"I work here, yes," he said. "In an advisory capacity. I am a professor in the College of Agriculture at U.C. My name is James Biddle. Is that all?"

The man seemed to have an overdeveloped sense of humor. He laughed too long and too loud.

"So you claim to be the guy who knocked Kelley for a loop last night," he chortled. "Well, then, I'm Napoleon!"

James began to see a light. Like the extinct quagga and the zebra, this man and Kelley, the man in the gray overcoat, had certain common characteristics. Shoes, for instance, and blue serge suits, and an appalling lack of finesse.

Very deliberately, James brought out his wallet and flipped back the cover to show his driver's license in its envelope of transparent celluloid.

"I'm just doing my job," the man apologized, reddening somewhat. "I was told to give the onceover, in a nice way, to anybody that started hanging around these olive trees."

"Yes?" James deplored his most unpleasant manner. He couldn't help it. Nerves, he guessed. He'd almost said, "Ye-e-ah?" he felt so mean.

Around the corner James found a gardener, who, fortunately, did not challenge his authority. The workman brought a spade along and dug, in the spots indicated, close around the base of one of the wilted olive trees.

James watched intently. Once he bent down, picked up a handful of earth, and held it near his nose.

"Does that smell queer to you?" he asked the gardener.

The gardener sucked in his nostrils and sniffed like a hunting dog.

"A little," he said, judicially. "If it was stronger, I'd say it had a stink like rotten eggs."

The shoveling went on. On the east side of the tree James stooped suddenly to pick up the heel of a woman's shoe. He examined it. It was high, of the French type, such as some of his students wore. It had not been buried long, for it still had a bright polish beneath the clinging earth, and there were no signs of mildew or decay.

James stuffed the heel into his pocket and directed the gardener to sink one last deeper hole. He already had samples of feeder roots, but he wished, if possible, to have a specimen of taproot bark as well.

The hole deepened slowly. It was difficult to dig in the narrow space between the tree and the enclosing rim of wood. The gardener was beginning to grumble audibly. Then his spade grated on something hard. He swore as the tool came up with its load of damp earth. Something round rolled free, and there was no mistaking it.

"Jeez!" he cried. "Can you tie that? A skull!"

But James gave it only a passing glance. He stooped to pick up a small enamel plaque threaded to a frail silver chain. It was antique, undoubtedly. Evidently it had once been suspended around the neck of this body buried beneath the olive tree.

But while the plaque was old, it was scarcely valuable. It had no jewel and the silver back was hardly as heavy as a dollar. And as James rubbed the dirt from the enamel, he saw that fine cracks marred the features of the woman pictured on the tiny disc.

She was of another century. Her coiffure was similar to that James had seen on family miniatures dating back to the early Napoleonic era. She was young and lovely and somehow familiar.

All at once James recognized her. This likeness had been buried in a forgotten grave long, long ago.

But James had seen the woman only yesterday. He was going to dance with her tonight in the Raleigh Rainbow Room. Feature for lovely feature, she was the Princess Tania Varnakov.

## CHAPTER 10

TAKING ACCOUNT OF HIS surroundings as one does when about to do something surreptitious, James slipped the small plaque into his pocket. Finders, keepers would have been his defense. But in spite of himself he had a guilty feeling. The feeling even developed to the point that he was sure he had been observed. So it was almost reflex action that caused him to look nervously directly behind him.

There he encountered the gnarled old face of Isaac Werner with the right eye screwed up into an omniscient wink.

"Hello," said James. "I didn't hear you come up."

"Saw you folks digging under my olive trees," said the old man. "Thought I'd take a look. See you found a bone." He didn't mention the pendant, but James was sure he had seen it.

"Yes," James said. "Probably an Indian."

"More likely that old Russian," said Mr. Werner. "Always did hear tell of an old Russian being buried in the olive orchard. Never took any account of it till this minute. Don't take any account of it now. A dead Russian is a dead Russian, that's all."

"Yes," said James. "But a dead Russian couldn't kill a live olive tree."

"I noticed how a couple of trees started withering up," said Werner. "What do you make out of that? Too much water, maybe. Water can kill an olive tree."

Inspector McDuff himself appeared at this moment.

"Morning, Professor," the officer greeted, a malicious glint in his eye. "I thought you'd be nursing a slight indisposition!"

James flushed. He was getting pretty bored with that joke. And if the inspector was going to be so funny he wasn't going to see the miniature. Not yet, anyway.

"Listen," said James. "Have you got any more bloodhounds tagging about that I'm likely to run in with?"

McDuff laughed. "Only that guy over there." He indicated the talkative individual James had so narrowly avoided resenting. "Don't tangle with him, Professor. He's an ex-prizefighter."

James shuddered. His head was better, but it wasn't well. And he didn't want to tangle with any prizefighters. McDuff was a reincarnation of old Johnnie Appleseed. McDuff planted coppers everywhere he went.

"Thanks," James said. "Thanks for the warning. I wondered how you happened along so promptly on the heels of a dead Russian. But I suppose you were informed."

"I heard there was a little digging project down here," the inspector said, grinning, "but a dead Russian is velvet. I didn't count on that."

"The world is full of dead Russians," said James. "But who would want to murder one of my olive trees?"

The inspector was bending over the skull. He was evidently deeply interested. The gardener stood nearby, leaning on his shovel. James approached him.

"When was this ground last watered?" he inquired.

The gardener shrugged his shoulders with a motion of only slightly guarded insolence. "Not my department," he said. "I dunno."

James went over to the Administration Building in search of a telephone. He was beginning to feel almost normal at last, and with it came the desire to forgive. He telephoned Kay.

"Hello," came her dulcet voice.

"Good," said James. "I'm lucky to find you home." He allowed his tone to be mildly disgruntled.

"You call it luck," said Kay. "And here I've been, pining by the telephone since sunup! And what's more, I've turned down at least one date."

"Your conscience must be hurting you," deduced James.

"Never," Kay denied. "I take my fun where I find it, Professor, and no time for vain regrets."

"How's for a little fresh gossip about mystery and murder?" offered James. He must tempt her. "Could you get yourself to the magic isle? I'd come for you, but I have to see a man about watering a tree."

"I'll make it if I have to come on water-wings," Kay promised. "Be seeing you under the olive trees."

"Under the olive trees," said James. He hung up the receiver and pranced joyously off between beds of varicolored ice-plant to the cave of Mr. Krantz, the head gardener.

He propounded his problem to that overwrought gentleman.

Mr. Krantz went into a feaze. "We only have sixty thousand trees and shrubs to take care of," he wailed, "and you come asking me when was watered the ninth olive tree from the corner of California Avenue on the left hand side of Clipper Way going south!"

"You know which one I mean," said James. "It's one of those that started shriveling up."

"Ho," cried Mr. Krantz, his integrity injured to the quick. "So, Professor Biddle, like everybody else, you think that I—"

"No, no," James interrupted in an endeavor to allay Mr. Krantz's ire. "You misunderstand me. It just happens that I must know when the ground was watered under that tree. It has nothing directly to do with the tree's dying, I assure you, although with the correct information from you I may be able to locate the culprit."

Mr. Krantz favored James with an air of judgment postponed and consulted his charts.

"One, two,...eight," said Mr. Krantz. "Would be this tree. Four o'clock yesterday afternoon. That's the time, Professor."

"That's when it was supposed to be watered, no doubt," said James. "But was it actually watered at that time?"

Mr. Krantz wagged his head with the expression of a man who had endured more than anybody ought to be expected to put up with, but he summoned the appropriate subgardener.

"Pedro," said Mr. Krantz, "did you possibly have too much work to do yesterday? Were there any trees on your division you could not get around to?"

James noted with what tact Mr. Krantz had angled for the truth and felt extremely grateful to the worthy man. "No, sir," said Pedro. "I didn' have no trouble. I did like every day."

"That row of olives along Clipper Way, by the Hall of Air Transportation, you got around to them about four o'clock, as usual?"

"Yes, Mr. Krantz," said Pedro. "Juss before quitting time. That's right, sir."

"All right, Pedro," said Mr. Krantz. "That's all." Pedro went out, and James extended his hand. Mr. Krantz gave it a horny shake.

"Most obliged," said James. "I'm sure you're very methodical, Mr. Krantz. Nothing could convince me otherwise."

"If you'd put in a good word for me with Mr. Sperry," said Krantz wistfully. "It couldn't do any harm. I know it looks bad, two of those olive trees withering like they are. It looks bad for me, but—"

"You couldn't have had any guilt in the matter," said James positively. "That ought to be evident to anybody. But I'll speak of it to Mr. Sherry if you wish."

"Thank you, sir," said Mr. Krantz gratefully.

James took his leave. That was interesting, about the tree being watered at four o'clock. Almost incredible, even. From his pocket he drew out the French heel. It was an intriguing little bit of evidence, all feminine. How charming women were, with all their special paraphernalia, their high heels, their powder-puffs, their lipsticks and hairpins and seductively scented hankies.

The heel had pulled loose from a single central screw about three-quarters of an inch long, judging by the depth of the hole and the markings. In addition there had been glue. The glue still retained fluffy bits of leather.

How assiduously women associated themselves with all that was delicate and fragile. Dime-sized Swiss wristwatches. Orchids. Musk. Lace and tulle and tortoiseshell. Pearls, amber and ambergris. Even their shoes. Imagine, for instance, a man trusting himself three inches off the ground on a heel attached by one small screw and a dab of glue.

It was time, James reflected happily, for him to expect his own fluffy little feminine baggage. He made his way to the olive trees. Among the Sunday crowd, homeward bound under the arching, gray-green leaves, was still old man Werner. Black-garbed, cocky, he resembled an old crow, strutting up and down under his migratory trees.

There was, James observed with amusement, more than a little jealousy between himself and Werner over those same trees. Both of them said, "My trees." And, ridiculously enough, the trees belonged to neither of them.

James forgot Werner and everything else when he discerned Kay slipping quickly past the strolling groups. He hastened to meet her.

"Gee, you look good," he said. He grabbed her hands and looked anxiously into her eyes to try and make out how much of this evasive personality was his and how much Harvey Bell's.

"And you," she laughed up at him, "you look like a freckled-face kid that's been playing hooky and loving it."

He swung around and she took his arm. They skirted the azure fountain at the center of the Magic Carpet and trespassed happily through the Court of the Moon. Black sentinels of Spanish yew guarded this temple of the night's queen. James felt too happy to talk.

"Did you see the man about watering a tree?" asked Kay and in the same breath added, "I'm sorry about last night."

"Well," said James, "that handsome young cravat-ad got ahead of me, that's all. Served me right. We get behind the times, we bearded old faculty. We're slow-moving."

"But hell when you get started!" said Kay, laughing. Evidently she, too, had read the morning paper. "Remember what you promised? You said you'd give me some new gossip about bodies."

They were stemming the tide in the Court of the Seven Seas, Kay's staccato little heels tapping a quick metronome to James's largo.

"So I will," said James. "In the first place I must tell you that we have a dead Russian."

"Heavens!" exclaimed Kay. "Not Tania, I hope!"

"No," said James. "A very old, very dead Russian. One of Tania's ancestors, possibly."

"It isn't him wrapped in that newspaper, is it?" asked Kay with a delicious shiver.

"No," James explained. "This bundle is a section of taproot. You see the plot thickens, Miss Ritchie. There has been another double murder."

Kay stopped in her tracks. "No!" she gasped. "Quick! Tell me! Who were they? Where were the bodies found?"

"Under the olives," James answered rather truthfully, pleased with a fiction that would bring such a charming face to peer up into his with wide-eyed awe.

"Who were they?" whispered Kay. "Was it poison?"

"It may have been," James conceded. "And as to who they were, my dear, they were two old and valued friends of Isaac Werner and myself."

"Oh, now I know you're kidding me. Come clean, James. What's the truth of the matter?"

"Two fine old olive trees have been ruthlessly murdered," said James. "It makes my blood boil."

"Yes," said Kay. "I can feel it, right through the sleeve of your tweeds, James. But you're fudging, Professor. I'm very much put out with you. You said there was some new murder gossip, and I thought it was something important. Who cares if two old trees kick the bucket?"

"You ought to care, for one," said James. "It's important, I tell you. If we knew who killed those trees I'm not saying we'd know who killed the two Japanese, but I'm saying we'd be one hell of a lot nearer knowing."

"Honestly?" Kay was almost impressed. "So I suppose that's why you're carting off a sample of the taproot. For a post-mortem, so to speak."

"Exactly," said James. "And I thought you'd like to sit in on the inquest."

Kay twisted her face into a *moue* for his benefit, and James resisted a temptation to plant a kiss.

"Cheer up, James," Kay prattled on, all unawares, "two hundred yards more."

They reached the parking lot and James installed the siren in Xantippe. It was appropriate. Xantippe had always needed a siren, a permanent accessory. Now Xantippe was complete.

James couldn't face an inventory of the present. Better wait. Let time clarify things. Time, the magic clarifier. Time, the precipitator of solutions. Stir in a little, as you stir the white of an egg into a cask of cloudy wine, and wait, and everything becomes clear.

They drove to Berkeley and James evoked his graduate student factotum, Barnes, to make a microscopic examination of the piece of root.

"Let me know what you find," James said. "I'll be home." Xantippe, in fine fettle, pulled up Euclid in high gear.

"I like bringing you to my house," James said. He swung into his driveway and stopped. "We might as well be here till we get a report on that root. I wish I could offer you supper, but I gave Mrs. Pringle the evening off."

They went in James's front door without a key.

"Goodness, how trusting!" exclaimed Kay. "Don't you ever lock it? Any tramp could just walk in and help himself."

"I haven't anything very valuable," James explained. "except books. Tramps aren't interested in books. Only my friends steal books. And they always do it when I'm here, so why lock the house when I'm away?"

He helped Kay off with her coat and stood and watched her while she doffed her hat and smoothed her hair with deft, expert little motions of her butterfly hands. There was something that got you, watching a girl in front of a mirror. And if it was your own mirror in your own hall then it made you want to keep her there, somehow, and have her to look at every day as her twinkling fingers busied themselves correcting an infinity of invisible faults.

The process was finished as abruptly as it began. Kay spun about and caught the pleasure in his eyes. He could tell by the teasing way she said "There!" Maybe it was all an act, that intimate little fussing that girls went through. Maybe they knew how men loved it and did it instinctively, just as birds sing.

Kay tiptoed into the living room in a way which was more than feminine, a way all her own. James had noticed that she always entered places as though by silently appearing she might surprise some new and miraculous manifestation of life, something, anything. It didn't matter.

"I think your tomatoes look grieved, James," she observed. "I'm afraid I've been distracting you quite a lot on account of all this sleuthing."

"More than you suspect, my dear," thought James. But his habitual caution only allowed him to say, "They probably need nitrates."

He lowered his hydrometer into the tank. How careless he was getting about his tomatoes! He couldn't understand. It was deplorable.

"I'm exploring, James," Kay's voice sounded unexpectedly from another room. "I hope you don't mind. I so love houses. Especially your house."

"If you had come last night when I asked you, there would have been supper," James reminded with a suggestion of "serves you right."

"I said I was sorry," Kay repeated tranquilly. Her voice was from the kitchen this time. "He was a lovely man, James. I'm not so very sorry."

"Oh," said James. He was being weighed, along with Harvey Bell. He recognized it.

"I bet his house isn't as nice as this," said Kay. There was a note of defense in her words. As though she was arguing with somebody. Perhaps herself.

"If she really loves him," thought James, "I can't stand it. I don't know what I'll do, but I know I can't stand it."

"I guess he's probably a pretty good dancer," said James unhappily.

"Divine," Kay agreed. "And you, James?"

"I can't dance very well," said James unhappily.

He was adjusting the mixture in the tank. He tested it with a little ribbon of litmus paper. Just on the tart side. Correct, for tomatoes.

"You can learn," said Kay. She was suddenly standing close beside him, and James started so violently he knocked over his hydrometer. Its eggshell glass shattered into fragments. The little shot weights rolled in every direction. He said "damn," not very passionately.

"Goodness," said Kay. "You are jumpy, James. You don't a bit look like somebody with nerves."

"I haven't nerves," James denied. "But when somebody pussyfoots about like a disembodied spirit—"

Kay went off into a peal of joy. "Oh, thank you, Jamesie dear! That's what I'd rather be than anything else in the world! In gold letters on my office door! KAY RITCHIE: DISEMBODIED SPIRIT. ENTER. Or would you prefer: PRIVATE?"

James chuckled. He loved her, damn it.

"I'm sorry I made you break your thing," said Kay. "But I'll not have you holding it against me. I'll buy you another first thing Monday morning. What was it called? Where does that woman keep the dustpan, James?" This last from well on the way to the kitchen. Then, still in the kitchen, "James, this is the most lovely stove. I want to cook. May I cook supper, James, and we eat it?"

A lump came in James's throat. He didn't have any control over it. He wanted that girl. The whole thing. Every scrap and crumb of it. And in eternity, when and if, he couldn't think of anything nicer to have about than a disembodied spirit, so long as it was hers.

The telephone rang then, and James came back from eternity to answer it. Root quite normal, factotum Barnes reported. No chemical reactions of sufficient strength to analyze. Only characteristic at all unusual was what seemed a slight preliminary decomposition, as though root might have been frozen.

James hung up the telephone. Very peculiar, that. He must confide in Kay.

He found her happy as a lark, supper already in its first stages. Bright blue tongues of flame were licking at the bottoms of Mrs. Pringle's pride, her stainless steel saucepans.

"It's such a lovely kitchen, James," breathed Kay. "Was the telephone about the root?"

"The olive tree died of frost," said James impressively.

"Oh, now come, James." Kay stirred something briskly in a yellow bowl. "Even I know that in sunny California—"

"And with the lowest temperature last night only fifty degrees Fahrenheit," continued James. "Nevertheless, my dear, I repeat. Those two olive trees died of frost, of frozen roots. They were murdered."

"I see," said Kay brightly. "By a man named Jack."

"I'll tell you about wild morning glory," said James.

"I love flowers."

"This wild morning glory is a weed. A very stubborn and disastrous pest to the California rancher. Once well started it chokes his orchards and bean fields."

"Poor man," said Kay sympathetically. "Now you've got me worrying about him, James. Can't he do anything to protect himself?"

"Yes," said James. "He can. He can freeze the stuff out."

"Not in California."

"Yes, in California. By pouring into the ground an extremely explosive and volatile and evil-smelling chemical called carbon bisulfide."

"I catch," said Kay triumphantly. "Sabotage! International jealousy in the olive industry. Who else has olives? Italy! Russia! Greece! France! And maybe Japan, James. It all ties up. Don't you see? It ties up with the spy ring. And the International Exposition. And two murdered Japanese. Oh, James! You're so wonderful."

James couldn't be a killjoy, not in the face of those shining eyes. He didn't point out that freezing two ornamental olive trees would not exactly devastate the California olive industry.

He wanted to take another look around the bottom of that tree where he had found the heel. He took the heel out of his pocket, and with it the silver chain and miniature pendant.

"Take a look at this face," he said. He handed the plaque to Kay. She took one swift glance at it. Her chin lifted an infinitesimal degree.

"When did Tania give you her portrait?" she asked coolly. "And I see you also have the heel of her shoe. Strange what big feet Russian women have, even the so-called nobility."

James grinned. "This might be Tania's heel," he mused. "I hadn't thought of that. It doesn't quite fit. Tell me, Kay. Does a girl sometimes kick off a heel purposely? I mean, do you think that would occur to one?"

"Certainly," said Kay. "She probably buys heels by the gross. Then she took your arm, I suppose. Or maybe even you had to carry her."

"Hmmph," said James. "But I do think it likely that she sat down. What would you do if you lost your heel, Kay?"

"I'd wait for a dashing gentleman in a cream-colored roadster to come and get me," said Kay acidly. "By the way, I have a telephone call to make. I must call Harvey. Will you stir this till I come back?"

James closed his ears to the words that would have been audible to him. Why should he listen to Kay's voice light up when she spoke to her lovely Harvey Bell?

In a moment she was back again. Her face was flushed with triumph. "If I told you I had put five dollars, twenty to one, on a horse named Carfare, what would you say, James?" she demanded.

"Nothing," said James. "Because it's none of my business. But I might think it had been rather a silly speculation."

"Well, I did," triumphed Kay. "And now I have a hundred dollars. Silly speculation, James? Yes?"

"Hmm," said James. "Getting sort of thick with Harvey Bell, aren't you! Carfare. His horse, I suppose?"

"No," Kay corrected. "A horse belonging to a man named Pudge Larraby."

## CHAPTER 11

KAY HAD DISCOVERED THE remnants of Saturday's roast shoulder of lamb and served it in small, irregular chunks with a delectable caper sauce.

"The thing about caper sauce is to use plenty of butter and very little cornstarch and thin it with the juice the capers came in," Kay explained.

James smacked his lips. "Whatever you did to this, it's right," said the professor.

There were also some tender and succulent bits of celery root and mashed potato light as foam.

"What's for dessert?" James demanded, fork poised over a possible further indulgence in the entrée.

"Winter pears and Camembert," said Kay. "You'll be stuffed with caper sauce if I don't warn you. And the Camembert is heavenly. It's soft as a persimmon and it has a lovely barnyard smell."

She jumped up. "Sit still," she commanded. And James sat, enjoying a sense of guilty luxury. It was so swell having this cute kid pirouetting out through the swinging door with two well-mopped dishes in one hand and the gravy boat in the other, to have her instantly reappear with a platter of frosted pears, to have her mesh into the machinery of his house as if she belonged there and would stay forever.

"Heavens!" she exclaimed, a half-peeled pear arrested *in statu quo*. "I almost forgot we were asked to Tania's tonight."

"I didn't forget," said James.

"Woe is mine," Kay grimaced. "And me hoping that my tempting supper would drive her from your head for a few brief moments."

"You don't understand," said James. "Something will happen tonight. I'm trying an experiment."

"On the princess? But James, a gentleman never tells."

"It'll be very interesting," said James. "I think I'd better get dressed. You're all ready, aren't you?"

"Heavens, no!" cried Kay. "To dance? At the Raleigh? I should say not. It'll take me hours!"

James pushed his chair back from the table with an energetic shove. His life had never seemed so full of everything a life should have. He was in love. He was untangling a fascinating problem. He had just finished a perfect meal. What more could a man ask of fate?

"I'll just dash into my tux," said James. And then he said, "damn!" because he suddenly remembered that Paul Hyman still had his evening wear. Well, perhaps it would be better if he dressed over at Hymie's, anyway. A man couldn't be too careful. People were forever misunderstanding the simplest, most innocent acts.

"Look, Kay," he proposed. "If you don't mind staying here alone I'll dress over at Paul Hyman's. My tux is over there, as a matter of fact. You'll be cozier here than sitting outside Hymie's in the car. And I'll drop by for you in twenty minutes. Half an hour at the most."

"I'll love it, James," Kay admitted. "I think your house is the nicest one in the world and I'll be happy as a clam."

"Well, make yourself at home," said James. "I won't be long."

He stepped into Xantippe with the feeling that there had been something incomplete about his leave-taking from Kay, as though an unkissed kiss had been left dangling in midair or a sentence broken off in the middle, leaving people annoyed. The casual comings and goings of daily life had their subjects and predicates and punctuation. To have left Kay without a kiss was more than ungrammatical. It was positively boorish.

Coupled with this dissatisfaction was the uncertainty of finding Hymie at his room. A shaded light in the window dispelled the latter fret.

Hymie answered the knock and hello with a quick "Come in," and James entered.

Hymie's room was bare as a monk's cell. There was something ascetic about Hymie, anyway. And he owned nothing. Books he either borrowed from friends or from the library. His most important possessions were his violin and a fine Staunton chess set. These he had bought without counting their cost, because they were tools. With the chessmen he developed his mind. With the violin he expressed his soul. But there was no rowing machine in Hymie's room. He didn't do setting up exercises or go for constitutionals, because to him the body was not important. Clothing it correctly in James's tux was necessary for reasons of prestige, that was all.

"I'm sorry," said Hymie. "I thought Monday I'd take it by my tailor and get it fixed up. I didn't like to return it the way it is. I never thought you'd—"

"That's all right," said James. "I'll just slip into it here, if you don't mind."

James dressed rapidly while Hymie stood about waiting for it to be over, making perfunctory conversation.

James rarely came to Hymie's room because he always felt, in spite of Hymie's politeness, a faint restless unwelcome.

The room was a personal thing with Hymie. It was very clean, noticeably free from the stale tobacco aura of college living quarters. James felt that Hymie actively didn't want anybody else in it or that if somebody must come, then he should go as soon as his business was concluded. When Hymie played chess it was always at somebody else's house, with Hymie carrying his fine Staunton men along under his arm together with the folding, spacious, baize-backed board. He always apologized. "You don't mind?" he would say. "I am so used to my own men." And nobody ever did mind, because they all hoped when their ship came in that they too could afford a chess set like Hymie's.

Half an hour had passed before James reached home again. Kay was not waiting in the living room, but entered it from his sleeping quarters just as he arrived.

"Beat the deadline, I did," she triumphed. "I can dress in a minute now, if you'll drive me by the apartment. You'll never guess, James. I took a whole, all-over, luxurious, wonderful bath while you were gone."

"Here?" said James. Good Lord! What if the scandalmongers got hold of that!

"Think of all the time I saved us, James. Wasn't I clever? Wasn't I a good girl?"

"Splendid," said James. It would never do to let Kay know how startled and even horrified he was. Or, for that matter, how secretly and scandalously pleased.

"I washed behind my ears," said Kay, "and I didn't leave a ring on the tub. And now let's go. You never told me your theory about the old dead Russian. I was thinking in the hot water. Hot water always makes me think. Tell me your theory, immediately. Why do you keep things back from me, James?"

That was Kay. Kay all over. What could a man do? Laugh and love it. That's what James did.

"It all hangs on a heel and a silver chain and a rubber band," said James. "And it won't be long now. We're getting to the heart of the matter, my charming sleuth. And forget your international spy ring, because you're barking up the wrong olive tree."

"That's not funny," said Kay, piqued at the pricking of her spy plot balloon. "I thought of a much better one about your seductive continental princess. It goes something like this: 'Never look a gift Russian in the teeth or you'll find the Tartar.' "

"Hmmph," said James. "Before we go I must feed Cinders."

"All right, all right," Kay tossed her head. "We'll call it quits."

Presently they were spinning along the gleaming trestle of the Bay Bridge. Xantippe was at her best. The mild night spilled in over the top of the windshield with a soft, rushing sound.

"Oh," said Kay. "I love this bridge, James. And I love driving over it at night. It's just as though we were living a thousand years from now. They'll never have anything any more wonderful than this! We needn't be afraid to die!"

"We came pretty near it, five nights back, at this very spot."

"Your good driving saved us, James," said Kay. And she said it with just the right note of humble adoration calculated to make a man spread his feathers like a peacock. James glowed. What a girl! What a night! What a world!

What a priceless possession life was!

And yet there were dark and guilty souls who would snatch the lives of others and cut them down ruthlessly for some sordid grudge or fancied advantage. These somber spirits looked like ordinary men and women. They were hard to distinguish, hard to convict. But they had to be hunted down and brought to bay and destroyed. Humanity must be rid of these heartless culls. Each man must help for mankind's need to lessen misery for all time.

Such were some of James's thoughts as he sped past the night-blooming miracle that was Treasure Island, the magic fairy city, towering iridescent into the dark star-scattered sky.

"I want to find who killed those Japanese," James said. "I want to track the devil down, Kay. And I'm going to do it. It can't be as difficult as it seems."

They drove on in silence, thinking companionably along lines that James knew were parallel in purpose, if not in approach. They threaded the maze of San Francisco's tilted streets and arrived at Kay's apartment.

"You'd better come in," Kay said. "It'll take me a little while, you know. I don't want to think of you sitting out here where you might be stabbed in the dark, or something. Life is so dangerous."

They climbed out of Xantippe.

"I'd love to go in," James admitted, "if you're quite sure it's all right."

"Nobody will see," hissed Kay. "Oh, James dear. You're such a hopeless prig! Honestly!"

Thus dared, James entered. He was really most anxious to see Kay in her proper frame. It gave you a slant on people.

She led him up two flights of balustered stairs to a small, neat apartment that overlooked the immediate neighbor to the north and commanded a narrow glimpse of the Embarcadero and bay.

"Sit in that one," Kay commanded, "but don't sit down too hard because it isn't as soft as it looks. I'll be out in no time."

Kay disappeared. Instead of doing what he was told, James wandered about the room piecing together bits of Kay's past.

The richest discovery was Kay's desk. Its spinet recess harbored a gentle mob of monochrome two-dimensional people. Some of them were obviously Kay—Kay with the basketball team, all in bloomers, Kay on a hayride, Dad teaching Kay how to keep right side up on her new bicycle, Kay in a family group on the front steps of Grandpa's farmhouse on Thanksgiving Day.

James realized that Kay kept these pictures before her eyes because of the other people, her friends, her family, the dear, the absent, or the dead. But James saw only Kay. In all the pictures he looked for her, and if he couldn't find her he was disappointed.

From the desk he went to her bookshelf. It was a meager little library. There were some schoolbooks, even. Quite an up-to-date armful of the better crimesters was its chief backlog. But James was pleased also to find the *Oxford Book*, Stephens' *Crock of Gold*, Robert Nathan's *One More Spring*, and several other special favorites of his own.

He had been so absorbed in his investigations that when Kay herself was suddenly at his elbow with her old apparition trick it gave him the impression that no time had elapsed, and yet there she was, completely transformed. It was a pretty thrilling Kay who posed demurely for his inspection. She was a vision in coral chiffon velvet, the low, square-cut neck revealing more than a little the white secret slope of breasts. Small tip-tilted feet in velvet-to-match turned the model slowly before James's eyes. Arms slight and childish curved deliciously into smooth level shoulders.

James was speechless.

"Don't you like my dress?" Kay asked with a hint of a catch in her voice.

"I've never liked a dress so much in my life," said James unsteadily. "I just didn't know what to say."

"Well, that's all right then," said the vision, smiling and evidently vastly relieved. "I made it myself to go out with you. Special." Then a note of transient worry. "It isn't too low, is it? I mean, this is how they're wearing them, but you're so proper, James."

That would never do. He had to manage somehow to correct that impression. But the worst of it was that it was true. At least it always had been true. He wasn't so sure, any more. He wasn't sure of anything except that in the last five days he had suddenly begun to live. He had but now been thrust full-fledged from the brow of Jove. Or was it Jove? Everything had become so uncertain, even the classic myths.

"A girl has to compete somehow," said Kay, sighing. "That Tania, she'll be showing everything. You just wait and see."

"I won't look," said James. "I'm not interested. But about your dress being that low. I think it's just exactly right, Kay."

Kay picked up her familiar little brown fur coat and James held it while she slipped her arms into the sleeves.

"Wait a sec," she fussed, "I'm lost somewhere in the lining. Oh dear."

James had seldom seen Kay at all fussed, and she was so completely childish and appealing right at this moment. His arms, already halfway about her, longed to join and clasp her tight against him. And imagine her having to wear this everyday fur for evening! What a joy it would be to dress anyone so lovely in the most beautiful evening wrap Post Street could produce. What a privilege it would be for some man. What a wonderful way, for instance, for a stodgy, stick of a professor to spend a month's hire.

They went down the carpeted stairs in silence and out the door. Xantippe seemed to be waiting motionless at the curb, but James knew the old thing better. He knew that Xantippe somewhere in the depths of her molybdenum heart was chaffing at the bit, pawing like a stallion.

"The Raleigh, James," Kay commanded.

And humbly James obeyed. He asked nothing better of life than to be at the beck and call of those imperious little crimson lips, forever and ever. Amen.

Xantippe had her good points, indubitably. But open cars, James found, are not held in high regard by young women carefully accoutred for an evening's dancing.

Long before Xantippe reached the Raleigh, Kay wailed that her coiffure was ruined.

"It's a perfect fright," she said. "I look like the Witch of Endor."

"Leave it alone," directed James. "It's perfect."

They laughed. But James had suddenly lost his carefree mood, somehow. He was glad that Kay was content to sit there silently and dabble at her hair. His mind had gone back to the Bay Bridge wreck.

They could ignore it, he reflected, he and Kay. They could carry on their ordinary pursuits as if it had never happened. They could laugh and dance. But it was not banished. It was still there. Like a rock tossed into a pool, it disappeared, but the ever-widening ripples went on and on into infinity.

And those ripples were not diminishing properly in their force. Imperceptibly but actually they were multiplying their initial energy. They were mounting into waves. And somewhere close beneath the surface, there was menace and greed and fear. And he and Kay were floating chips, without any real knowledge of the hidden currents, without real volition of their own. They were powerless to defend themselves against hazards unknown.

Kay reached across his arm and pressed the horn button. The echoes bounced back and forth between the walls of the Grant Avenue tunnel. James smiled contritely.

"I forgot," he said. "I'm sorry."

"Don't forget again," Kay warned him. "It's important, James. It's why I liked you the other night so much better than that unpleasant Professor Biddle."

"So you had me under the microscope?" said James, grinning.

"Men are always under the microscope," the girl confided. "But there are really just two kinds. The realists, and the ones who blow horns in tunnels."

"I'm glad," said James, "that I did horn in on Professor Biddle." He laughed. He liked his pun, and his good humor came rushing back.

An attendant took charge of Xantippe at the Hotel Raleigh's portico. Di Piazzi came bustling up while James was checking his coat and hat. There was the customary sulky expression on Rubio's pale face, but he was affable enough.

"Tania," he said, "she will join us presently. That is her message. It may mean anything. I think we should, perhaps, take seats."

But Tania Varnakov appeared almost before di Piazzi had finished his apology. An elevator door slid open silently and she was there, approaching from the far end of the marble foyer. She wore a collar of seed pearls and a severely plain velvet gown that looked black but was probably dark blue. Simplicity created for her the most theatrical of effects.

James understood the trick. In essence, the campus coeds employed it every day. The radiant ones invariably chummed up with drabs. But Princess Tania was truly beautiful and charming. She greeted her guests cordially, especially James.

"Your coming has made me happy, very, very happy," she said, with a sidelong glance of her tawny eyes. "I have found that the continental men, the Latin type especially, lack inspired rhythm. Their dancing reflects an unhappy decadence." Her laughter, soft yet tinged with derision, brushed aside di Piazzi's swift low-voiced oath. "Shall we go to our table now?" she asked.

The Raleigh Rainbow Room greeted them with a blast of hot slippery syncopation. The waiter, escorting them to a reserved table beside the crowded dancing floor, was sleek and deferential and efficient. The decorations were colorful and lavish. Long drinks were ordered and appeared too quickly.

It was a pretty blatant business, James decided, show business. It was all right for youngsters. But when you passed that age, it was just a shot in the arm for unhappy extroverts. He didn't think he was going to enjoy the evening very much.

But Davy Doolittle's Dizzy Drudges were going to town tonight. They were putting it in the groove, as Kay observed. They popped up and down, grinning, grimacing, brandishing their instruments. A tall boy with a sensitive face slapped a bass fiddle fervidly. The drummer slugged out a fast primitive tempo. A couple of violins made a gallant stand against a massed attack of trombones, saxophones and clarinets.

James danced. He danced first with Kay. He didn't know any tricky stuff, but he was steady and reliable. And it was an excuse to clasp her, yielding and responsive, in his arms. She was so little. She followed so perfectly. She enjoyed it all so much. James tried an original step in half-time and got away with it. The music definitely was improving!

He danced with Tania, and that was something, too, something else. She wasn't decadent. She affected James like the sound of a tom-tom far away at night. He had never heard a tom-tom far away at night, but he was sure it would be like that, restless, disturbing, reaching out, reaching out to possess you.

There didn't seem to be much to say. Speech didn't seem necessary. But when he returned with Tania Varnakov to their table he felt a silly unaccountable impulse to apologize to Kay.

The Dizzy Drudges swung into another set. They were broadcasting on a network hookup now. They were hot. Davy Doolittle was singing into a microphone.

But Kay shook her head when James suggested that they follow Tania and di Piazzi out onto the dancing floor. She had become quiet, suddenly, aloof and pensive. James had seen her dancing with Rubio only a moment before. She hadn't looked tired then, but she was now, she said.

James mulled it over while he smoked a slow cigarette. It was just a whim, he guessed. At least, women had whims in something or other he had read.

"Look!" Kay cried abruptly. She was all smiles again. Her whim had vanished magically. She wasn't tired any more.

James followed the direction of her nod. Over by the entrance to the lounge he saw a group of four men waiting to be conducted to a table. None of them was in evening dress. Three were huddled in a tight triangle, laughing a trifle noisily.

The fourth, glancing casually around the Rainbow Room, marked the table of Tania Varnakov. His face lighted with pleasure. James waved politely, but he realized that it was Kay who had drawn the salute from Harvey Bell.

After a word to his companions, Bell came over to greet Kay. He was glad to see them both, he said, and apologized hastily for his companions.

"It's one of those victory celebrations we're having," he explained wryly. "You'd be surprised how much time I have to waste keeping up the goodwill of our farm. If a colt I sell doesn't pan out well, the owner has to be consoled. If the colt wins, I'm in for a victory powwow."

The music stopped. James had risen to present the princess and di Piazzi as they came off the floor. But they seemed to know Harvey Bell already, as it happened. Tania looked pleased to find him here, but her manager glowered more than usual as he shook hands, James thought.

"Yes, we have met," said Tania, smiling. "Down at Mr. Werner's very interesting farm. If you are free, we would like to have you join us, Mr. Bell."

"I'm sorry. I'm with a stag party," he explained.

"A stag? Oh, yes, I see." There was an infectious ripple to the girl's laugh. James smiled, but he noticed that Kay did not. She was looking at Harvey Bell.

"I'm sorry I can't join you," he was saying, "but there's a real character with me tonight. I'll bring him over for just a minute if you don't mind."

"By all means," said Tania Varnakov.

Bell returned in a moment with a short barrel-chested man. The newcomer was almost entirely bald, but his eyes, peering out from beneath bushy brows, were alert and young. A long cigar tilted aggressively upward from between strong, white teeth, and a diamond horseshoe stickpin gleamed like a major galaxy in a cravat of martial hues.

Harvey Bell presented Pudge Larraby, and the little man shook hands effusively all round. He was pleased to meet everybody and offered cigars to James and Rubio.

"It's my night to howl," he expanded. "I guess Harvey's told you, Princess? No? Well, Harvey's too modest for his own good sometimes. He don't blow his horn enough. He bred that little mare I started in the fifth race this afternoon. And she can run a bit. It surprised everybody, but she can—she can really run a little bit—and I had five C's riding on her nose."

Pudge Larraby tapped the long ash from his cigar and looked complacently from face to face.

"Five C's," repeated Tania Varnakov. "Your American slang—it's so quaint, but so very cryptic!"

"Five centuries," explained Larraby. "Half a grand. That's what I bet she'd come romping home. And she made it, going away. You can have your Seabiscuits, but I'll take Carfare. She's going to be news before she's a three-year-old."

"She's already good news to me," said Kay. "I won a hundred dollars on her at twenty to one this afternoon." Larraby looked at her approvingly.

"Good for you," he said. "Smart girl."

"I don't know anything about racing," admitted Kay. "I just wanted to make a bet for fun, so I asked Harvey for his advice."

Pudge Larraby slowly removed the cigar from between his teeth. His lips puffed out a thin stream of smoke.

James, watching Carfare's owner with amusement, saw the face of a benign Billiken become fleetingly hard and sinister.

"You're running a breeding ranch, Harvey," said the turfman. "You're doing all right there. Stick to that, feller, and keep your friends."

Whereupon Harvey Bell behaved excellently, James thought. He didn't lose his temper or his smile.

"I'm afraid you're going to lose some friends, Pudge," he said, "if you don't get back to our table and tell the boys to quiet down. They don't seem quite at home here. Perhaps it was a mistake to bring them to this sort of place."

"Sure, Harvey," Pudge agreed. As quickly as it had gone, the warm twinkle returned to Larraby's eyes. "I'll make 'em pipe down. Anything you say, Harvey."

Harvey Bell had the excellent taste not to apologize for the choleric turfman. James admired him for it, even though a moment of awkward silence followed the departure of Larraby.

A burst of applause terminated the hush. Davy Doolittle was back again, taking an amber spot to announce a brand new selection he hoped the folks would go for in a big way.

"It's just an original little ditty of my own, girls and boys," he said modestly. "It's called *Why Can't We Try It Again, Again?*"

"Well, I have to be running along," said Harvey Bell. But Princess Tania reached out a detaining hand.

"Please! At least not until Professor Biddle and I have finished our cigarettes."

Di Piazzi led Kay to the dance floor. James and Harvey Bell were left in attendance on the princess. It was the opportunity James had hoped for. Indeed, it was better than he had hoped for.

He said, "I suppose the stolen ikon has not been found or we would have heard."

"No." Tania raised expressive hands in a gesture of feminine helplessness. "It may never be returned."

The moment was propitious. James brought out the enameled plaque he had found on Treasure Island and laid it on the tablecloth. Tania Varnakov picked it up curiously. Her breath came in a little gasp.

"Where did you ever get this? It is antique, is it not? Russian, surely."

"We had to bare the roots of an olive tree," said James. "I happened to find this in the loose earth. I brought it along because the face so strikingly resembles yours, don't you think?"

The princess examined the antique carefully.

"Perhaps I should not agree too readily," she said. "The lady is so beautiful. What do you think, Mr. Bell?" Harvey Bell inspected the plaque and returned it to Tania.

"A resemblance," he admitted, "which falls short, my dear Princess."

Tania Varnakov accepted the compliment gracefully. "Could I borrow it?" she begged. "I would have it photographed by Rubio."

"By all means," James consented. Things were working out admirably.

It was not until later, after much dissonant syncopation of the Dizzy Drudges, that James remembered apprehensively that tomorrow was another day. And a busy day. Monday.

But by then Xantippe was gallantly scaling the last steep hill west of Kay's apartment, and James refused to be intimidated by the thought of consequences. He whistled *Why Can't We Try It Again, Again,* but he cut it off to look down at Kay and smile.

"I had a swell time tonight!" he said. "You follow so wonderfully. Much better than Tania. Because you're more psychic, of course."

"James," she said, "could I see that little plaque again that you found on that very dead Russian?"

"No," said James. "I lost it."

"Lost it! But James, how careless of you! How on earth did you lose it, and where?"

"On a live Russian," said James. "A very live Russian, my dear."


## CHAPTER 12

IT SEEMED TO JAMES THAT HE had hardly closed his eyes when it was already morning and the telephone was ringing again like a thing possessed. These morning incursions of the outside world were becoming as regular and dependable as an alarm clock.

James stumbled to the offending contraption, still half asleep. "James Biddle speaking," he indicated for the benefit of the as yet unknown who had been so brash as to harass him out of slumber.

"This is McDuff," said that Highlander.

"I might have known," James yawned. "Now what?"

"How soon can you get over here?" McDuff wanted to know. His voice was harsh with fatigue. Its very sound made James feel much less abused to have been roused so early.

"Some time this afternoon," said James. "If that—"

"No," vetoed the inspector briefly. "This morning. Nine o'clock?"

"Ten," bargained the professor. "You don't seem to realize I'm a teacher. And this is Monday."

"Ten, then," came the tired voice of McDuff. "And don't be late. This isn't only Monday, Professor. This is murder."

"More murder?" asked James. He found he was wide awake now.

"Of course, more," said McDuff crossly. "There's always more, Professor. Murder loves company, Professor. You show up at ten."

James dressed as rapidly as possible. Mrs. Pringle had just come in and it never took her long to fling his breakfast on the table. The kindling had already begun to crackle its first warning.

James disposed of his breakfast absentmindedly and went out to Xantippe. He was still pretty full of memories of the evening before. It seemed very recent to him and very real. To have danced awkwardly with Kay, to have held her own perfect self in his arms for the duration of several haunting tunes, that was an experience an inexperienced academician couldn't easily forget.

He cranked up Xantippe with a couple of prods at the starter and headed over toward the city.

There was a stop to make at the Exposition. He wanted to investigate the ground at the base of the two dead trees. If carbon bisulfide had been applied to them, according to his theory, then there must have been holes in the ground. He remembered with interest how that heel had seemed forced down into the soil somewhat, possibly plugging a hole by which the chemical had been applied. But if so, why? Evaporation caused the cooling which produced freezing temperatures. Then why would a tree murderer have stoppered the hole? Ah. The odor. The permeation of rotten eggs. Memories of lab days, H2S, and all that. Perhaps an interruption...

James pulled off the Bay Bridge onto the timber viaduct leading down to the Fair. He flashed his pass at the gate and took a chance on finding a parking place in front of the Administration Building. It was still early in the day.

There was a place, and James left Xantippe. A brisk three minutes took him to his olives. He wanted to see if there was a deep hole at the base of the tree, a hole by which carbon bisulfide could have been administered, a hole in turn which might in case of an unforeseen interruption have been stoppered with a heel.

James reached the spot. He was examining the foliage overhead as a means of identifying the first of the two ailing trees. To his mystification he didn't immediately spot the dead leaves. Counting from the end of the double line he located the site. But the dead tree?

It was gone.

In its place, looking exactly as though it had grown there, was what James now recognized as a younger and inferior tree. His eye crossed the walk to the location of the other wilted tree. That one, too, had been removed and replaced by another. What admirable organization. But by what authority? It didn't seem possible Mr. Sperry would have rushed through such a considerable task without first having consulted him.

There was one way to find out. James sought out Mr. Sperry's office. Yes, said Mr. Sperry. He had authorized the replacing of those two olive trees. A prominent citizen had happened to notice that they were either dead or dying and had insisted out of the kindness of his heart on replacing the trees during the night with a pair from his own ranch.

Yes, a very prominent citizen. Being disturbed to have visitors see any tree wilting in California, this generous man had undertaken the replacement entirely at his own expense. What could be more convenient? Well, he had asked that his name be withheld. But surely he wouldn't mind being known privately to the professor. The philanthropist was none other than Mr. Cartwright himself. Yes, Mr. Porter Cartwright.

"But damn it!" James exploded, "I wasn't finished with those trees. I'm not through with them at all. I'm particularly interested in finding out the cause of their death!"

"They aren't dead, in Mr. Cartwright's opinion," Sperry explained. "He thinks his gardeners can restore them with proper treatment and care. But you understand all about olive trees, Professor Biddle, much better than I do."

"Or Cartwright, for that matter," James mused.

With that thought he left Mr. Sperry. It was approaching ten o'clock. McDuff was an ally now. It wouldn't do to keep him waiting. And, damn it, the inspector was baiting him with news of another homicide.

The victim couldn't be an acquaintance, James decided, as he pointed Xantippe's blunt nose toward San Francisco. It couldn't possibly be Princess Tania, or Cartwright or Rubio, or Doreen. McDuff wouldn't hold back news like that.

When a traffic light held him up, James dug out a lone nickel and whistled to a newsboy across the street. But before the boy could reach him, a bell clanged. The light turned green. Horns blared. A bumper nudged Xantippe in the rear, and James perforce was swept on with the current.

He was in an advanced state of curiosity by the time he reached headquarters and was admitted into the presence of the McDuff.

"Who was it, Inspector?" he demanded. "I mean, who's been killed? And where does it tie in?"

McDuff motioned to a chair. His eyes were grim and tired. His voice sounded half asleep.

"Sit down," he said. "And keep your shirt on, Professor. It's only the man with the cauliflower ears."

"Only!" James gasped the word. "Why, that's the most unbelievable thing that's happened."

"Nothing ever 'happens,' " snapped McDuff. It was a favorite theme of his. He believed in it, apparently. "We haven't got to first base with this new stiff. In fact, he's blasted hell out of the theory I was working on. All we know so far is that he's been identified by that guy, di Piazzi, and the Rooshian princess, and I wouldn't risk a dime on their identification."

"But if they both recognized him, Inspector—"

"We'll see if you recognize him. You talked to the guy. You gave him a real onceover because he made you sore. Di Piazzi and the dame could be wrong. There's a thousand slug-nutty pugs with tin ears." McDuff shrugged. "I think he's the same hood myself, being that he was in the gang that tried to hijack Cartwright's truck. But that hypodermic outfit he was packing got me down."

"The man I saw didn't look like a dope fiend," said James.

"Who said he was?" rasped the inspector. "This outfit was the kind Boy Scouts carry for snakebite. Get me?"

"Only the gent with the cauliflower ears wasn't a Boy Scout, either," James stoutly maintained. "But get on, Inspector. What's your angle?"

"It's like this," said McDuff, nodding. "I had a hunch about that long hole beneath the olive tree. If it wasn't a grave, it was something else. People dig holes to put things in, don't they?"

"Dogs do, anyway," James conceded.

"Well, I suppose you've been around enough to have run across rumors about Porter Cartwright's famous Black Room. Or have you?"

"I've heard it referred to once or twice, Inspector. The Sargasso Sea of missing masterpieces? Oh yes. I've treasured the phrase. The alliteration is topnotch."

"Anyway, you know the story," McDuff went on. "You know it's only an easy sprint from the Fine Arts Exhibits at the Fair to the hole that was ready and waiting beneath that olive tree. You know that money couldn't buy some of those loaned exhibits, and that Cartwright would give his eye teeth for that kind of junk. It could be stolen, probably, if it was done quick enough. But it would be too risky trying to get it off the island while it was still hot."

"It sounds pretty theatrical," James objected.

"They got the Mona Lisa, didn't they? Cut it out of the frame and rolled it up." McDuff spread his hands. There was a regretful expression in his tired eyes. "That's what I was waiting for. Something like that. I've been keeping a man hanging around in Clipper Way all the time. And when Cartwright's truck showed up last night and took away two olive trees, I thought I had hold of something at last."

"Cartwright wouldn't be so obvious," said James.

"Now we can say that," McDuff admitted. "But last night it looked certain. We made a quick check on the important stuff in the Fine Arts Building, and it was all there. So we didn't bother to trail the truck. But someone did. We got an earwitness report that a sedan rolled out of a side street onto Bayshore Boulevard just as Cartwright's truck went by. And another closed car came roaring up from nowhere and tangled with the first sedan. They traded shots and then lit out, both of them. But they left this mug with the cauliflower ears behind. He stopped a slug from a .45. That's the story, but you won't find it all in the papers."

"Cartwright denies all, I suppose," said James. Inspector McDuff did a deadpan.

"What's Cartwright got to deny?" he growled. "He can't help it, can he, if some gangsters want to put on a show alongside his truck? We quizzed his crew, a Dago and a Jap. Had to let them go. That angle isn't even news." He stood up ponderously. "So now, Professor, if you'll just take a run over to the morgue..."

"Okay," James agreed. "But you can help me too, Inspector. I want a note to that man of yours on Clipper Way. I want you to make it good and strong. I'd like to know what he's seen without having to chip it out with a nutpick."

"If you'll stick around you can third-degree Pohlemus here," McDuff promised. "I'm going to pull him off the island. We're all washed up on the great olive-tree mystery."

"On the contrary!" protested James. "You've got to keep a man there from now on, Inspector. It's vital."

The inspector reached for a scratchpad and scrawled a brief note on it.

"Here," he said. "I don't take any stock in your hunch, Professor, but I'll string along for another day or two. What the hell." He added a doubtful compliment. "You might turn up something in a screwy case like this."

James phoned the inspector from the morgue.

"It's that fellow," he said. "What does Kay know about it?"

"More than's good for her," said Angus McDuff, "but no more than she read in the papers, probably."

"Then she has no way to know it's the man with the cauliflower ears."

"Till you tell her," said McDuff.

"We won't tell her," said James. "Right?"

"Right," agreed the inspector. He hung up. They understood each other.

James headed back toward Treasure Island. By the time he reached the olive trees his lungs were full of fresh sea air, and his mind was full of cheerful conjectures. He could even smile as he accosted the stocky Mr.

Pohlemus and handed him McDuff's note.

"I'm Biddle," said James. "Remember me?"

"Sure." Pohlemus looked up after a glance at the note. He didn't seem particularly impressed. "What's on your mind?"

James drew the French heel from his pocket.

"This is a French heel," he said.

"Okay, it's a French heel," Pohlemus agreed. "So what?"

"Has anybody been injured along this avenue during the last few days? While you've been on duty here, I mean."

"Nobody. Nothing happens here. It's enough to give a guy the megrims." Pohlemus tucked a cigarette between his lips. "Got a match, maestro?"

"A pretty girl, for instance," persisted James. "One who tripped and hurt herself when her heel came off. And she had to lean against a tree or sit down in the grass, maybe, for a while."

"Oh, yeah!" Pohlemus's moonlike face brightened suddenly. "Sure. That could be the little stenographer who twisted her ankle the other afternoon. She was a nice dish, that one. She had to lean against a tree for quite a spell." Mr. Pohlemus refreshed his memory. "It happened on account her heel came loose," he announced brightly.

"Well, well," said James. "And was she carrying anything?"

"Sure. An umbrella."

"That's all?" James was disappointed.

"Well, she had her portable typewriter, of course. I told you she was a public stenographer, didn't I? And it ain't right," said Pohlemus, gallantly, "for a little dame like her to be lugging around that heavy case. I told her so when she stopped here a couple of minutes for a rest this morning."

"Here?" James was standing beside one of the replaced trees.

"No. That's where she got hurt, hooking her heel on that wooden rim." Mr. Pohlemus indicated the casing, several feet square, set in the walk to form a shallow watering basin around the tree. As far as James could see, it offered no more hazard than similar casings surrounding other trees.

"Next time she shows up, see where she goes," James commanded. "But don't carry her typewriter, if you know what I mean."

"Okay," agreed Pohlemus sulkily. "But she's no suspicious character, Professor. She's a nice girl."

The morning was shot, but James had an afternoon class at two and an office hour for conference with students from three to four. He picked up a quick lunch at one of the restaurants on the lagoon. Then, a little self-consciously, he telephoned Kay. He was rushing things, he knew. And what if she refused? But what if she got a call instead from Harvey Bell? Or what if she was in danger from the sender of the anonymous note? The danger might be real. It was real. A frightened murderer might do anything. Anywhere. At any time. You couldn't tell. The fat's in the fire the second you become a problem to a desperate man.

"Society item!" James spoke into the phone. "Miss Kay Ritchie is having dinner tonight with James Biddle at Joe DiMaggio's. Miss Ritchie will take a taxi to Fisherman's Wharf and arrive at seven sharp. Or am I wrong?"

"That's news," said Kay. "We'll run it as it reads. I'm standing by for a call from Mrs. Morgenafter, James. She threw a soirée last night and ought to be coming out from under the ether any minute now. Goodbye."

So much for supper. But James lingered in the booth. He came to the decision slowly, but once he had made up his mind, he looked up the proper number and dialed it before he could have time to falter.

"This is James Biddle," he announced, when his call was answered. "Professor James Biddle of the University of California. I wish to speak to Mr. Cartwright, please."

He waited, and presently the brisk feminine voice addressed him again.

"I'm sorry, Professor Biddle. Mr. Cartwright is just leaving for lunch. Can I take your message?"

"It's personal and important," said James. "If you can catch him, please tell Mr. Cartwright that I would like an appointment with him late this afternoon, to discuss some olive trees on Treasure Island."

He waited again. More successfully.

"Mr. Cartwright will see you at four-thirty," he was told. "Please be punctual."

It was the admonition which practically spoiled James's afternoon. His two o'clock class, where he was breaking new and exciting ground in agricultural practice, was a fizzle. He was even unkindly brusque, he regretted afterward, with a promising junior student in an office conference. But he was on time at Cartwright's at four-thirty sharp. He entered the financier's reception room high up in the Russ Building, identified himself, and was told to sit.

He sat. He waited, while a woman with pince-nez sniped away at a noiseless typewriter. This den of entrenched wealth was distinctly disappointing. It didn't seem at all the sort of place in which a tycoon would barricade himself for a long siege by the New Deal. The furniture wasn't even number one Grand Rapids. It was all antiques.

At five James was finally accorded his interview. He entered the inner sanctum, seething.

Mr. Porter Cartwright failed to look up at once from the single sheet of paper he had before him on an enormous desk. He was a tall man, massive and beetle-browed. His hair was gray but thick and curly. He glanced up finally and said, "Well?"

It wasn't an ingratiating salute and in response James on his own part discarded the polite approach he had planned.

"I came to find out, if possible," he confessed frankly, "just what use you intend to make of two dying olive trees, Mr. Cartwright?"

The financier looked James over slowly from head to brogues.

"All right," he said. "All right, Biddle. I think we can understand each other pretty quickly. I think we should understand each other, too. That's why I allowed you to come here. I want you to know that I'm not flattered by your curiosity. And when I want to talk to you about olive trees, Biddle, I'll come to you."

"But perhaps you're making a mistake," James suggested mildly. "Perhaps my curiosity has unearthed a few more facts than you realize, Mr. Cartwright."

"And you," returned Cartwright, rising from his chair, "may not realize a thing or two. For example, has it occurred to you that a university might not appreciate having a generous donor annoyed by an intrusive faculty member? Has it escaped your attention that people of influence could, possibly, affect the future of such an individual, especially one who allowed himself to be publicized in an inexcusable tavern brawl?"

Two hours later, James was still angry when he joined Kay at Fisherman's Wharf. Kay was in good form, but James ate little and talked less. It would be better, he decided, not to discuss Cartwright just yet. But he couldn't forget him.

"It's just a tantrum I'm having," he tried to apologize with a laugh. "One of my black moods. Let's forget it and take in a show."

"No," Kay said. "You're all wrinkled, James. I think you're tired out." A cool finger smoothed his forehead with a soft swift touch. "You're keeping something from me, James. You are."

It wasn't any good trying to hold out on the girl, so he told her how Cartwright had used him for a doormat. Then he had to tell her why he had gone to see Cartwright in the first place. And then he had to tell her about the gun battle around Cartwright's truck. And before he knew it she had wormed it out of him that the victim of the night's killing was the man with the cauliflower ears.

"But don't tell Angus I told you," pleaded James, "because we agreed that you shouldn't get mixed up in this any worse than you are, and here I've gone and spilled the beans."

"You were a dear," consoled Kay, "and don't be having it on your conscience, either, because I'd have got it out of you sooner or later, and if you hadn't told me then Angus would have. So there. And don't ever try to keep anything from me again."

"All right," said James meekly.

And presently he left Kay at her home and went home. He was tired, oh so tired.

He didn't even bother to turn on the light in the hall because he would have to walk back and turn it out again. He went straight through the dark house to his bedroom and fumbled under the shade of his reading light for the pull-chain switch.

His fingers came in contact with the unlighted globe and for an instant he stopped breathing. The globe was hot.


CHAPTER 13

CHILLS CRINKLED DOWN JAMES'S spine. His fingers closed over the elusive pull-chain but numbed into dizzy indecision. Instantly he must do one of two things: either pull on the light and go carelessly about his business as though he had noticed nothing, or else keep the room in its present half-protective darkness. One of those courses he must decide on instantly. The least hesitation would betray him.

If he pulled the light on he would become an illuminated target for the intruder. If, on the other hand, he kept the room in darkness the unknown menace might suspect himself to have been discovered by the hot lamp globe and might forthwith assume a deadly and directed initiative. It might be a fusillade from an automatic, perhaps, or the ripping load of a sawed-off shotgun, discharged at this very spot, at any moment.

In the breathless blackness there was the slight unmistakable sound of a stealthy motion. It might have been the brush of sleeve against coat as an arm straightened and tensed to aim. It might have been the whip of one pants leg past another in the taking of a hurried, stealthy step.

But whatever the sound was, it was filled with an almost intolerable menace. James felt the imperative need to move away from the spot with which he had obviously, by this hesitation, identified himself. He crouched to the floor. If he only had a weapon, any kind of weapon, he could at least go down fighting. He remembered the doorstop. His groping fingers followed the bottom edge of the door, making grateful rendezvous with the small cast-iron damsel with the basket of flowers. His fingers closed, and he waited, feeling the goose-pimples prickle in waves from his knees to the roots of his hair. Having a weapon in his hands seemed to have the effect of filling him with righteous anger. His body tensed and his pulse pounded. There was no such thing as soundless motion in that still blackness. The slightest breath, the merest inter-friction of moving cloth was audible.

The electric tension had reached an arcing point. It was unendurable. Another slight sound sent it off. With a beast-like roar that horrified even himself, James lunged into the dark.

"Who's there?" he shouted. "Drop that gun! I've got you covered!"

Instantly the room seemed filled with plunging enemies. One of them James knocked cold and then identified with a sweep of his hand. It was his faithful Morris chair.

But even as the tumult momentarily subsided, a foot tripped over his own extended leg, and there was a brief, violent scuffle in the dark. James caught at the foot with his left hand and swung the iron lady lustily over his head. She struck something a glancing blow and followed through to terminate her brief orbit abruptly against James's knee.

The intruder's ankle twisted away from James, and running footsteps ended their audible progress with the bang of the kitchen door.

Shakily James turned on the bedroom light. A search uncovered nothing missing. But the room had evidently been thoroughly ransacked. Thoroughly, but not carelessly. There seemed to have been some effort on the part of the intruder to leave no trace of trespass.

James postponed an investigation of the rest of the house. He thought it would probably be a good idea to call McDuff immediately.

"And you're the wise guy that could get along without a tail," McDuff reminded over the phone. "Just sit down, now, and try and keep body and soul together till I get there. Don't busy yourself opening and closing all the drawers, thus messing up our best chance at fingerprints. Or did you do that already?"

"Of course not," James denied guiltily, then thought it best to add, "Just the bedroom drawers. I did glance in them a little."

"Oh. Just the bedroom drawers," mimicked the inspector. "Well, sit down now, Professor, and fold your hands. That will help us the most, if you don't mind." And the discouraged McDuff hung up.

James didn't mind the letter of the inspector's law, but he refrained from touching anything more. In a surprisingly short time the doorbell rang and James admitted the person of the law.

"This is Sergeant Ashley, Professor," McDuff said, introducing his companion. "Champion paddy man on the force. He'll want your finger-prints first."

"If you please," said Sergeant Ashley. He unpacked his little kit of fingerprinting paraphernalia and with a medium of some dark and oily pigment placed James's natal John Henry permanently in the public records. He then offered James a little dab of tissue moistened with cleanser to restore the digits to their former impeccability.

"Is there anybody else has the run of the place?" McDuff asked.

"Only Mrs. Pringle," said James. "But I would hesitate to send for her this time of night. She doesn't live here, you know."

"Funny," said the inspector. "Everybody else's sleep seems to be practically sacred. But they rout me out of bed if a branch scratches the side of a house."

"This wasn't any branch," said James. "I had him by the ankle once. Only he twisted loose."

"I'll show you the toehold," promised McDuff. "Next time you can use that."

"Mrs. Pringle is the cook?" inquired Sergeant Ashley. "It won't be necessary to disturb her. I'll pick her up on the frying-pan."

James winced at this shockingly cannibalistic picture of Mrs. Pringle, but Sergeant Ashley went on to explain.

"Cooks seldom wash frying pans," he said. "It's on account of the grease. They lay them away in the cooler or set them in the oven out of the dust. It's convenient that way. We can nearly always pick up a good right hand on the handle of the frying pan."

With this final frank revelation of the ways of fingerprinting experts, the sergeant disappeared, kit and boodle, through the kitchen door.

"Just my luck," sighed McDuff heavily. "Just the one night when I figured to catch up on a little shuteye, and you have to go and get yourself attacked in your own bedroom."

"I attacked him," James corrected with some dignity. "Furthermore I put him to flight with a small cast-iron lady."

"Somebody he brought along, no doubt," deduced McDuff.

James ignored the pleasantry.

"So I took the fifty grand," said McDuff, "and I came over to Berkeley to play nursemaid to a Ph.D. Why the hell don't you keep out of this,
Professor?" James glanced into McDuff's bloodshot eyes and saw that it
wasn't a rhetorical question he had been asked. But it was a hard question
to answer.

"Well," James said, and even in his own ears his voice sounded apologetic, "Kay was interested. And that got me started thinking about it. And
then trouble began to threaten my olive trees. And I had to protect them.
And then, damn it, I got interested."

"Listen," said McDuff. "You're paid for a job, aren't you? And well-
paid, too, no doubt. And what's that job? It's a job developing bigger
crops so the government can have more to turn under. Doesn't that keep
you busy? Can't you get along with that and not have to go messing
around with murder?"

"I thought you appreciated my help," said James, finding his feelings
hurt in spite of himself by the inspector's evident disapproval.

"Maybe I did, and maybe I didn't," said McDuff. "But we've had
another murder now, and it links up. And Miss Kay is a friend of mine,
and you're a friend of hers. And if you had more sense maybe I wouldn't
even mind calling you a friend of my own. Do you think I want to be
calling up a cute little happy-faced kid one of these days and breaking the
news to her that her buddy's run into something that came out the other
side? Not my dish, Biddle!"

"I think you exaggerate my importance to the underworld," said James.
"I've just been adding up what little I know."

"And that's probably what the guy with the cauliflower ears was
doing, too," said McDuff. "And he won't do it any more. Nobody gave
him a nice warning the way I'm giving you. But listen, Professor. Just
before you quit this business, would you mind telling me this—if the guy
with the cauliflower ears bumped off that guy that was murdered in the
car, then who killed the guy with the cauliflower ears? Or did somebody
else do both murders?"

"You mean all three murders," corrected James. "The man with the
cauliflower ears is one, and two in the car makes three."

"Oh, nuts, Professor!" wailed McDuff. "Do we have to go through
all that again? A car doesn't drive itself. One of those guys had to be
alive!"

"You forget the rubber band," James reminded.

"Then what's the answer?" queried McDuff weakly, and James realized with a shock that the great McDuff, for all his pretense of assurance

and authority, was really sending out an SOS.

"We'll find the answer when we know the whole truth about those olive trees," said James. "And when we know about the heel of the pretty steno. And Rubio di Piazzi's phony camera. And that Tartar skull, and the locket—"

"Hold on there," interrupted McDuff. "What camera?"

"A tripod outfit that redheaded Italian had down under my olive trees," said James. "Claimed he was taking pictures."

"Probably was," groused McDuff. "Can't see any connection between that and two murders."

"Three murders," said James implacably. "And there is a connection. There has to be, when you add that up with the locket."

"Listen," said McDuff. "Have you got a lot of new clues you're holding out on me, or what? What locket?"

"Well, I did hold it out on you for a few hours, Inspector," James confessed. "It was around the neck of that very dead Russian. I kept it because I wanted to flash it at Tania last night."

"Ah-ha." The inspector raised his eyebrows. "Last night you flash it on the princess. Tonight somebody ransacks your house. You don't see any connection, I suppose."

"Not the one you think," said the professor, grinning. "Tania didn't send a burglar for the locket, Inspector, because I loaned it to her."

"You loaned it to her, and you wouldn't even show it to me. But of course I suppose I'm expecting too much," growled the inspector. "Would it be unreasonable of me to ask why you loaned her a bit of so-called evidence?"

"Because Rubio di Piazzi was going to photograph it," James explained. "At least that's what she said."

"Who else knew you gave it to her?"

"Kay, Harvey Bell, and Rubio."

"Did anyone else know you had it?"

"No. Except—well, I think old man Werner saw me find it and put it in my pocket. He winked at me."

"Oh," said McDuff. "He winked, did he? May I ask why you wanted to show it to the princess?"

"Well, in the first place I wanted to see if she really would recognize a genuine Russian antique if she saw one, after that phony publicity stunt about her ikon."

"Nothing phony about that," said McDuff with unexpected conviction.

James pricked up his ears. "I'm afraid I never even gave the princess the benefit of the doubt," he admitted. "It sounded fantastic. What makes you so sure her St. John Chrysostom wasn't a publicity stunt?"

"I saw all his pedigree papers," said McDuff. "He's been in the Varnakov family since Catherine the Great was in didies."

"Possibly," conceded James, "but his value must have been exaggerated. Who would hash up a saint in a mosaic of rubies and sapphires and canary diamonds?"

"Some former Rajah of Peshawar," said McDuff. "That's what the princess claims. Hid out with the Varnakovs during a local revolution. Caught up on his church lore. And when things settled down back home he had the boys turn out a really nice knick-knack, probably not so much out of gratitude as to show that he was the big cheese in his own home town."

"Very interesting," said James. "I compliment you, Inspector."

"Not that it has anything to do with our two murders," said McDuff apologetically.

"Three murders," corrected James. "And on the contrary, Inspector, it's much the most pertinent bit of information your department has produced."

"You're joking, Professor." McDuff sighed. "And I'm too tired to laugh."

James drew a match from his pocket and relit his pipe. "Teachers have no sense of humor, Inspector," he confessed. "If we did have it would prove fatal. We would undoubtedly die laughing at ourselves. So being devoid of a sense of humor we try to achieve an impervious dignity."

Sergeant Ashley, who had crossed the horizon several times in the hurried manner of a springer off the scent, now approached, exuding triumph.

"I've got it, all right," he said. "Most of them were carefully rubbed off. But I found one distinct right thumb and a corroborating similarity in a left."

"What type of man, roughly?" McDuff inquired.

"Not a man," said Ashley. "A woman."

"Tania Varnakov," guessed McDuff. "Bound to be."

"It might be," James conceded. "I can't imagine what she'd have been looking for."

"Surely she doesn't think you've got her ikon."

"I'm not so sure," said James. "Maybe that's what she does think."

"Where did you find the prints, Sergeant?" McDuff asked.

"In the bathroom," said Sergeant Ashley.

A sudden dizziness overtook James. He cleared his throat.

"Ah, I think you can disregard those," he croaked rather feebly. "There was a lady. Ah, I forgot to mention her before. She took a bath. I wasn't here, myself. That is, I wasn't here at the time. She wasn't authorized. I—"

McDuff's cheeks bulged up under his eyes in an ominous and enigmatic manner. "Get those prints, Charlie," he commanded. "Check them against the one on Miss Ritchie's automobile operator's license. Good night, Professor Biddle."

## CHAPTER 14

THE DISTRACTING OCCURRENCES of Monday night lopped three from James's customary eight hours of sleep and shunted him into Tuesday's obligations ill-conditioned to cope with them.

He found the undergraduates in his ten o'clock class more than usually irksome. And what was worse his mind continually wandered from the job he was hired for to business that was none of his.

What sort of girl was the pretty steno with the French heel? Or rather, without the French heel? What was her connection with the man with the cauliflower ears? Why would Mrs. Porter Cartwright be cruising about the bay in the dark? And why, if she had a mink coat, wasn't she already wearing it at ten minutes before eight, instead of just at that moment putting it on? Surely the orchidaceous Doreen would have felt the chill bay mist earlier than 7:50.

As soon as he could decently dismiss class, James set Xantippe's course for Treasure Island.

He arrived at the exposition parking lot in advance of his date with Kay, so he approached the olive trees by the roundabout route of the Gayway. It was too early to find a crowd in the zone, and there was a relaxed, rather pleasant air to the gaudily faced concessions.

The attendants at the shooting gallery were having a contest amongst themselves. The barker for *Leda and the Swan* was sitting on the rail of his little pulpit meticulously peeling an orange. A confectioner was busily occupied molding a huge tray of popcorn balls, and a pair of midgets from Lilliputia watched the process with grave, ageless eyes.

James didn't know what had drawn him to the Gayway, but he was glad he had come. It was interesting to see the place with its hair down, so to speak.

As he approached the lurid facade of *Neptune's Mermaids,* his attention was attracted by a couple engaged in conversation at the small private entrance to the concession. A lady with dark sunglasses was talking earnestly with a thin, energetic-looking young man of the typical barker type. The girl was obviously beautiful in spite of the goggle-eyed effect created by the glasses. The man's eyes never wavered from her face. He was handsome in a hawklike way, and there was a hypnotic quality to his gaze which was undoubtedly his stock-in-trade in the show business.

James was not at first aware of why his attention had been drawn and held by this couple. They both glanced sharply at him, but that was only as he drew squarely abreast of *Neptune's Mermaids,* and something urgent in their manner with each other had impressed him strongly before this.

James's eyes were turned away as the couple looked up, but he felt the brief scrutiny like a slight electric shock, or perhaps it was the shock of his own recognition. A breath of expensive perfume had reached him. Then he knew. The woman was Doreen Cartwright.

Without looking back, James left the Gayway and quickened his pace toward the olive trees. Kay ought to be there by now.

He had a lot to tell her. The intruder of the night before, the embarrassing discovery of her fingerprints (to be dished up with a little homily on conventional behavior), and now, the running onto Mrs. Porter Cartwright in such an unexpected moment, place, and company.

Kay was under the olive trees already, and the inevitable Mr. Pohlemus had already dutifully engaged her in conversation.

At James's appearance Mr. Pohlemus assumed the role of bearer of important tidings, a role which necessitated such chest-expansion as might easily have been fatal, James thought, to that well-developed personage.

"Well, Professor, it's happened!" announced Mr. Pohlemus.

But James was holding Kay's hand at this moment, savoring the allure of her smile, and losing himself in her velvety brown eyes, and other matters became momentarily slight.

"I've got lots to tell you," he promised. And then he became aware of the insistent Mr. Pohlemus and said, "What has happened?"

"Two more olive trees dead," said Mr. Pohlemus cataclysmically.

"It seems just too fantastic." Kay at least was impressed. "Why don't you gasp, James?"

"I'm put out about it, but it's what I expected," James confessed.

"But that's not all, Professor Biddle," said the plainclothesman. He looked questioningly at Kay.

" Go ahead," directed James. "Miss Ritchie knows the whole deep and dark secret."

"Well, then," said Pohlemus, "the girl came by again today. The steno. You know, her that lost the heel?"

"Yes, yes," said James. "You followed her to her work. Where did she go?"

Mr. Pohlemus became confidential. His voice lowered to a mere whisper. "I stayed about a hundred yards behind her," he said, "so's she wouldn't suspect nothing. Well, she went up California Avenue and turned at the corner of Pacific Promenade and went past the restaurants and the lagoon—"

"Never mind all that," said James. "Where did she end up?"

A guilty look came into Mr. Pohlemus's honest face at  this point. "Well," he admitted, "I was scared I'd lose her, so I kept pretty close behind. She looked back a couple of times, but I wasn't the only guy on the walk, so I figured she wouldn't notice me. Well, she suddenly stopped over by the Japanese exhibit and set down her typewriter on the step and took to powdering her nose. Then she left her typewriter standing there at the side of the step and went into the Japanese exhibit. So I figure to myself 'she'll be right out' and I wait for her. After about fifteen minutes I thought I'd better go in and see, and she wasn't in there at all. She must of just walked right out the other side of the building."

"She had her back to you when she was powdering her nose," James suggested. "And you stood there ogling at her."

"Why, yes," said Mr. Pohlemus uncomfortably.

"Girls use mirrors when they powder their noses," said James with fortitude. "Especially when they're just pretending to powder their noses. Well, at least you got the typewriter."

"Yes, I got that," said Mr. Pohlemus. "But there wasn't any typewriter in it. I took it to the police station here at the Fair. I didn't know if I ought to open the case or not. But I stayed by when they opened it."

"Was there a can in it?" asked James.

"Yes," admitted the bewildered Mr. Pohlemus. "How did you know?"

"Tell them it contains carbon bisulfide," James directed. "That will save me a trip. Thanks."

"You're so wonderful, James," breathed Kay, her arm linked in his as they started down the path of olives.

"Let's get somewhere," said James. "That man drives me to drink."

"You can't expect him to be as bright as you are, James," Kay argued contentedly. "Nobody is."

"Anyway, let's get off by ourselves," said James. "I've got at least three major links for your chain-gang."

Their progress was halted and their privacy destroyed by the sudden appearance of old Mr. Werner in his shiny black mohair suit. He looked more like a crow than ever, James thought, standing there cawing a good morning at them, his flapping black sleeves spread out genially to bar their way.

Kay and James admitted that it was a good morning, and then James said, "By the way, Mr. Werner, I'm much obliged to you for letting me get away with that locket. But now I feel guilty about it. It should properly belong to you. It's your land they brought up here with these trees."

"I noticed you picked up some trinket," said Werner. "I said to Harvey last night how that old Russian had turned up. He thinks like you do, that any such souvenir as that trinket ought to go to me. But I don't care. I'm an old man. What do I want with such nonsense? Keep it and welcome. Might show it to me, if you have it on you."

"I haven't the locket at the moment," James said apologetically, "but if you're going to be down on your boat tonight I'd like to drop by with it."

"Sure," agreed the old man. "And you come too, Miss Ritchie. Maybe we can have a little party. I'll see if I can get Harvey to come over. Folks sure have a high old time on that yacht, the *Iolanthe.*" The *Iolanthe* was visible from where they stood, as she rode at anchor, in the Port of the Trade Winds. "That's Cartwright's yacht," Werner added. A sneer marred the generally benevolent face of Isaac Werner as he mentioned the capitalist's name. "He's got more than any one man has a right to."

"We'll stop by tonight," Kay promised, and they left the old crow under his olives. "At last," she breathed. "Now we can talk. Tell me quickly."

"Hush," said James, attempting to concentrate.

Kay gave a discouraged little sigh. "First you tell me you've got three new clues and get my curiosity all whetted, then you carry on interminable conversations with a cop about a lady who all you can prove against her is that she lost a heel, and then old man Werner comes along and feels chatty, and then when at last we're alone you tell me to shush."

"I'm sorry," James apologized. "I thought there were fifty olive trees, but I just wanted to make sure. I was counting."

"As if anybody cared how many olive trees there are." Kay's patience was at the breaking point. "Are you going to tell me something important, James, or are you a mystery four-flusher? Clues, James. Put up or shut up!"

"Well, in the first place, you don't seem sufficiently impressed with the fact that we've found out who was murdering the trees," James observed.

"You mean the pretty steno."

"Yes. But be impressed."

"I'm afraid I just can't take the trees seriously enough, James. I try, but I just can't."

"That's why women don't make good sleuths," said James. "They have to find the murderer dripping gore before they see any connection. But you might be slightly interested in the fact that I went to the mat with a mysterious intruder last night."

"You don't mean literally?"

"Don't I," said James.' "I'd show you my scars if I knew you better, Miss Ritchie! As a matter of fact I believe the intruder got the worst of it. The iron lady bounced off the side of his head, unless I'm mistaken."

"You'll drive me wild, James. What iron lady?"

"The iron lady who stops my bedroom door," James explained. "I was alone in the dark with a desperate criminal. I was unarmed. What could I do? I took the iron lady and after a brief scuffle the rascal fled."

"I haven't any idea whether you're telling me the truth, James. I think you're joking."

"People always think I'm joking," James complained. "I protest that I don't know how. But if you don't believe me you can ask your Angus McDuff. He came over, fingerprint expert and all. Whose fingerprints do you suppose they found, by the way?"

"Heavens," said Kay. "I'm terrified, James. Suppose it was some phantom slasher and he had harmed you!"

"Fingerprints were discovered and identified," said James. "They were found about the bathtub. They were yours."

Kay gave one horrified gulp and then went off into practically hysterical mirth.

They reached the parking space and made their way to Xantippe.

"I expected you to be decently embarrassed, at least," said James. "When Sergeant Ashley appeared with word of his discovery it was a very trying moment for me, in front of Inspector McDuff and all."

Kay wiped tears of joy from her face and made a charming effort to appear mortified. "There was one other clue, you mentioned," she reminded him, "if one could change the subject."

"Yes," James agreed. "Presently." He curved Xantippe around the causeway toward Yerba Buena. On their left was the Port of the Trade Winds with its myriad small boats lined up at parallel anchorage. Werner's boat was indistinguishable from a dozen others, but the *Iolanthe* rode aloof, shining and queenly, clearly Park Avenue.

"Why would Doreen Cartwright of the matchless legs and the chewing gum choose to harbor the *Iolanthe* indefinitely at the Port of the Trade Winds?" James demanded. "You're a woman. You tell me."

"I rise to a point of decency, James. A gentleman shouldn't criticize a lady's legs. But if they are matchless it's undoubtedly because through an active life of putting the right foot foremost the right leg has become overdeveloped. To get around to your question, I would say she probably has a heavy on the fairgrounds."

"Very astute, Miss Ritchie," said James. "You get off the track occasionally on international tangents, but when it comes to the sex you're tops."

"Thanks, James," Kay said, very demurely.

They were gliding down the bridge slope into San Francisco now. "Being only a man, I would never have suspected such a starry-eyed matron as Mrs. Cartwright. You think of everything. How could I get along without you, Kay?"

"Nobody asked you to," she said. "It was only a guess."

"But a remarkably lucky one, my dear, because I saw the man."

"No!"

"Yes. Less than an hour ago. Cutting through the Gayway to kill time till you should be at the olives, I found the guilty lady. She was inadequately disguised by a pair of sunglasses and fragrant to heaven of expensive perfume. And she was conversing with a man in a manner which was somehow very telltale."

"You're fairly observant yourself, James," Kay allowed. "You mean she was giving him the looks."

"That's it," said James. "She was giving him the looks. Even through her dark glasses I could see the adoration."

"A girl would have to be careful with you, wouldn't they, James."

"*She* would," James corrected instinctively.

"What kind of a guy was he?"

"A slicker, if I know. Sharp and energetic. May bark out one of those shows. May own some concessions."

"Where are we going?" Kay demanded suddenly.

James drew Xantippe to a standstill at the red-painted curb before the Raleigh. "Stay here and keep me out of trouble," he ordered. "I'll be back in a moment."

"I should mind the car while you call on your girlfriend!" he heard over his shoulder in a sweetly disgruntled plaint.

At the Raleigh desk he inquired for di Piazzi.

"Just checked out," was the response.

"And Princess Varnakov?"

"Also checked out."

James muttered savagely to himself. He should have foreseen this. Of course, they would check out. It was small use asking for a forwarding address, but he did ask.

"They left none," said the desk clerk. "Mr. di Piazzi mentioned Hollywood as their destination but said he had not decided as to a hotel."

James thanked the man and returned to Kay.

"See?" said Kay. "No ticket. When they wanted to haul Xantippe off to the boneyard I just told them my friend was Angus McDuff, and you ought to have seen them turn pale."

"The birds have flown," James announced. He slid into his seat and cranked up Xantippe. "They mentioned Hollywood vaguely as their destination. At least that is one big place, then, that we don't have to look for them."

"Oh, dear, James. You're so obscure. You mean Tania and Rubio slid down the fire escape? And if so, what of it? I'm glad to be rid of that white-hot Russian, myself. She was stealing Harvey Bell from me."

"We've got to find them," said James. "We're heading south, Miss Ritchie. Maybe you don't want to come."

"Listen, you can't leave me on a street corner. Of course I want to come. Where are we going? What are you trying to do, overtake Tania and Rubio?"

"No," said James cryptically, weaving a dizzy warp through traffic. "I'm trying to get ahead of them."

"Of course it's none of my business," Kay shouted across the whistling wind, "but what do you want of them?"

James was busy driving. "I'm not quite sure," he admitted. Xantippe went like the wind. "I want to get back my locket, for one thing. They can't do this to me. I trusted them. (Like snakes!) And I think, Miss Ritchie, that I want to see if *My Rubio* has a bump on the head."

"Why, you're a perfect daredevil, James," Kay cried, as Xantippe rounded a corner on two wheels. "Who'd ever have thought—"

"Keep your eyes peeled for cops," James shouted. "This is life and death, but it might take a lot of time to prove it."

The wind whistled over Xantippe's safety glass as James swept down the Bayshore Boulevard. They passed two motor cops idling along in the opposite direction. James applied the brakes, but they were still traveling. "Sister Ann, Sister Ann," James agonized, "see if they turn around."

"They haven't yet," Kay answered. "But James, supposing Tania and Rubio took the other highway, through Burlingame?"

"That's what I'm banking on," James shouted. " I don't think that pair of four-flushers could resist traveling by way of the finest residential district!"

"But then we'll miss them."

"If they don't come where we're going we don't mind if we do miss them," James proclaimed with royal authority.

He slowed down. The turn was near now. They took it gently enough. "If we're still ahead of them we have plenty of time," he said. "If they're ahead of us, it's already too late."

Kay's mystification was a joy and a delight to any masculine soul. James nourished it with all the loving attention he had once given to his now neglected tomatoes.

He drove in at the Werner gateway and down the shell-bordered driveway beside the disintegrating old house. At the stables he waved briefly to Reed, whose dun-colored form busied itself in the shadowy stalls. Xantippe didn't stop, but rounded the corner of the stables and headed straight for the site of the old olive orchard.

James gave an exclamation of satisfaction. "We're here," he announced, "and they aren't." He pulled Xantippe to a standstill and dismounted.

At the edge of the ravaged orchard he stood wagging his finger methodically down the rows.

A little moan of distress was audible from Kay. "Really, James," she cried, "if I'd known criminology was going to unhinge you so frightfully I'd never have consented, never! Much less encouraged you! What on earth are you making that perfectly silly motion for? I'd tell you what you remind me of if I'd ever seen anything like it in my life, but I never have!"

"Hush," James directed. "I'm counting. Forty-nine, fifty, fifty-one."

"Isn't that pretty elementary?"

"It is," James acquiesced. He had finished the roll-call. "It's something I should have thought of a week ago. Now we're working against time."

There was the faint guttural murmur of an open cutout, and an ox-blood phaeton of foreign make, with silver exhaust pipes springing from the hood, rounded the corner of the stable and coasted down the lane. At the wheel was Rubio di Piazzi, and beside him, leaning forward with urgent feline tenseness, was Princess Tania Varnakov.


## CHAPTER 15

"GUARD YOUR JAW, AS WE SAY in the ring," James whispered, "and let the other guy do the leading."

He waited while Tania and her escort, with rather forced smiles, clambered from their foreign equipage. And Kay, bright girl that she was, seemed to understand the game as well, James observed, as Princess Tania.

It was Rubio who broke.

"To find you here," he said, "what a surprise."

He bowed stiffly to Kay and removed his gray Homburg. A dark bruise, partially concealed by hair, showed in the vicinity of his left temple. If it hadn't been made by the iron woman, James stood ready to be called a grassroots Republican

"We have come to take pictures of spring blossoms," Tania explained easily.

As if the princess had not indubitably established the point, Rubio reached into the tonneau and brought out his leather camera case. He laid it ostentatiously on the running board.

James had an irresistible desire to be nearer that leather camera case. And by way of developing a little business to make it seem natural, he rummaged in the rumble seat of Xantippe, and emerged with an "Ouch!"

"Damn," he complained, squeezing his thumb. "Too bad the automobile manufacturers can't be bothered to plane the floor boards. Have you a pin, Kay?"

Did he get a splinter, Kay had to know. And then she must have a look. "I don't see a thing, James," she repeated for a second time.

Very obtuse Kay was, for a stooge. "It's under my thumbnail," James explained stoically. "Now, if you will just let me have a pin!"

"Never," said Kay. "It's very bad to take out splinters with a pin, James. It must be a needle. And I haven't got a needle. You'll have to leave it there till we get back to town. It's much better, James. People get lockjaw around horses. And here we are on a horse farm. I wouldn't think of letting you have my one and only pin. Besides, it would leave me all undone."

"But I have a needle," offered Princess Varnakov unexpectedly, and produced one triumphantly out of her handbag. Fate was on his side after all, James congratulated himself. He sat on the running-board of the di Piazzi car and casually laid the needle on the leather camera case while going through the difficult maneuver of locating a splinter which did not exist. In picking up the needle he allowed it to slip from his fingers and fall against the side of the camera case. The needle hung suspended against the leather. So there was a magnet in the case, a compact and powerful electromagnet.

Di Piazzi snatched up the contraption, giving James hardly time to recover Tania's needle.

"I'm afraid it's too deep for me," James observed whimsically. He returned the needle with thanks and apologized for their imminent departure.

"We have a busy day," he said. "But how nice to have seen you."

Princess Tania turned on the charm. It enveloped them all, James felt, even the sullen Rubio. "Could you meet me for tea, Miss Ritchie?" she begged. "If we could get away from these men we would have so much to talk over together."

Kay glanced questioningly at James. "Of course," she accepted promptly. She wasn't being obtuse any more. "At the Raleigh?"

Very clever of her, James observed. The princess would thus not be aware their departure from the hotel had been discovered.

"Of course," said Tania. "The Raleigh. In the lobby, my dear. At five."

A cordial waving of hands terminated what might have been an embarrassing occasion, and James rolled Xantippe swiftly away. "When is a camera not a camera, my dear sleuth?" he demanded.

"When is a splinter just an excuse to get a princess to hold your hand?" Kay retorted.

"But she didn't hold my hand," James pointed out. "You did."

"Well, she would have if I hadn't," said Kay. And James was willing to let it go at that.

A half-mile from the Werner ranch, James turned sharply to the right onto a branch highway.

"I thought we might take a run over to Medbury Landing," he said, "and have a look at the place where Werner usually keeps his boat."

But he drove at a moderate pace which permitted him to look searchingly from side to side of the right of way.

"What are you hunting for?" asked Kay.

"Lunch, for one thing," said James truthfully. He looked back over Xantippe's booted top and accelerated the motor. "Tania and Rubio will be coming after us," he prophesied mysteriously.

"I do hope not," sighed Kay. "They seem so unwholesome."

Xantippe reached Medbury Landing, however, and there had been no sign that they were being followed by the oxblood phaeton. James's disappointment increased as he walked along the shore of the dredge-deepened slough.

There was nothing here. Nothing significant. An old building served as headquarters for a small yacht club. A gasoline pump was prepared to service the few motorboats moored in the basin alongside several sailing craft. The landing might accommodate a lumber schooner, and had even, James remembered, been boomed at one time as a potential port. Now it just slept, without dreams or illusions, in the sun.

James turned Xantippe around and started back. Kay tried to conceive a conversation, but it died aborning.

"I see," she prodded, maliciously. "You're in a brown study, aren't you, James? You're still working on those murders. You've given me all the facts, but you won't interpret them. And you have all the answers, except for one little elusive point. Isn't that right?"

"That's about it," said James. And he managed a smile because he knew it was expected of him. He retraced the road toward Isaac Werner's ranch, still hunting along the highway, but without success.

It was not until Xantippe approached a narrow bridge that James permitted his attention to be distracted.

"Here come Tania and Rubio," he announced. "What did I tell you?" Di Piazzi's phaeton was traveling at high speed, its silvered exhaust pipes shining in the sun as it came roaring toward the bridge.

It occurred to James that the car was the sort a criminal would be able to depend upon to make a getaway, the powerful, underslung speedster of newspaper accounts. A first-rate killer would lose caste, James supposed, dashing off in a mere Chevrolet or Ford. He might escape, but his press notices would be bad.

James crowded Xantippe over to the shoulder of the road and eased up on the foot throttle. It was fortunate that he did. He was only a few yards from the bridge and there was room for two cars to pass slowly.

But the Piedmontese was not slowing down.

The phaeton surged onto the bridge. It swerved, as if the new, loose gravel had thrown the rear wheels into a skid. The tonneau swung round. The heavy body missed Xantippe by a matter of scant inches before Rubio regained control and went racing on.

"Damn fool!" James burst out impulsively. But he wasn't so sure of that. A light blow could have sideswiped Xantippe into a canyon full of live oaks. But it did not follow necessarily that the heavy phaeton would likewise be wrecked, not with a skillful driver. And in that helpless split second when a crash had appeared inevitable, James had glimpsed di Piazzi's set face. The fellow might be a coward, as Tania habitually insinuated, but just then he hadn't looked like a frightened man.

"Well," said Kay, tremulously, "I hope you're not too disappointed, James. If that's what you were hunting for, I think you picked an ideal place for a wreck."

She was evidently trying to make a joke of it, but James doubted if she realized how closely they had grazed tragedy. Her newspaper work, thank God, had not sharpened her toward life.

That was undoubtedly one reason the *Sun-Telegraph* employed her: for her naivete, for the new, fresh slant. Innocence sold down the river by the headline hunters. It was a hell of a note, James thought.

He quickened Xantippe's pace and at the main highway headed her north.

"It's past one," he remembered. "And I'm a hungry, desperate man, Miss Ritchie. I want a big, rare steak and a side of mashed potatoes and asparagus. I want—"

"I want a hot dog," said Kay unequivocally. "You see, we happen to be right near the San Marcos track, James. And Carfare's running again. Harvey Bell wanted me to go with him, James. Now can we? Please?"

So James had his hot dogs at the San Marcos track. Hot dogs and coffee. An attractive café offered better, but there wasn't time for that. Carfare was running in the fourth race and the second was already over.

James bought programs and a bulletin that the vendor called a dope sheet. A trumpet sounded as he and Kay took their seats in the long grandstand. In single file, seven or eight sleek thoroughbreds minced out onto the wide, oval track, their implike jockeys resplendent in bright stripes and satin.

James gave only passing attention to the horses. They were magnificent high-strung beasts, and he admired them without being interested in any special one. But he found it more intriguing to watch the crowds with their pencils and dope sheets. Their strained, intent faces were flushed with excitement and cupidity.

And there was something called the totalizer, which was a giant board, intricate as the human brain, that kept constant tally of the wagers in the betting booths, showing what one might win, insidiously tempting one to gamble. By the time James had ceased to marvel, the third race was over. A horse named Martinez seemed to have won. A "mudder," somebody said. And it shouldn't have won, according to the prophecy James had purchased for a quarter.

"James," said Kay, "will you take this money down for me and bet it on Carfare? To win!"

Five crisp new bills, folded once and perfumed faintly, were in James's hand. A hundred dollars on a horse!

"I'm sure Carfare will win again," she said defensively. "And today she's a favorite. If I want to win a lot I have to bet a lot. Besides, it's just velvet."

When James returned from the betting booth he had some trouble at first in locating Kay. He was looking for a lone woman, and she was no longer that. She had been joined by Harvey Bell.

Werner's nephew offered his hand with a friendly smile, and James tried to hide his own annoyance at being forced to share Kay's attention.

"I was crossing over to the clubhouse," Bell explained. "Kay spotted me. I've been scolding her for betting on Carfare. She's up against two fast horses today."

"I know Carfare's going to win!" Kay insisted.

"Well," shrugged Harvey Bell, "anything can happen in a horse race, but I'm afraid it's in the bag for Ontario. Even though Carfare's ready, and she's drawn a post position. And Jack Paulin's up. He's the best apprentice riding at San Marcos. Sandalwood and Carfare ought to trail for place and show. That's my book, anyhow."

"They're at the post," a loudspeaker blared from the infield. "Paulin is having trouble with Carfare."

Bell lifted the binoculars dangling from a thin strap around his neck. He stared through them for a long moment, then passed them along to Kay.

"It's funny," he said. "That filly has never been a bad actor before."

Kay handed the glasses to James. He took them perfunctorily but was surprised to find himself getting excited. Inside dope made all the difference. The thoroughbreds were no longer merely horses. Three of them at least had names that meant something to him. Larry's bay mare Carfare;

the lanky, honey-colored Sandalwood; and the black Canadian entry, Ontario.

James had finished identifying them by their numbers when the loudspeaker blared again: "Carfare is still giving trouble."

"If you don't mind, for just a minute," asked Bell, extending his hand for the binoculars. His voice was low, but there was tension in it.

"They're off!" the voice announced. "Carfare is leading."

Far off, beyond the clipped green of the infield, James saw a blur of moving, straining bodies. Kay had gripped his arm. Her shoulder pressed against him.

"At the eighth! Carfare out in front. Ontario a length behind. Sandalwood is moving up."

The roar of voices blurred against James's eardrums. He felt the pull of it, the noise and the conflict, the mass excitement. And he could easily distinguish the favorites now: Larry's bay filly, leading by two lengths, and Ontario and Sandalwood, driving along almost side by side. The other entries seemed hopelessly outclassed. Harvey Bell knew his horseflesh, sure enough.

At the half another black was nosing up to challenge Ontario. Sandalwood had closed in a half-length on Carfare. But Larraby's jockey, Jack Paulin, was riding a cool race. Hugging the rail, he didn't once look back as he swung into the stretch.

Perhaps Jack Paulin could distill the roaring tumult of the crowd, James thought, as the massed voices chanted their supplications to Ontario and Sandalwood and Congola. The Canadian horse had again forged into second place, tight against Carfare's withers. Congola, the other black, was half a length behind, neck and neck with Sandalwood. All three were running wide. Larraby's two-year-old no longer held any advantage at the rail as they crept up on her.

Then Jack Paulin began to use his bat. His arm lifted and fell as he began to whip Carfare home. For a dozen strides, Ontario's nose barely held even with his stirrup.

James saw what could happen in a hundred feet and a matter of two short seconds. Carfare was faltering. Had faltered. Ontario swept past her, followed by Sandalwood and Congola. Larraby's mare finished out of the money, a bad fourth.

Guiltily, James remembered Kay. A moment ago she'd been shouting with the rest of them, with him, too, one time and another, but now she was silent. He looked down at her. She tried to smile, but her eyes were blurry.

"Easy come, easy go," she rallied. "But it's nice of you, James, not to point out that I was asking for it."

"I'm sorry, Kay," Bell intruded awkwardly. "Keep a stiff upper lip. I'm going down to the stables now. I want to have a look at Carfare."

"We'll go with you," James suggested blandly. He took Kay's arm under his. Kay was very quiet.

Bell led the way past the paddocks to the long rows of low-roofed and scrupulously neat stables beyond the infield. It was a hive of activity now, for these few brief hours of the afternoon. Jockeys. Swipes. Handlers. Thoroughbreds. But it was all orderly. There was no confusion. Big business managed and championed this sport of kings.

Pudge Larraby was loitering outside the quarters when they arrived. He greeted them all cordially. If he was downcast he didn't show it. Indeed, it seemed to James that the turfman was in one of his best moods.

"Somebody's got to lose," he said, philosophically. "I'm running eight nags here, and they can't win every day. I'll save my fretting until I'm too broke to buy oats."

"Carfare looked bad this afternoon," Bell said, bluntly. "Do you mind, Pudge, if I take a look at her?"

"Go ahead," invited Larraby. "Go right ahead. You know where to find her, Harvey, down the line there, in number four."

But he accompanied them to the mare's stall, James observed, and he stayed right there as they leaned over the closed lower half of the stall door.

A couple of swipes were working on Carfare. One rubbed her down. The other sponged her foam flecked mouth with a damp cotton swab. She accepted the ministrations with complete docility.

"She's O.K.," said Larraby, "and she should have won. Jack Paulin's a good boy, but he didn't go after the bat soon enough."

"If you're finished with it," intruded James, "I'd like a little piece of that. Yes, you." He wasn't addressing Larraby. He was speaking to the boy who held the swab. Larraby whirled on him.

"What's that?" he snapped.

Regretfully, James emptied a half-full tobacco tin and tossed it to the boy.

"You can put it in that," he said.

"What's the big idea?" demanded Larraby. His voice was getting louder. He crowded close, belligerently. "What's on your mind?"

"A test," said James, blandly. "A very simple test I happened to remember about just now. I think I ran across it in *Time*. A test to tell if a horse has been doped."

The squat little man drew back a fist that was out of all proportion to his size. If his anger was simulated, as James suspected, there was still no fraudulent intent as to his course of action.

"Say that again!" he challenged.

"Hold on, Pudge," Harvey Bell interposed. "Don't bite off more than you can chew. No one's accusing you of anything. Not yet. You're taking the wrong attitude."

"Yeah? Well, there's just one way to handle these bellyachers that yell you're crooked the minute they drop two, three bucks!"

Harvey Bell persisted in the role of mediator.

"Blame me, Pudge," said Harvey. "I know Carfare, and that fourth race didn't look right to me."

"The judges and the track stewards didn't kick," snapped Larraby. "Why should you raise a howl?"

"I'm not howling," explained Bell, patiently. "I'm trying to keep it quiet, do you understand? I want this test made privately. I want to be wrong and have to apologize to you, Pudge. But I'm going to blow the lid off if you won't cooperate."

The little man thought the matter over at some length. Then, with a sudden burst of energy, he gestured to one of the boys.

"What are you standing there gawking for?" he snapped. "Didn't you hear what the professor said? Wrap up that tin and bring it here." He waited until his orders had been obeyed. Still smoldering, he presented the specimen to James. "I'm not doing this for you, Professor," he pointed out. "I'm doing it because I'll get a real kick when you come crawling back to apologize."

"It's a simple test," said James. "I think I can do it this afternoon."

"The white mouse test," nodded Bell. "I've read about it, too. It's supposed to be reliable. I'll be in my apartment around six this evening if you should have anything to report by then."

They were well out of the crowded parking zone and heading north when James confessed his perfidy.

"I suppose we'll have to go through with the test," said James. "I've got to have something to tell Harvey Bell when he calls up at six o'clock."

"But I thought you were the one who wanted to make the test."

"I was experimenting on our fat friend, Pudge Larraby," James confessed. "He was the mouse of the moment. As you may have surmised, the experiment was a complete success!"

"Well, I'm much more interested in Mr. Larraby's horse than I am in Mr. Larraby," Kay admitted. "And I think you said a mouthful, James, when you said you'd have to go ahead with that test. How about me? Don't I deserve to know if that horse was doped? Don't I get anything for my money?"

In the nick of time James remembered Kay's date with Tania. "You see," he pointed out, "there isn't time. I must either deliver you in San Francisco, which is important, or I must be sticking things into white mice. I have nothing against white mice, Miss Ritchie. In fact I always rather liked them."

"There's plenty of time, James," Kay was adamant. "You will loan me Xantippe. I will go to Tania's. And you will attack the mouse."

Reluctantly James crossed the Dumbarton Bridge, which from that point provided the nearest approach to Berkeley. At San Leandro he stopped and telephoned Barnes. The admirable Barnes indicated neither curiosity nor surprise as he checked back the items he was requested to procure.

"Yes, sir," he said. "A hypodermic syringe. A white mouse. I'll deliver them to your house, sir."

Half an hour later they drew up at James's curb. "You can take Xantippe," he said. He liked the picture of Kay driving around in his car. It made another bond between them, one of those clinging, practical bonds which mesh so insidiously about the heart.

"Put gas in it if you use it much," he cautioned. "My credit card is always in the glove compartment."

"I want to come in, for just a minute," Kay insisted. "There's time enough. What's more I'm going to see that you go through with that white mouse thing."

But on James's living room table there was only a syringe and a small wire cage, empty. And there was a smile on the face of Cinders.

"Oh, James!" bewailed Kay. "Now we'll never know. And that poor little white mouse went for nothing."

"Jungle law, my dear," said James. But he was relieved. Now he had something whimsically indeterminate to tell Harvey Bell. And to appease Kay there was a satisfactory method which he had postponed until just this most suitable moment.

He had placed Kay's bet—in his pocket. He now removed and returned it. "I suppose it wasn't ethical," he admitted. "But here it is, at least, and that's something."

Kay spread the bills fanwise in her hand and her eyes were round and glistening.

"But James…" she whispered. "Suppose…suppose Carfare had won?"

"In that case," said James, "I would have lost."

## CHAPTER 16

PROMPTLY ON THE DOT OF SIX o'clock James phoned Harvey Bell and confessed his lamentable failure and Cinders' howling success in the matter of the mouse.

"No kidding, Professor," came Harvey's disappointed voice, "didn't you prove a damn thing?"

"Not a damn thing," James admitted.

"Because you've got me all hopped up, now. If there's dirty racing going on down there I'm washed up with those tracks."

James rang off a few moments later and breathed a sigh of anxiety. That young Bell had a way with him. You couldn't blame Kay for falling under the spell of it. Why, James demanded of himself, when he had never fallen in love with anybody before in his life, did he have to do it in the face of such serious competition? James didn't respond to the spur of rivalry. He wanted a clear field. This lack in himself, he feared quite frankly, probably sprang from an inferiority complex, a basic and profound humility. How could he persevere against a bronzed god like Harvey Bell? But doggedly he knew that he had to, somehow.

After polishing off his supper with a dish of Mrs. Pringle's thoughtful prunes, James stepped out to the garage to mount Xantippe. Xantippe was gone. His first fleeting impression that he had been robbed gave way to embarrassment. Was he a doddering old fool? Was his mind incapable of grasping the fact that he had loaned Xantippe to Kay?

He called Kay, but her apartment didn't answer.

Via the Euclid Avenue streetcar and convenient connections to the ferry, James arrived at the Port of the Trade Winds and boarded the *Corsair,* moored in her snug berth at the far end of the dock.

The cabin ports were brightly yellow and a riding light glinted from the diminutive masthead. A shout sounded in answer to his hail, and presently James saw the figure of old man Werner shamble from the cabin.

"Figured it was about time for folks to get here," Werner said. "But where's the young lady?"

"She'll be here soon," James promised hopefully.

Nonetheless, he had an uncomfortable moment of wishing that Kay wouldn't be so independent. She oughtn't to be out alone with no one to escort her along the narrow catwalk so close to the dark, lapping water.

But that fear gave way to what was almost a worse one. She would probably come with Harvey Bell. That's why she hadn't answered when he rang her apartment. That explained it.

"I'm evidently the first," said James.

"Well, not exactly," the old man denied. "There's a young fella happened to drop in a bit ago."

To James's surprise the young fellow was Rubio. Following brief salutations an uneasy constraint seemed to settle on the cabin. Even old Werner's habitual joviality seemed to fail him and his sallies lacked their usual convivial ring.

James had no warm feeling for the redheaded intruder, especially since the episode of being so nearly crowded into the ditch.

As for Rubio, his surly manner changed remarkably little at any time. There was something bothering that man, James decided. Nobody he had ever met had shown upon further acquaintance such a consistent lack of manners, such a boorish disregard for others, a quality even too mean and cold to deserve the label of malevolence.

There was the unmeasured menace of the unknown about Rubio. Well, at least the camera pretense had been exploded.

Werner's radio was already playing softly, and he turned it up louder, with the idea, James thought, of substituting noise if there could not be conviviality. On other occasions James had seen nervous hosts resort to this device.

"Doggone," remarked the old man. "Missed my Crime Crusaders again."

"A program you listen to frequently?" asked James.

"Every night," said Werner. "Whiskey or rum, Professor? I got both."

"I'll try the rum this time." James was gambling, as he already knew the whiskey. Evidently Rubio had been here half an hour, if he had compelled the old man to miss his favorite program. What had brought him here? And what kind of a hobby was this for the old man to have? Crime, was it? Well, maybe the old fellow could provide some useful information.

"That was a puzzling murder they uncovered on the bridge last week," James broached boldly. "if anybody's interested in that kind of thing. Miss Ritchie and I were on the bridge at the time. We narrowly escaped being hit by the death car."

"Cuckoo," offered the old man moodily. "Hell of a place to take a body, right by all those bridge coppers. Guy must have been dead drunk."

"Not dead drunk," said James. "Dead. You see there had to be a third man, a man to set the car in motion and leap off, leaving the throttle arranged to accelerate the car to top speed and cause what would appear to be a fatal crash."

James felt the old man's eyes searching his face keenly. "That's not a bad idea," he said. "But what's your proof?"

"There was a rubber band on the steering post," said James. "It was attached to the throttle in a manner to accomplish such a result. But there seems to be a missing link. A pedestrian on the bridge would have been very conspicuous because they are not allowed, leaving as the only solution, the possibility that the killer leaped from the bridge."

"Suicide?" suggested Rubio unexpectedly.

"Not necessarily," James argued. "There may have been a boat waiting below to pick him up. It wouldn't be a difficult feat for a good diver. And it would leave a trail so thoroughly broken as to be practically impossible to follow. Do you recall the night?" James directed the question at the old man.

"I remember when it was," said Werner. "It was the evening of the same day I cruised up here from Medbury Landing. Harvey wanted me to take him bass fishing up at Antioch. I told the boy we could go bass fishing later on and I wanted to see the World's Fair."

"If you were here that night you were right near the scene of the killing," said James. "One of those Japanese had cyanide gas in his lungs. There was cyanide equipment right out here on Clipper Way."

"Yes, I read about the murder," said Werner. "Saw that tent, too. Remember? I was real interested, on account of their stealing Harvey's car, and then all of a sudden they quit running anything about it in the paper."

"They stopped publicizing the killing because the cyanide outfit found on the Fair grounds is said to have belonged to the skipper of the *Iolanthe*," James baited.

The old man's face grew hard. "Those big shots, they can get away with anything," he snarled. "They can get away with murder."

James began to wonder about Kay. Why didn't she come? And what was Rubio waiting for? Why did he sit there sullenly sipping at a glass of the old man's rum?

The rum, as a matter of fact, was worse than the whiskey. If he had to accept another James had already decided that it would be the whiskey next time. But meanwhile there seemed to be interesting crumbs of information available out of old Werner's memory.

"I saw the *Iolanthe* come in to mooring that night," said Werner. "I remember well, on account of it being the first time I ever saw her. I didn't know what she was, at the time, but it didn't take me long to find out she belonged to that hijacker. She cruised in and tied up, and I'd missed my Crime Crusaders that night too, so I got in the skiff and sculled over to see if I could make out her name. It was too dark for me to read it, but when the crew piled out to go ashore they told me she was the *Iolanthe*."

"Mr. or Mrs. Cartwright must have been aboard, you'd think," James suggested. "Did you see either of them?"

"No, I didn't," said Werner. "Just five Japanese or Filipinos. Dark little fellas. Piled into the dinghy like kids outa school. I guess they were headed over to spend the evening at the Gayway."

"You wouldn't remember what time the *Iolanthe* came in to mooring," James challenged cunningly. "That was almost a week ago."

"Yes, I would, too," contradicted the old man. "She come in not long after Harvey had his car stolen. Maybe an hour after. And Harvey's car must have been stolen just before that crack-up on the bridge, because he hadn't hardly left it before it was gone. He was over here worrying about my stuffing box. Said I'd wake up in Davy Jones's locker. And I said, shucks, it could wait till morning. But nothing would do but he must cinch up on it then and there, and that's how I happened to find out his car was stolen."

"How's that?" James asked for clarification.

"It's a measly job working on a stuffing box," the old man explained obligingly. "Got to work up to your chin in water, with no chance to see where your hands are working at. But Harvey said he wouldn't feel safe to have me spend the night with water leaking past the propeller shaft the way it was. So he put on a pair of my old pants and rigged a bight of rope to stand in over the stern. Then I showed him what I had for wrenches and he said he'd try with those, but he wished he had the crescent wrench out of his car. But he hated to have me miss my Crime Crusaders. There!" exclaimed the old man triumphantly. "That must have been seven-thirty, right then, because the theme song was just starting in. Must have been near half an hour before I got back from the parking lot."

"So what time is it that you estimate the *Iolanthe* came in?" James prodded gently.

"That's what I'm coming to," said Werner. "You said I'd forgot, didn't you? Well, just wait and I'll tell you on the dot. So Harvey told me right where his car was parked, and I went up to the parking lot. It's quite a stretch. Must be three-quarters of a mile from the cove here. When I got there I went straight to where Harvey told me, and his car was gone. So I didn't know but what I'd made a mistake, on account of there being a lot of cars there. And I went back to tell Harvey I couldn't find it.

"He said it didn't matter about the wrench, because he fixed the stuffing box all right with my old Stilson. But he was upset about his car, and he went right ashore to report it. So then I turned up the radio, but Crime Crusaders was over already. Eight o'clock, see? Well, then, it couldn't have been an hour later when I was just about to fix for bed, I saw Cartwright's *Iolanthe* pull in with green and red riding lights and enough brass to sink a battleship."

A halloo from the dock interrupted the old man's recitation, and he left the cabin.

James saw no reason to make conversation with Rubio, whom he fervently detested. A surlier individual would have been difficult to imagine. Neither did Rubio, for his part, attempt to break the inimical silence. The thump of footsteps was the first sound to vary the pulse-like beat of bilge against the keel.

Harvey Bell was the new arrival, and in spite of jealousy James couldn't resist a sense of grudging welcome as the young Apollo ducked to come down the companionway.

"Hi, Professor," he saluted James, "the party's ruined. Kay Ritchie can't come. She called me up just after you confessed about the mouse. She had to console Tania. She wanted me to tell you. Hello, Rubio." Harvey turned to the latter. "I thought consoling Tania was your job. How about it?"

Rubio gave a shrug of shoulders and a grunt. If the combination represented his current feelings toward Tania they were not chivalrous.

"I was just telling the professor how the *Iolanthe* came in to moor not long after those murders last week," said Werner. "The professor's got a hunch. He thinks there must have been another guy besides the two stiffs in your car, Harvey. Guy that got the car rolling, stepped off the running-board, and then dove off the bridge to where there was a boat waiting below. Might have been picked up by the *Iolanthe*. What was she out cruising for? It was two Japanese that got murdered, and the crew of the *Iolanthe* is all Japanese or Filipinos or something!"

"Good sleuthing, Biddle," Harvey addressed James genially. "I'd sure as the devil like to nab the guy if there was one. I took a beating on the insurance settlement on my car."

Old man Werner croaked on. "I was telling the professor how I went up to the parking lot that night and came back just when Crime Crusaders was finishing their theme song. That means the *Iolanthe* must have come in to mooring at around nine o'clock, maybe an hour after the wreck up on the bridge. You can bear me out, Harvey. You just finished working on the stuffing box. Remember? And you said it was too bad I missed my program."

"That's right, Uncle," Harvey agreed. "Then I beat it ashore and reported my car stolen. I'll bear you out on that." He grinned at James. "Uncle Ike's not going to have any holes in his alibi, is he?"

"A great disappointment," said James. "I just about had it pinned on him. Incidentally, he saves your skin, too."

A faint hail from shore took Werner out on deck. He poked his head back in. "I'll have to go ashore," he said. "There's some guy shouting at us."

The old man had no sooner gone than James began to wish he had thought up some quick excuse to accompany him. This wasn't much of a party without Kay. He had gotten to depend on Kay to the point where he couldn't have a good time without her. And why on earth was she suddenly so solicitous about Tania? He wanted her near him, safely near him.

Harvey Bell also seemed subdued for that young man, undoubtedly because he also depended on Kay for the stimulus only a pretty girl could provide. Desultory conversation between the two of them seemed unnoticed by Rubio.

Old man Werner ducked agilely down the ladder with a piece of paper in his hand and passed it to James. "For you," he said. "I asked the messenger if there was any answer expected, and he said no."

James opened and read. It was a brief note dashed off on a typewriter, and the signature was Kay's.

"James," it said, "come to 123 North Nopal Street at once. I don't expect you really to believe me, but the ikon has been found. I need you, and I'm counting on you definitely to come."

James chuckled. "Looks like a break for you, Rubio," he announced, and read the note aloud. "Anybody know where North Nopal is?"

An extraordinary change had come over Rubio. His eyes were bulging and he was leaning forward, evidently to try to check up on the authenticity of the note with his own eyes.

James passed it to him.

"Is it Miss Ritchie's signature, correct?" Rubio demanded thickly.

"Certainly," said James. "I'd offer to take you, if I had my car." He doesn't, James observed, offer to take me.

There was a short silence.

"I suppose you want to be off, Professor," Harvey suggested. "If you don't mind, I'll walk a little way with you."

"I must go, too," said Rubio. "It's late. Good night, Mr. Isaac Werner." There seemed to be a note of malice in Rubio's meticulous farewell. Or, James wondered, did he imagine it?

There was a series of brief good nights and then the unbroken silence of the walk ashore. Rubio disappeared the moment they passed the toll station at the shore end of the pier. He grunted a barely intelligible good night and was gone.

"I wanted to get a word in edgewise to you," Harvey said in a low voice to James. "They've split up, those two."

"The princess and Rubio?" James asked. "How did she stand him this long?"

"That's why Kay wanted to stay with Tania tonight," Harvey explained. "I couldn't very well tell you in front of him, but that's how it is. And Kay wanted me to explain to you."

James took leave of Harvey Bell and walked rapidly to a telephone booth in the lobby of the Administration Building. He called police headquarters and was plugged through to the inspector's office.

"Hello," he said. "McDuff? Listen to this!" He read the note over the phone and followed it immediately with his own instructions. "Meet me right off at the San Francisco end of the Bay Bridge. And send some coppers out to trace Kay. She left me to meet the princess at the Hotel Raleigh at five o'clock."

"I'll trace her if you say so," drawled McDuff tantalizingly. "But why, if you're going to meet her now? And why should I come to where the princess is if she's got her jewels back?"

"You meet me, McDuff," said James. "And bring two revolvers with you."

"What?" demanded McDuff's astonished voice. "One for you, Professor?"

"One for me," said James shortly. "And step on it."


## CHAPTER 17


MCDUFF WAS WAITING AT the appointed spot. James paid off his taxi driver hurriedly and transferred to the police coupe. As he clambered in, he handed Kay's note to the inspector.

"Here's the address," he said. "It's 123 North Nopal Street."

"I'll find it," nodded McDuff. "North Nopal isn't far from where they rubbed out that bird with the cauliflower ears."

He stuffed the note into a pocket. The car started with a rush. It was at once evident that the Highlander was used to getting places in a hurry. His hairy paws, resting lightly on the wheel, had a way of finding traffic holes. And while Inspector McDuff drove, he talked.

"So the princess has found her jewels, eh?" he began. "And now she needs protection from di Piazzi. I'm thinking that'll be the angle, anyway." He shrugged. "Well, she won't have to worry long. Things are beginning to move at last. We've got more than larceny against that redheaded gent."

He glanced with evident expectancy at James, but James ignored the overture. He was trying to concentrate on a problem of his own. Di Piazzi didn't interest him at the moment.

"It's one up for you, Professor," went on McDuff. "There was a third man in that crash car on the Bay Bridge after all. He did dive off. He left marks on the fresh paint, and he got paint on his shoes. And we found those shoes."

James stirred restlessly.

"The man who did those murders," he said, "was too smart to leave his shoes lying around for you to find."

"Killers aren't smart," contradicted the inspector. "We found the shoes all right. And they're going to be a close fit for a friend of yours. We found them in the luggage di Piazzi left at the Raleigh to guarantee his unpaid bill. He's blown, but we'll locate him. And when we do those moccasins'll be a tight fit."

"He tried to run my car into a ditch this afternoon," said James. "He looked desperate, if that's any help to you."

"We can handle him," said McDuff. "And he's got plenty to answer for. The princess swore out a warrant for him late this afternoon on account he helped himself to her dough to play the gee-gees. And we'll rap him for the bridge murders before we're done. He was tied in with the guy with the cauliflower ears on some kind of a race track squeeze, I'll bet my shirt. Him and another slicker named Larraby."

"Larraby!"

"Yes, Larraby. We shipped the tin-eared guy's prints to the Washington Bureau, air mail, and the identification just came in. His name was Seifert, a race track chiseler and needle man. He's a two-time loser. And he used to pal around with a lug named Watson, who beat a forgery rap two years ago and came out west under the name of Larraby. And there's a Larraby running gee-gees at San Marcos track."

"I've met him," said James. "He's a smooth little thug."

"I don't know," growled McDuff. "I'm only telling you what they said. But we'll have this Watson's prints from D.C. tomorrow, maybe. Then we'll round up Larraby. And it won't hurt my record, will it, if I solve three murders and blow the lid off some crooked racing business at one swoop. It's tough on San Marcos. They run that plant on the level. But once in a while the crooks get on the inside of every track."

James saw no immediate reason to mention his little experiment of the afternoon. He was worried about Kay again, more worried than he would admit to himself. Fortunately the inspector's driving was some distraction. James closed his eyes every time they rounded a bend.

"And that, Professor, is the way real coppers work," McDuff expanded. "Organization. Detail. A hundred discouraging blind alleys, perhaps, without finding one worthwhile lead. Then, suddenly, things begin to mesh and make sense, like today. And a lot of imagination and this scientific hooey didn't have one damned thing to do with it. We cracked the case with nothing but old-fashioned sweat!"

"But about Rubio," said James. "If he was bilked by that cauliflower-eared fellow, Seifert, how could they have worked together on the Bay Bridge murders with Larraby? And what about Doreen Cartwright swearing that she saw no one dive into the water when she stood on the *Iolanthe's* deck? You've got hold of something, I admit, but as it stands, your theory's full of holes."

"Wait till we get hold of di Piazzi," growled the inspector. "He'll fall apart when we stand him in those painted shoes. And when he talks, he'll fill the holes. And what's more, you and I are going to pick him up tonight."

James shook his head dubiously.

"Of course, I may be wrong," he admitted, "but I don't think our principal concern tonight is going to be with Rubio."

"Well, we'll soon know who's right or wrong," said McDuff. "I took a gander at a street map, and North Nopal cuts off to the left somewhere along this big bend in Bayshore Boulevard."

"It must be a short street then," James guessed, "lying between the boulevard and the bay. So don't drive into it at all. If they spot the car, there'd be no chance to sneak up on the house from behind."

"Why sneak up on it?" demanded the inspector. "Miss Kay's note didn't say anything about playing Indian."

"You see," said James, "Kay didn't write that note."

James had a feeling that the inspector was clenching his teeth in a formidable and uniquely McDuffian way.

"This is a hell of a time to tell me that, Professor," he said. "I could of called out a squad car just as well. And I'd a damn sight rather be a live cop than a dead hero." McDuff swung the coupe around in the middle of a block and stopped it beside the curb. "Well, it's too late now," he said. "That's North Nopal back there. Come on!"

North Nopal Street was an outpost of a subdivision that hadn't moved very well. From the boulevard a single house was visible in a virgin expanse of steep brush-grown lots. The shades were drawn. Two cars were parked in front.

"That ain't the place," growled McDuff. "Numbers on that side aren't odd."

They passed the house, and James checked up. The number was 32. But in the next block North Nopal took a sharp left bend around a hill. Number 123 must be somewhere beyond that turn. It couldn't be very far.

McDuff led on. It grew darker as they went farther from the illuminated boulevard. There were no street lamps here. The brush, as they cut crosslots, was scarcely distinguishable from the ground. But beyond the bend a bright light gave them direction. It shone from the front windows of a lone, stuccoed bungalow.

The inspector closed in boldly. It kept James scrambling to keep up. He was relieved when the dark bulk of the bungalow loomed close ahead.

"Here, take this," whispered McDuff, and James felt the cold weight of a revolver pressing into his hand. "I'll be right back."

The inspector seemed gone a long time. But he returned at last, a hulking shadow, moving with caution but speed.

"Something screwy around here," he whispered. "Lights on but not a sound in the whole damned place. Come along."

James followed him to the kitchen door. McDuff tried the knob. There was a faint click as the tongue released. The door opened and James followed McDuff into the silent house.

McDuff led the way from the dark kitchen into what might be a dining room. There was some illumination here, a few stray beams entering through the arched doorway leading to the hall. There was furniture and a rug, but there was no intimate sign of a tenant. There was still no sound.

The inspector proceeded stealthily to the door. Suddenly he cursed aloud, and beckoning James to follow, he went on, letting his shoes scuffle on the hardwood floor as he crossed the hall. There were sheets draped over a davenport and a wing chair in the living room. A gasoline mantle lantern, with good air-pressure in the reservoir, glowed brilliantly from the center of the floor.

"You've been hoaxed, Professor," grumbled McDuff.

"Of course," said James. "But why?"

The inspector tried a light switch with no result. Taking up the lantern, he took a quick look into the two bedrooms and bath opening off an extension of the entrance hall.

"Nothing doing," he said. "Let's go. But wait." He turned out the lantern and waited until the glow was gone before he said, "Okay." And James opened the front door.

"You can't tell," McDuff apologized, apparently for his caution. "We might as well spread out to go down those steps."

James led the way. He believed the note had served its purpose. It had lured him to this remote spot where, for the moment, he could intrude on no one's plans. But supposing those plans from which he had been so deliberately excluded—suppose they affected Kay?

James began to walk a little faster along the dark shrub-bordered walk leading to the street. But he stopped presently. There was an obstruction blocking one side of the path.

James knelt beside it and struck a match.

"What the hell!" McDuff burst out wrathfully from the steps.

"It's a man," said James. "Dead, perhaps by stabbing. It's Rubio."


CHAPTER 18


JAMES OPENED HIS EYES TO THE light of day and the horrible problem of having to remember where he was. It took him several frenzied moments. Then it all came back.

Rubio was dead, dead as could be. And McDuff's tired eyes had said good night over a thick-rimmed mug of coffee at some lunch stand out on Bayshore Boulevard.

"I'll take over," were McDuff's words. "Maybe if I don't get some sleep Thursday I can arrange a nap for Friday or Saturday. You run along, Professor."

So James had run along. He had to find Kay. Then he had come straight to Kay's apartment and Kay wasn't there. But here he was lying on the couch. It was morning, and Kay had not come in.

Terror struck through him to his very bones. Why hadn't she come in? What could he do now? Where could he go to look for her? He stood up dizzily and then sat down again.

Why had they ever gotten mixed up in this gruesome murder business? What satisfaction to one's curiosity could ever compensate if harm came to Kay, if harm had already come to her?

She was so small, so fragile, so lovely. And she was caught already in the merciless cogs of a murder machine, perhaps drawn in and destroyed, with all that ripe promise unfulfilled. A total loss to him, and to the world. He couldn't bear it.

He leaned forward with his elbows on his knees, his face covered with his hands, and tried to think. What harmless and unexpected occurrence could possibly have prevented her from coming home last night?

There was the throb of footsteps on the carpeted stairs. Or was it in his head? The doorknob clicked as the door opened.

James raised his head, and there she was, alive, wide awake, and not a little startled to find him.

"Heavens!" she gasped. "I thought I was seeing ghosts, James, and you certainly look as though you are seeing ghosts, too! What on earth are you doing here?"

The anguished lump in James's throat was changing character.

Kay was safe now, and that was an established fact. But what she could never do was retract the gray hairs she had given him. Anger welled up deep and strong.

"What do you mean by not coming home last night?" he demanded. "I suppose it never occurred to you that I might be scared to death."

Kay gave a startled laugh with an edge of outraged femininity to it. "Since when do you check up on my comings and goings so intimately?" she demanded. "And by virtue of what misconception do you start talking like a husband, Professor?"

"By virtue of common decency." James retorted, ceding not an inch. "You promise to meet me at Werner's. You don't go. You send a silly excuse by another man. I have a telephone myself. Why didn't you phone me? Devil a bit you care how the message may be garbled in transit. You stay away from your apartment all evening. You stay away all night. And you breeze in in the morning making wisecracks."

Kay's sense of humor evidently got the upper hand of her ego at this point, for she made a sort of explosive sound and started busily rolling the rubber band off the morning paper.

"What's more, I'm not assuming any but the most normal human prerogatives," James asserted hotly. "If you'd been a stray cat I've have worried about you."

Kay made another explosive sound and covered it with a hasty unfolding of the newspaper. "I was at Tania's," she said, in firm but conciliatory explanation. "Rubio cleaned her out of all her money betting on the ponies."

"You're nobody to criticize that," groused James.

"I'm merely stating a fact," said Kay, with extraordinary good temper. "Or at least, if my tone was critical, I was not resenting the fact of Rubio's betting on the ponies, but the fact of it not being his money that he was betting."

"I suppose Tania will even miss the surly so-and-so," James presumed moodily.

"Never," Kay denied. "She'll take him back, the goose."

"Not this time she won't," said James. "Take a look at the news."

A low and expressive whistle escaped Kay's lips as she read the front page. "Ouch!" she said. "Poor Rubio." And then, "I don't like it, James." And her eyes, full of concern, turned to him. "That lightning is striking too near, James. I'm frightened. I'm scared to death. Why, it might have been—"

"Saddest words of tongue or pen," James quoted nonsensically.

Kay didn't smile. "You're in it up to the hilt, James," she said. "And I got you in. And now I wish I hadn't."

"If I had to change it all, I wouldn't change any part of it," said James.

Kay's eyes had returned to the paper. "It says here they're looking for Tania. She isn't in hiding. Do they think she killed him, the dopes? She's at the Russell Hotel. She's just out of dough. She isn't on the lam."

The telephone rang and Kay answered it. "I certainly was," she said with considerable spirit. "And I thought better of you, Angus! Now you're being perfectly ridiculous."

But in answer to further arguments she finally said, "All right, then. We'll be down."

And again. "Yes, of course *we* means the professor."

After sharply replacing the telephone receiver, Kay said, "Sometimes I think you're right about Angus, James. He's really being very impossible right now. And if we don't want Tania to go scooting off to the death cell we've got to go down and alibi her out this minute."

From Angus on the telephone to Angus in the flesh was a mere miracle of modern transportation.

The inspector was in a stern and impersonal mood, the mood of patriotic presidents who stand by without a tear and see their only sons shot for treason.

"Is it true, Miss Ritchie, that you spent the night at the Russell Hotel with Miss Varnakov?" McDuff intoned majestically.

"Yes, Inspector," said Kay. "And you needn't pretend that you don't know who I am. You're trying to be dignified and you're just being silly."

"Did you spend the whole night?" demanded McDuff inexorably.

"Yes," said Kay. "That is—"

"Go on," commanded the grim McDuff.

"Well, about nine o'clock Tania was feeling better and I thought maybe I would go down to the party at Mr. Werner's boat, for just a little while. And Tania said she didn't mind, so I went. But the boat was all dark and everybody must have gone, so I went right back to Tania's."

"Werner was gone, too?" James interrupted.

"I'll handle this, Professor," McDuff reminded. "Just what time would that be when you came back to the Russell Hotel, Miss Ritchie?"

"Ten o'clock," said Kay in a small voice.

"Just to go to the island and back it took you an hour or more?"

"I...I ran out of gas," confessed Kay.

"I gave you my credit card," said James. "I told you the gas was low."

"Yes, James," Kay responded meekly.

"Hold Miss Varnakov on an open charge," the inspector directed his sergeant in a cold voice.

"Oh, Angus!" pleaded Kay. "Don't be like that. How could you possibly think that Tania would do such a thing as murder? You haven't the least sort of proof at all, and the idea is perfect nonsense."

"There's proof enough to make it an open and shut case," said McDuff more informally. The three of them were alone now, and he evidently didn't have so much public dignity to sustain. "Di Piazzi shoots the princess's dough on the ponies. Yesterday afternoon they have a big blowup and he walks out of the wigwam. She figures to get even. She rigs herself up a feeble alibi by getting you to stay all night. When it comes time she suddenly feels better so you can go to your party."

"But she didn't even know about the party," Kay pointed out.

"That's what you think," said Inspector McDuff. "She wrote a bait note to the professor and signed your name to it. You didn't write this, did you?" McDuff held before Kay's eyes the note James had given him the night before.

"No," Kay admitted, somewhat baffled. "I certainly didn't write any such note as that."

"Exactly," said McDuff. "The princess wrote it. And she knew where to send it, too, didn't she? Right to the party. Who says she didn't know about the party? So then the professor reads it in front of di Piazzi."

"But Tania didn't know where Rubio was. She couldn't have known he was down at Mr. Werner's boat." Kay was having a tough time squeezing back tears of exasperation, James thought.

"That's your guess," said McDuff. "Rubio beats it out to the deserted house and gets a shiv in the ribs. Or maybe," suggested McDuff, "he's only playing possum."

James had to choose between leaving the inspector without adieu, and losing sight of Kay forthwith. That stormy lady had gone out like a March lion, tempestuous at least, if not roaring.

James chose the lady and the lion. He could be polite to an inspector any day. And Kay *did* stop at Xantippe. Evidently she was sure of him, James realized, with a warm feeling in his heart.

He thought it best not to talk for the present, so he drove at a modest speed in the direction of Berkeley. He had it in mind that tonight might be a good chance to repeat that pleasant evening they once enjoyed when Kay stood in for cook, hostess, and mermaid.

At the end of the Yerba Buena tunnel James flicked the wheel suddenly into a right turn and they coasted down the ramp toward Treasure Island. He wanted to check up on something.

Then he realized that actually he had done it for another very good reason. He had done it because Kay needed fun and fountains and flowers.

There was room for Xantippe in front of the Administration Building, and James pulled in and waited. He reached in front of Kay and opened Xantippe's door for his stormy petrel. Finally he gave her a little shove.

"I don't lose my temper very often, James," she promised. "I really can't, because when I get angry I get so terribly angry. Do you suppose Angus will ever speak to me again? And will you? What can we do about Tania ? I'm frightfully jealous of her, of course, but I don't want her to hang."

They were walking past Treasure Garden and in the center of its myriad flowers the fountain shimmered a celestial blue. In the background the sheer walls of the Machinery and Homes exhibits flanked the Court of the Moon with the gargantuan masses of modern architecture.

"Tania's all right," James assured Kay. "As a matter of fact, she might not be if she was out of jail. So I thought I'd just let your Angus keep her there for a day or so. I only wish you could be locked up as safely."

"Do you mean the killer may be found in a day or so?" demanded Kay, suddenly taking a new lease on life.

"Finding a killer is one thing," said James. "That's not so hard. But pinning it onto a killer is something else again. I think, though, that we can do that, too."

"You mean you already guess who..."

"I know," said James. But his eyes wandered out over the boat-speckled expanse of the Port of the Trade Winds. "Hello," he said. "Werner has piloted his Corsair out of these waters. What do you make of that?"

"Nothing," said Kay. "You certainly don't suspect that nice old dodo, now do you? But James, look!" She pointed. "The *Iolanthe* is gone, too!"

"Hmmph," said James. "Inconsequential. She'll be back. I was wondering if anything in my power would persuade you to cook supper for me tonight?"

A crafty and calculating look crept into the hazel eyes of the society byliner. "I could be persuaded, yes," she ventured cautiously. "That is, I have my price."

"And what would that price be?" asked the professor.

"A complete confession, James," said Kay. "You're to tell me every single one of your hunches, your deductions, your suspects, and finally who done it."

"Give me twenty-four hours?" James haggled.

"Twenty-four and not a minute longer."

"It's a deal," said James. "Provided you come to Berkeley with me now and stick around where I can watch over you. You might even come to some classes. I have an assortment for you to choose from this afternoon."

"I'm too old to soak up any more schooling, James," Kay decided. "But I'm no piker. And if you're going to come through I'll owe you a real dinner. Get me to that kitchen, James."

So James inveigled Xantippe across the bridge and deposited Kay at his house. He was a little nervous as to how Mrs. Pringle would take the interference, but he needn't have bothered. She was apparently delighted, not only to take the rest of the day off, but to see him bringing home such an evidently eligible young woman.

James snatched a pineapple malt at Dad's and hurried on to his two o'clock. Part of the afternoon he speculated as to what particular items of scrumptious food Kay was going to serve him, and occasionally he let his mind drift away to the absorbing topic of crime. But by far the greater part of the intervening hours he spent thinking about Kay herself and wondering how she would act if he asked her, very humbly, to come and live with him, to see if they could make a go of it.

If you thought cold-bloodedly about marriage, your emotions were immediately trapped into all sorts of conventional pitfalls. You remembered the high incidence of divorce, and that vague bogey, incompatibility. But if you thought merely of a legal transaction by which you could arrange to be as near somebody as possible for as many hours a day as possible, and if you substituted Kay for X, then you couldn't see anything the matter with the idea, if only the person you wanted would sign on the dotted line.

It was dusk when James turned Xantippe homeward. The curfew note of the campanile chimes overtook him with a heart-rending and nostalgic sound. He was going to his home, and in it was the woman he wanted to have for his woman. He felt at once terribly happy and terribly frightened. Suppose he couldn't have her? Suppose something cataclysmic should happen? Life was so fragile and time so evanescent. Already they had squandered a whole week of it interfering in other people's affairs. That was more than enough.

Kay was right. The other business must be settled immediately, within twenty-four hours. And then they would be free, free to take their crime in small, carefully considered, fictional doses. Let red blood do the beating of their hearts for them and call it a day.

James found a car already parked in front of his house, so he pulled Xantippe up behind it. Why couldn't the people across the street park on their own side? But he wasn't very annoyed. He was too happy to let small matters worry him.

He was climbing the porch steps when the door opened, and Kay stood there. She was smiling. And as he took three paces toward her he knew he wasn't going to be able to resist. He stooped and kissed her, and her lips were just as he had always known they would be, sweet and pliant and thrilling. She didn't step back and slap him, either. She acted as though he had done no less than was expected of him. Why, he asked himself angrily, hadn't he done that before?

"There's company for supper, James," she said.

"Company?" said James. "Who, Hymie?"

"Mr. Cartwright," said Kay.

## CHAPTER 19

IT WAS AT HIGH NOON THE following day that Cartwright's surrender became the most significant.

In the quarter-hour preceding noon James had made a quick tour of the *Iolanthe*. When would he ever be on a yacht again, unless some canny millionaire, for exemption purposes, selected him as suitable camouflage on a scientific expedition to the Galapagos Islands or the Beaufort Sea?

It was all very spic and span, with the brass polished till it had that rare white sheen of green gold. But there was an impersonal aura to the ship. How could any man feel that he really owned such a splendid thing? And if you had a stethoscope, wouldn't you find the shell-crusty heart of the great Cartwright himself quaking a little with awe at the glamour of his own surroundings?

James went back to the saloon, where the inquisition was to be held. It wouldn't be long now. The great Cartwright was pacing nervously to and fro on a port and starboard tack.

Tania and the jail matron had already arrived. Tania was sleek as a black leopard in a svelte ebony creation, which begged the question nicely as to whether she should be in mourning for one or on the make for another.

Reed, who had smelled faintly of manure all the way up in James's car, and his wife, Werner's dour housekeeper, were sitting stiffly just where James had plunked them down.

Imura, the steward of the *Iolanthe,* entered the saloon and announced "Mr. Frank Tevis." Mr. Tevis was the owner of *Neptune's Mermaids.* He looked distinctly out of place on a seagoing yacht.

Mr. Cartwright approached him and shook hands stiffly. "I don't think I have had the pleasure," he said.

Pudge Larraby was the next arrival and, James felt, an unwilling arrival. He trudged in in the manner of a very plump and breathless prisoner with a bayonet at his back. Actually at his back was Harvey Bell, and behind him old man Werner.

They were coming thick and fast now. Cartwright bowed briefly to each quasi-guest.

Mr. Sperry, of the Exposition administration, drew a handshake. Krantz, the head gardener, looking more perturbed than ever, followed at Mr. Sperry's heels but sat down at a sufficient distance behind him not to claim social acquaintance.

Then entered Mr. Pohlemus, and McDuff, escorting a pretty young woman James had never seen before. Brave McDuff. What a dependable man. The girl took in the occupants of the room with a swift glance, and then, with quite an enchanting smile, accepted the red leather armchair proffered her by Cartwright.

But James's interest in the steno of the French heel was interrupted by the breezy arrival of Kay. She slipped into a seat beside him and whispered, "Have I missed anything, James?"

"A lot of interesting tidbits of human nature," James answered, also in a whisper. "I hope the beauteous Doreen doesn't stand us up."

"She'll be here," Kay prophesied, "if it costs her her neck. She's too much of a showgirl to keep the audience waiting any longer than enough to build her a good entrance."

Presently, as Kay had foreseen, the lovely Doreen Cartwright swept past her husband to a seat near Frank Tevis, of mermaid fame. She drew, as always, the appreciative appraisal of the men and the critical acknowledgment of the women.

"There she goes," sighed Kay, "and she has it with her. She takes it everywhere."

"I think we can start," said James. "My star witness hasn't arrived yet, but he's somebody I can count on."

With a questioning lift of his eyebrows in the direction of McDuff, and an answering nod from the latter, James stood up and faced the group.

There was a sudden hush, which called attention to the fact that there must have been a preceding murmur of voices, whispering voices. And in the hush the well-bred throb of the *Iolanthe's* diesels could be faintly distinguished. They were moving.

"You all know why you're here," James said, "but it would seem unorthodox to begin an inquisition without a preamble. Also I have hopes of speeding the issue by a frank warning. You are here, each of you, because you have had some connection, serious or slight, with the murder of two Japanese laborers on the Bay Bridge. I myself was inextricably connected with the problem by being present at the discovery. Inspector

McDuff has asked me to conduct this informal questioning in his presence, and Mr. Cartwright kindly consented to provide these comfortable surroundings.

"You all have information that it is in your power to give or withhold. I assume that only one of those present has done murder, and that therefore only one of you has a fundamental reason to withhold the truth. With that thought in view, let me suggest that any divergence from fact will appear suspicious and is therefore to be avoided."

Doreen Cartwright swept to her feet with a rustle of heavy silk. "I object!" she cried. "How dare you address me on my own yacht as if I were a common murderer!"

"My yacht," corrected Cartwright, without humor.

"How dare you," continued Doreen, ignoring her husband, "insinuate that there is a murderer present!"

"That is not an insinuation," said James. "I know there is."

The lovely showgirl collapsed into her seat and instituted a series of nervous glances at her neighbors.

"Since most of you are aware of the superficial circumstances of the finding of the bodies," said James, "I will not recapitulate that story at this point. I prefer to begin my investigation at the outer fringes of evidence and work from those toward a common center."

He turned abruptly toward the pretty steno. "Miss Peterson," he said, "several olive trees on the Exposition grounds have died of poisoning by a chemical. You were observed to leave a portable typewriter case at the door of the Japanese exhibit. The case contained not a typewriter but a gallon can, such as could be used to transport a liquid chemical in a sufficient amount to poison a tree. You were further observed by Mr. Pohlemus, here, to stop under the olive trees.

" Allow me to reconstruct your behavior at that time. With the point of your umbrella you had poked a hole in the soil at the base of a tree. Into this hole you had managed to pour enough of the evil-smelling carbon bisulfide to damage the tree, and you were about to depart when Mr. Pohlemus approached. You wished to explain your prolonged presence there in case it had been noticed. Furthermore, you feared Mr. Pohlemus would detect the chemical by its odor. So you kicked the heel off your right shoe and stuffed it into the hole in the ground, thus plugging off the chemical and allowing the odor to dissipate. When Mr. Pohlemus spoke to you you were able to show him that the heel was broken from your shoe and thus arouse everything in him that is chivalrous."

The girl was eyeing James defiantly. "That account is largely true, isn't it?" he asked.

"And so what?" the girl asked, her voice breaking slightly. She seemed to have grown pale, but perhaps it was the motion of the boat. They were outside the protection of the Port of the Trade Winds now, and there was a slight swell.

"I just wanted to establish your responsibility in the matter of the carbon bisulfide," said James. "It has recently been discovered by Inspector McDuff that you are in the employ of Mr. Frank Tevis, owner of *Neptune's Mermaids,* a concession at the Gayway. Do you acknowledge this?"

The barker jumped to his feet. "I never saw her till last week," he claimed sharply. "She came whining around for a job. Said she'd work for just enough to buy her food, said she was starving. So I let her do the bookkeeping. I don't know anything about her. She's no business of mine."

Mr. Tevis sat down with the air of somebody who's spiked that gun. The pretty steno also sat down.

"Since you intrude, Mr. Tevis," James acknowledged willingly, "I have a few questions to address to you. Where were you at ten minutes to eight on the night of last Wednesday?"

"Search me." Tevis shrugged insolently. "How can I remember where I was a week ago?"

"Perhaps you'll want to remember," said James. "You should know that the throttle of the wrecked car in which the two Japanese were found was held open by a rubber band, indicating that a third person had stepped from the running board of the machine before it picked up speed. And since no pedestrian was seen on the bridge, it is assumed the killer must have dived seventy feet into the bay. You formerly did a diving act in the Roos Brothers circus, did you not?"

Frank Tevis showed signs of considerable nervousness at this point. "Listen," he said. "If you mean by that that I had anything to do with croaking those two guys, you're barking up the wrong tree, mister."

"You'd better remember an alibi," said James. "That will be the easiest in the long run. I repeat, where were you at ten minutes to eight last Wednesday, at the moment this yacht, the *Iolanthe,* cruised under the scene of the Bay Bridge wreck?"

"I don't know," said Frank Tevis doggedly. His face was white. His hand shook as he lit a cigarette.

"He was with me!" The four words tumbled out in a low, trembling voice. All eyes turned to the lovely Mrs. Cartwright, all except Cartwright's eyes. And he looked stolidly away.

"But at ten minutes to eight you were on the afterdeck of this same ship, all alone, except for the steward, Imura, who was putting your mink coat about your shoulders."

"Imura corroborated that story," broke in McDuff. "I quizzed him before the inquest."

"It isn't true, anyway," said Doreen sulkily. "I wasn't on the afterdeck and I wasn't putting on my mink coat, but Frank Tevis was with me, and I can swear to that."

"Imura," James addressed the Japanese, "do you wish to change the story you gave Inspector McDuff?"

"No savvy English, velly good, please!" said Imura. His attempt at pidgin was deplorable.

"Funny how one forgets the mother tongue," came an aside from Kay. "He talked American like a whiz when I was on the boat last week. I believe he told me he was a Stanford graduate."

James rejoiced loyally that Imura wasn't any son of the U.C. Golden Bear, misrepresenting facts and all. But Cartwright was speaking, and letting the beans out of the bag, from his tone of voice.

"Let's have an end to this nonsense," Cartwright demanded angrily. "Mrs. Cartwright wasn't on the *Iolanthe* at all last Wednesday night, and you know it, Biddle. She was over at Tevis's concession with him. I bought some information from that blackmailer, di Piazzi. That started me thinking."

"Surely you didn't take di Piazzi's word in calumny against Mrs. Cartwright," said James.

"He had all the dope," said Cartwright sullenly. "He found out somehow that she was supposed to be on the boat. He found out where she was and he also proved that she wasn't on the boat. He had a signed affidavit from Isaac Werner that she didn't leave the boat that evening on its return to the Port of the Trade Winds."

"And it was as a result of that information that you hired Miss Peterson to seek a job with Frank Tevis as a spy upon your wife?" James deduced.

"Exactly," said Cartwright doggedly.

"Then she was also carrying out your orders when she poisoned those olive trees?" asked James.

"I don't know anything about that," said Cartwright angrily.

"It would explain a recent purchase of carbon bisulfide billed to your

Hollyoaks farm," said James. "It's too bad you can't simplify matters by just allowing us to tie it up neatly. But no matter." He turned to Isaac Werner. "You signed a paper that was to be used for blackmail?"

The old man got to his feet with an angry gesture of his right forearm. "How did I know what that guy Rubio was going to use it for? I signed it, sure. But I didn't get any money. I knew he was going to use it to devil a rich guy that's deviled a lot of farmers out of their ranches. That's all I knew. So I signed it. Sure I signed it."

"By the way, Werner," said James. "According to your story you were on your way back from the Exposition parking lot at ten minutes to eight the night of the murder. But you can't prove that, can you?"

"Listen here, mister," came an outraged voice from an unexpected source. It was Reed. He was on his feet and his face was flaming. "You'd better not say any insinuations against my Mr. Werner. I've never been by and let anybody speak against him, and I won't start now."

"That's right, Reed," said his wife, up in arms with him.

"I saw Uncle start up to the parking lot," Harvey Bell offered. "That was at half past seven. And I saw him come back about twenty-five minutes later. Isn't that enough?"

James disregarded the latter intrusion, but turned on Reed. "You are a good swimmer, Mr. Reed," he recalled. "Is that not so? Don't you frequently go down to Medbury Landing after work and take a quick plunge in the bay?"

"Perhaps I do," said Reed defiantly. "There's no harm in that."

"Of course not," James conceded. "Well, we've got a lot of ground to cover. Princess Varnakov, could I ask you a few questions?"

The princess rose. "I am ready," she said. "But you will excuse—" She dabbed at her face with a very small, very perfumed handkerchief, but lightly, so as not to disturb the makeup.

"The so-called exposure meter of Rubio di Piazzi, what is it, really?" asked James.

"A sort of, what you call, divining rod," said the princess.

"Then evidently Mr. di Piazzi was looking for something," suggested James. "Did he once look for it in my house at Berkeley?"

"I believe so," admitted Tania. "Poor man. He is dead, now."

"But you had a falling out with him before his death," James reminded.

"Yes," said Tania. "But now I am sorry. He just took my money to place bets. It was not so very wicked. He thought to win."

"Ah," said James. "They all do."

"He would have won, perhaps. But he said the race was so crooked. He said the man who own the horses was a crook, a man by the funny name of Pudge."

"Pudge Larraby?" asked James with lifted eyebrows. It was embarrassing when these bits came out so rather baldly. Either the princess had forgotten that she was presented to Pudge in the Raleigh Rainbow Room, or else she was dissembling admirably.

"That was, I believe, the name," corroborated Tania.

"See here," broke in Pudge himself. "I don't see that anybody has any call to—"

"Pardon me, Pudge," said James. "Your last name is, is it not, Watson? I understand that at one time you were accused of forgery but not convicted. You might have been easily able to reproduce such a simple signature as Miss Ritchie's upon a typewritten note I receiver recently. You also had a friend named Seifert. He was very strong but not very bright, isn't that so? And his ears, they were cauliflower, weren't they? And if you wrote that note, then you know about the Ikon of St. John Chrysostom, isn't that so, Pudge? It all begins to add up, I think." St. John was the password. Where was Sergeant Chisholm? Didn't he hear it?

"Okay," sneered Pudge. "Add it up, then. It takes more than gab to convict a man."

"Ah," said James, "Sergeant Chisholm. Just in the nick of time." James greeted the handsome young police officer who entered the saloon at this moment. "Can you identify this gentleman, Sergeant?"

James had indicated Pudge, but Pudge was no longer there. With extraordinary celerity for one so pudgy he had made a dash for the saloon door. Harvey Bell, conveniently near the door, tackled and held him. Handcuffs were forthcoming from Sergeant Chisholm and promptly applied to the squirming little turfman.

When a sort of calm had been restored in the *Iolanthe's* saloon, James continued. "We're not through yet," he said. "Mr. Cartwright, would you sketch briefly the history of the Ikon of St. John Chrysostom?"

"Certainly," acquiesced Cartwright. "From the beginning?"

"From the beginning," said James.

"In November, 1835," related Porter Cartwright, "Baron Wrangell, ex-governor of Russian America, sailed from San Francisco for San Blas, Mexico, ostensibly to treat for trade concessions, but actually with the hope of buying the San Francisco Bay area for the Imperial Russian Government. So much is common history. Most of the rest comes from family records still in the possession of the descendants of Prince Igor Varnakov.

"Prince Igor commanded another ship which appeared in San Francisco Bay shortly after Wrangell's departure from Mexico. It was a common thing at that time for Russian ships to winter in the bay. And it was also usual for these vessels to be manned, except for the officers, by a low and criminal class of sailors.

"Word came that Wrangell had been unsuccessful, that he had even been snubbed in Mexico, where it had long been suspected that the Russians in California were there under some secret agreement with Spain. Popular feeling turned against the Russians. Varnakov, whose ship had been anchored in the southern reaches of the bay, prepared to sail for Chile. Russian vessels had gone that far for wheat, as the Russian settlement at Ross could not provide the Alaskan posts with grain. But Varnakov's crew mutinied and were determined to return to Russia.

"On the eve of the departure, Prince Varnakov, fearing he would be murdered by his crew and his death blamed on Mexicans, fled ashore, gravely wounded, taking with him the Ikon of St. John Chrysostom, which had been brought on the expedition to give authenticity and impetus to the Orthodox Greek Church in America.

"Varnakov's ship sailed and was never heard of again. Igor Varnakov himself died at the ranch of a friendly Californian, after burying the ikon and entrusting a letter to his host. The letter reached Russia and the surviving Varnakovs by way of various whaling and trading ships, and was opened to reveal a map. The map located the ikon definitely in an olive grove, but it was not possible to discover where the olive grove was situated.

"It was not," said Cartwright, "until my agents in Russia came across a record of Varnakov's voyage written by a sailor and sent from San Francisco that a clue appeared. My agents located Princess Tania, the last of the Varnakovs, in Shanghai. She was given five thousand dollars and was to get fifty thousand more when she pooled her information with mine and the ikon was delivered safely into my hands. We successfully identified the Werner ranch as the location of the olive grove and obtained from Mr. Werner's nephew permission to search for treasure on the ranch and a contract from him abandoning all claim to whatever might be found. This transaction, with Mr. Werner's nephew, Harvey Bell, was perfectly legal in every respect, since the young man held his uncle's power of attorney. I also compensated Mr. Bell for the privileges he accorded us.

"Since a question had arisen between myself and Mr. di Piazzi as to the order in which Princess Varnakov and myself should reveal our vital information concerning the location of the ikon, Mr. Bell, who had already shown himself to be most cooperative, was selected and approved by both parties to umpire the transaction. To hold stakes, so to speak."

"Did you suspect that Mr. Werner had not been informed of the transaction?" James interrupted to ask.

"I suspected it, yes," said Cartwright. "But Mr. Bell had been thoroughly cooperative up to that point, and I was just as well pleased not to have to do business with an irascible old—"

Isaac Werner created a distraction by leaping to his feet and trying desperately to paw his way through the intervening company to get at Cartwright, but he was eventually subdued, if not pacified.

"Continue," said James. "Omitting personalities, please."

"Very well," said Cartwright. "Princess Varnakov contributed her information, which revealed the location of the exact olive tree by which the Ikon of St. John Chrysostom was buried. I considered the priceless art object practically in my possession. Imagine my consternation, then, to discover that fifty trees out of the grove had been sold to the Golden Gate International Exposition, and that the ikon was buried under one of the missing trees."

"Did you count the holes from which the trees had been removed?" asked James.

"No," said Cartwright. "But there were fifty trees bought by the Exposition."

"Pardon the interruption," said James. "Continue."

"Whereupon di Piazzi accused me of obtaining their information by misrepresentation, or something vague and typical, and demanded a cash bonus of ten thousand dollars which naturally rather burned me up. I felt it was Harvey Bell who had misled us, and I told him so. There was a general ruckus from that point on," Cartwright finished.

"Then it was the devil take the hindmost," said James, "with three factions devising ways and means of getting at the ikon and of frustrating each other."

"That was about it," said Cartwright.

"And the fumigating apparatus was yours?"

"Yes," said Cartwright frankly. "It was. I thought of that as being a possible way to dig about the bases of the olive trees unsuspected."

"And the two murdered Japanese were in your employ?"

"Yes," said Cartwright. "One of them was the father of my steward here, Imura. It was planned that one man would be in the tent digging, while the other kept watch outside and warned curious passersby away with the threat of poisonous gas."

"And you thought the sheer nerve of the expedient would allow the fumigation tent to go unquestioned by the Exposition authorities?"

"Something like that," said Cartwright, not without pride.

"Imitation is the sincerest form of flattery," said James. "Doesn't it seem reasonable, Mr. Cartwright, that another faction desiring the ikon might have hoped to destroy your men, substitute their own, and possibly discover the ikon before the substitution was noted?"

"I thought of that," said Cartwright.

"You also thought of poisoning the trees and replacing them at your expense, did you not?" James asked. "Hoping thereby to be lucky enough to acquire the soil in which the ikon was buried?"

"I'll admit it," said Cartwright. "I did poison the trees. But at least this confession should make it very clear that I am not implicated in the murders."

"I'm inclined to agree with you," said James. He faced Harvey Bell. "You had some rather gangster friends, Bell," he pointed out. "Such as Pudge Larraby, alias Watson, and Seifert, the man with the cauliflower ears."

"Well, hardly friends," distinguished Harvey Bell. "Seifert was associated with Pudge Larraby at one time, I believe. But there were lots of things Pudge and I didn't see eye to eye on."

"You yourself have two excellent alibis for the time of the wreck murder," James admitted. "You were just going into the water to repair your uncle's boat when he left for the parking zone at seventhirty. At eight o'clock when he came back you were just coming out of the water. The timing is your own, based on the program of the Crime Crusaders.

"But there's a hole in that alibi, Harvey. There's nothing to have prevented you from killing one of Cartwright's workmen *before* you went to the *Corsair,* say the guard standing outside the cyanide tent. Having killed him with a blow on the head, perhaps you pulled a piece of canvas over him. It was suppertime. There were only occasional passersby. And the man in the tent being unaware, there was nothing to have prevented your opening slightly the valve of the cyanide system.

"Then you could have gone to the *Corsair* to establish an alibi and get your uncle off the boat. I suppose the man with the cauliflower ears could have cruised the *Corsair* under the bridge as well as anybody. It would be a simple matter for you to load the bodies onto the handtruck, cover them with a tarpaulin, and haul them up to your car, which was not where you had told your uncle it was.

"From then to the time of the crash on the bridge was when you took your greatest risk. Somebody might suspect those two lifeless shapes beside you as you drove out the main gate. But everything went smoothly. You hooked the rubber band over the throttle. You were traveling at say, eight miles an hour, in high gear. You slipped out on the running board and stepped off. Immediately the hand-throttle snapped to its open position and the car picked up momentum. But you weren't worrying about that. You had to get off the bridge before you were seen.

"You looked down. The *Corsair* was down there. It wasn't a difficult dive, for you. Reed had taught you to swim and dive. You plunged. The *Corsair* picked you up. And by the time your uncle came back from looking for your car the boat was back at her moorings and you were changing into some dry things. How's that, Bell?"

Harvey Bell gave an easy laugh. "It's a pretty story, Professor, but there's something you forget."

"Ah, your other alibi," said James. "There's nothing like having two good alibis, in case one should fail. There's nothing like it unless they overlap by a few minutes, Harvey. At ten minutes to eight you were reporting to the Fair police that your car had been stolen."

"I'm not sure it was ten of eight," said Harvey. "But I reported it."

"That was the time," said James. "And that's where a friend like Pudge Larraby comes in."

"You needn't keep calling him a friend of mine," Harvey Bell denied sharply. "Didn't I catch him for you just now? Maybe he did kill the Japanese."

"That's not why he made a break for it," said James. "When your car was reported stolen, the report was made to Sergeant Chisholm here. The police assume the identity of a complainant is authentic. In this case the assumption was wrong. A man who called himself Harvey Bell reported your car stolen. But the man was not you, Harvey. That man was Pudge Larraby. It was a neat idea, having the police furnish you an alibi. But it's all over now."

Harvey leaped through the door. His foot touched lightly on the rail of the *Iolanthe,* and he was over.

"Observe the diving technique," said James. "Excellent."

But like a streak a dark figure followed him—Imura, the son of the dead Japanese laborer. He flashed through the water after Harvey and overtook him. And as the two swimmers drew together out toward Alcatraz, the *Iolanthe's* tender, Sergeant Chisholm and Angus McDuff were not far behind.

It took a few hours and a few tears to reconcile Kay to the truth about her lovely Harvey Bell. James took her to his house and was prepared to cut a whole slew of classes, if necessary, because now there was something really at stake. It was more than a mere matter of life and death.

"I suppose he has to pay," she conceded, "after killing those others. Do you think he killed the man with the cauliflower ears, James?"

"Yes," James guessed. "Seifert was too dumb and he knew too much. Harvey had to be rid of that guy at the first opportunity. The gun battle was his chance."

"There are so many things I don't understand," said Kay. "Why did Tania report her ikon stolen when she had never had it at all?"

"So that if Cartwright got hold of it she could collect her fifty grand or else claim that he had stolen it from her."

"How on earth did you suspect it was Rubio in your bedroom that night?"

"I had shown Tania the plaque and told her I found it under an olive tree at the Fair. Rubio would think I might have found the ikon, too. Anyway, he was going to have a look. Harvey also saw the plaque, but he knew from his uncle that nothing of value had been found. Rubio undoubtedly went to the *Corsair* the night of his split-up with Tania to try to get the old man to join forces against his nephew by telling how Harvey had been two-timing him."

"But I still don't see why Harvey was worried about Rubio. Why did he lay that complicated trap for him out at the deserted house?"

"He didn't." James could say it with composure now. "It was a trap for me, and Rubio walked into it."

"Oh, James! Goodness, it terrifies me to think of it. And that note? How did you know it wasn't mine?"

"Because," said James, with a grin, "there were two swell infinitives in it, and neither one of them was split, Kay." He took her small hand, now, and it lay in his without a struggle. "Wouldn't it be sort of swell to sit around the fire of an evening, drinking cider and splitting infinitives and all? How about it?"

"I'd be as bad as Cinders," said Kay. "I'd be jealous of your tomatoes."

"I don't give a damn about tomatoes," said James. "They're an insipid vegetable anyhow."

"I feel the same way about the *Sun-Telegraph,*" said Kay. "I ought to sit down and hack out a headliner for them. But I just don't give a damn. There's something the matter with us, Jim," she said. "It must be love. Because it's so nice just being here, you and me, alone."

She had called him Jim. To James it was more precious than anything he had ever imagined. One of those cold afternoons was blowing in over the barren hills. James had pulled down the shades and now he lighted Mrs. Pringle's fire.

"How did you know Tania and Rubio were going down to Werner's ranch when they checked out of the Raleigh?" Kay asked.

"It was about time. He'd had a chance to test all the olive trees at the Fair with his divining rod, so he would know the ikon wasn't on Treasure Island after all."

"You mean divining rods actually work?"

"For certain things, they do. Tania knew the ikon was in an iron box. A very simple little magnetic device will indicate the presence of iron a short distance under the ground, as that would have been."

"James, darling!" Kay's eyes were glistening. She was the most beautiful thing James had ever seen in his life. "James," she said, "you're so clever. How could you ever want me?"

James took a deep breath and showed her how he could want her.

"Just to think," said Kay. "Everybody might be happy, like us. And yet there was all that killing over a fantastic old bauble that probably never even existed."

"Yes, it did," said James. "You saw me counting. Remember? There were fifty trees, fifty-one holes. There was one tree damaged at that bridge on the road to Medbury Landing. The men just dumped it into the gulch, got another, and said nothing. I looked twice and didn't see it. But this morning I had better luck."

James tore himself briefly from the thrill of Kay's arms and opened the lid of a small iron chest that stood on the hearth. He lifted out something square and old and richly brilliant.

"Darling," he said, "I've wanted you two to meet. St. John Chrysostom, Kay Ritchie, formerly of the *Sun-Telegraph.*"

THE END

# About The Rue Morgue Press

The Rue Morgue vintage mystery line is designed to bring back into print those books that were favorites of readers between the turn of the century and the 1960s. The editors welcome suggests for reprints. To receive our catalog or make suggestions, write The Rue Morgue Press, P.O. Box 4119, Boulder, Colorado (1-800-699-6214).

## Rue Morgue Press titles as of July 2004

Titles are listed by author. All books are quality trade paperbacks measuring 6 by 9 inches, usually with full-color covers and printed on paper designed not to yellow or deteriorate. These are permanent books.

**Joanna Cannan.** This English writer's books are among our most popular titles. Modern reviewers have compared them favorably with the best books of the Golden Age of detective fiction. "Worthy of being discussed in the same breath with an Agatha Christie or a Josephine Tey."—Sally Fellows, *Mystery News*. Set in the late 1930s in a village that was a fictionalized version of Oxfordshire, both titles feature young Scotland Yard inspector Guy Northeast. *They Rang Up the Police* (0-915230-27-5, $14.00) and *Death at The Dog* (0-915230-23-2, $14.00).

**Glyn Carr.** The 15 books featuring Shakespearean actor Abercrombie "Filthy" Lewker are set on peaks scattered around the globe, although the author returned again and again to his favorite climbs in Wales, where his first mystery, published in 1951, *Death on Milestone Buttress* (0-915230-29-1, $14.00), is set.

**Torrey Chanslor.** Sixty-five-year-old Amanda Beagle employs good old East Biddicut common sense to run the agency, while her younger sister Lutie prowls the streets and nightclubs of 1940 Manhattan looking for clues. The two inherited the Beagle Private Detective Agency from their older brother, but you'd never know the sisters had spent all of their lives knitting and tending to their garden in a small, sleepy upstate New York town. *Our First Murder* (0-915230-50-X, $14.95) and *Our Second Murder* (0-915230-64-X, $14.95) are charming hybrids of the private eye, traditional, and cozy mystery, published in 1940 and 1941 respectively.

**Clyde B. Clason.** *The Man from Tibet* (0-915230-17-8, $14.00) is one of his best (selected in 2001 in *The History of Mystery* as one of the 25 great amateur detective novels of all time) and highly recommended by the dean of locked room mystery scholars, Robert Adey, as "highly original." It's also one of the first novels to make use of Tibetan culture. *Murder Gone Minoan* (0-915230-60-7, $14.95) is set on a channel island off the California coast where a Greek department store magnate has recreated a Minoan palace.

**Joan Coggin.** Meet Lady Lupin Lorrimer Hastings, the young, lovely, scatterbrained and kindhearted daughter of an earl, now the newlywed wife of the vicar of St. Marks Parish in Glanville, Sussex. You might not understand her logic but she always gets her man. *Who Killed the Curate?* (0-915230-44-5, $14.00), *The Mystery at Orchard House* (0-915230-54-2, $14.95), *Penelope Passes or Why Did She Die?* (0-915230-61-5, $14.95), and *Dancing with Death* (0-915230-62-3, $14.95).

**Manning Coles.** The two English writers who collaborated as Coles are best known for those witty spy novels featuring Tommy Hambledon, but they also wrote four delightful—and funny—ghost novels. *The Far Traveller* (0-915230-35-6, $14.00) , *Brief Candles* (0-915230-24-0, 156 pages, $14.00), *Happy Returns* (0-915230-31-3, $14.00) and *Come and Go* (0-915230-34-8, $14.00).

**Lucy Cores.** Her books both feature one of the more independent female sleuths of the 1940s. Toni Ney is the exercise director at a very posh Manhattan beauty spa when the "French Lana Turner" is murdered in *Painted for the Kill (*0-915230-66-6, $14.95) while she's a newly minted ballet reviewer when murder cuts short the return of a a Russian dancer to the stage in *Corpse de Balle*t (0-915230-67-4, $14.95).

**Norbert Davis.** There have been a lot of dogs in mystery fiction, from Baynard Kendrick's guide dog to Virginia Lanier's bloodhounds, but there's never been one quite like Carstairs. Doan, a short, chubby Los Angeles private eye, won Carstairs in a crap game, but there never is any question as to who the boss is in this relationship. *The Mouse in the Mountain* (0-915230-41-0, $14.00), was first published in 1943 and followed by two other Doan and Carstairs novels, *Sally's in the Alley* (0-915230-46-1, $14.00), and *Oh, Murderer Mine* (0-915230-57-7, $14.00).

**Elizabeth Dean.** In Emma Marsh Dean created one of the first independent female sleuths in the genre. Written in the screwball style of the 1930s, *Murder is a Serious Business* (0-915230-28-3, $14.95), is set in a Boston antique store just as the Great Depression is drawing to a close. *Murder a Mile High* (0-915230-39-9, $14.00) moves to the Central City Opera House in the Colorado mountains.

**Constance & Gwenyth Little.** These two Australian-born sisters from New Jersey have developed almost a cult following among mystery readers. Each book, published between 1938 and 1953, was a stand-alone. The Rue Morgue Press intends to reprint all of their books. Currently available are: *The Black Thumb* (0-915230-48-8, $14.00), *The Black Coat* (0-915230-40-2, $14.00), *Black Corridors* (0-915230-33-X, $14.00), *The Black Gloves* (0-915230-20-8, $14.00), *Black-Headed Pins* (0-915230-25-9, $14.00), *The Black Honeymoon* (0-915230-21-6, $14.00), *The Black Paw* (0-915230-37-2, $14.00), *The Black Stocking* (0-915230-30-5, $14.00), *Great Black Kanba* (0-915230-22-4, $14.00), *The Grey Mist Murders* (0-915230-26-7, $14.00), *The Black Eye* (0-915230-45-3, $14.00), *The Black Shrouds* (0-915230-52-6, $14.00), *The Black Rustle* (0-915230-58-5, $14.00), *The Black Goatee* (0-915230-63-1, $14.00), *The Black House* (0-915230-68-2, $14.00)and *The Black Piano* (0-915230-65-8).

**Marlys Millhiser.** Our only non-vintage mystery, *The Mirror* (0-915230-15-1, $17.95) is our all-time bestselling book, now in a seventh printing. How could you not be intrigued by a novel in which "you find the main character marrying her own grandfather and giving birth to her own mother."

**James Norman.** The marvelously titled *Murder, Chop Chop* (0-915230-16-X, $13.00) is a wonderful example of the eccentric detective novel. Meet Gimiendo Hernandez Quinto, a gigantic Mexican who once rode with Pancho Villa and who now trains *guerrilleros* for the Nationalist Chinese government when he isn't solving murders. At his side is a beautiful Eurasian known as Mountain of Virtue, a woman as dangerous to men as she is irresistible. First published in 1942.

**Sheila Pim.** *Ellery Queen's Mystery Magazine* said of these wonderful Irish village mysteries that Pim "depicts with style and humor everyday life." *Booklist* said they were in "the best tradition of Agatha Christie." Beekeeper Edward Gildea uses his knowledge of bees and plants to good use in *A Hive of Suspects* (0-915230-38-0, $14.00). *Creeping Venom* (0-915230-42-9, $14.00) blends politics, gardening and religion into a deadly mixture. *A Brush with Death* (0-915230-49-6, $14.00) grafts a clever art scam onto the stem of a gardening mystery.

**Craig Rice.** *Home Sweet Homicide* (0-915230-53-4, $14.95) is a marvelously funny and utterly charming tale (set in 1942 and first published in 1944) of three children who "help" their widowed mystery writer mother solve a real-life murder and nab a handsome cop boyfriend along the way. It made just about every list of the best mysteries for the first half of the 20th century, including the Haycraft-Queen Cornerstone list.

**Charlotte Murray Russell.** Spinster sleuth Jane Amanda Edwards tangles with a murderer and Nazi spies in *The Message of the Mute Dog* (0-915230-43-7, $14.00), a culinary cozy set just before Pearl Harbor. "Perhaps the mother of today's cozy."—*The Mystery Reader*.

**Sarsfield, Maureen.** These two mysteries featuring Inspector Lane Parry of Scotland Yard are among our most popular books. Both are set in Sussex. *Murder at Shots Hall* (0-915230-55-8, $14.95) features Flikka Ashley, a thirtyish sculptor with a past she would prefer remain hidden. It was originally published as *Green December Fills the Graveyard* in 1945. Parry is back in Sussex, trapped by a blizzard at a country hotel where a war hero has been pushed out of a window to his death, in *Murder at Beechlands* (0-915230-56-9, $14.95). First published in 1948 in England as *A Party for None* and in the U.S. as *A Party for Lawty*.

**Juanita Sheridan.** Sheridan's books feature a young Chinese American sleuth Lily Wu and her Watson, Janice Cameron, a first-time novelist. The first book (*The Chinese Chop* (0-915230-32-1, 155 pages, $14.00) is set in Greenwich Village but the other three are set in Hawaii in the years immediately after World War II: *The Kahuna Killer* (0-915230-47-X, $14.00), *The Mamo Murders* (0-915230-51-8, $14.00), and *The Waikiki Widow* (0-915230-59-3, $14.00).